RETRIBUTION

RETRIBUTION

Gwen Moffat

Chivers Press • **Thorndike Press**
Bath, England **Waterville, Maine USA**

This Large Print edition is published by Chivers Press, England, and by Thorndike Press, USA.

Published in 2003 in the U.K. by arrangement with Constable.

Published in 2003 in the U.S. by arrangement with Constable & Robinson Ltd.

U.K. Hardcover   ISBN 0–7540–8799–9 (Chivers Large Print)
U.K. Softcover   ISBN 0–7540–8800–6 (Camden Large Print)
U.S. Softcover   ISBN 0–7862–4771–1 (General Series Edition)

The text of this Large Print edition is unabridged.
Other aspects of the book may vary from the original edition.

Set in 16 pt. New Times Roman.

Printed in Great Britain on acid-free paper.

British Library Cataloguing in Publication Data available

Library of Congress Cataloging-in-Publication Data

Moffat, Gwen.
    Retribution / Gwen Moffat.
      p.   cm.
    ISBN 0–7862–4771–1 (lg. print : sc : alk. paper)
    1. Pink, Melinda (Fictitious character)—Fiction.
    2. Women detectives—England—Lake District—Fiction.
    3. Lake District (England)—Fiction. 4. Large type books. I. Title.
    PR6063.O4 R4 2003
    823'.914—dc21   2002028919

CHAPTER ONE

The cloud ceiling was solid around a thousand feet but there was no question of her getting lost, not on the ascent anyway, and even where the path crossed the boggy uplands it kept to the firmer ground and was marked by boots and the odd cairn. Not that you could spot the cairns at any distance in the mist, in fact there wasn't much the solitary walker could see at all; there should be butterwort and sundew here, even orchids, but no flowers would show up today until you were about to trample them. Miss Metcalf grimaced; if the cloud didn't lift she was going to miss the orchids. Never mind, the walk was exercise and she might detour and nip up Blaze Fell, test her navigation skills. She tramped on, peering close to make out the bootprints, hindered by her tinted glasses (but she'd see even less without them); on the other hand she didn't have far to look. Less than five feet tall, with a face like a shrivelled walnut under a baseball cap, wearing Austrian boots and carrying a neat rucksack, she would have occasioned more than a casual glance from anyone encountered in the cloud: a diminutive solo mountaineer moving with confidence, at least on the level. Had the chance-met stranger known that she suffered from cataracts and incipient arthritis, and was rising eighty, he wouldn't have believed it—but Miss Metcalf met no one and felt smug. She liked to have her mountains to herself.

She crossed the high moor and started down the other side to emerge below the cloud and see the pale stretch of Closewater below. Not a bird moved, even the sheep were silent. No sunshine showed anywhere. This was May in the Lake District. She snorted and dropped down the escarpment, not all that happily now because of the stiff knees, but her mood lightened when she saw that the beck coming down beside the path had plenty of water in it, cascades showing white among the crags. It made for a bit of excitement.

She came to the road beside the lake, turned right and reached the car park at eleven o'clock. Three cars were there, two with RSPB stickers, their owners no doubt looking for the red kite which had been seen here once—but surely not today. Miss Metcalf wasn't interested; she lived here, if she wanted to see kites she'd pick a good day.

Paths took off from the head of the lake, all neatly signposted in carved wood; this was, after all, a national park. Miss Metcalf nodded approval at the signs and turned to the Gowk Pass route. There was a faint drizzle in the air now. She paused to read a new notice at ground level, small, unobtrusive: 'Drivers of Off-Road vehicles are requested not to use

2

this track in wet conditions'. She frowned. That drivers of off-road vehicles could use tracks in national parks under any conditions infuriated her. Grudgingly she admitted that farmers might be excepted although she deplored the noisy little farm bikes, you came on their tracks everywhere, even on the tops. Time was when shepherds walked or rode a pony. And a lot more healthy they were then. She could hear an engine now, very faint, but in this amphitheatre of hills and muffled by the mist it was impossible to tell its direction.

She climbed the track at the pace of an old guide until her legs would accept the gradient, slow enough to become convinced, with rising tension, that there was a vehicle ahead of her. Its track showed: too wide for anything other than a Land Rover, and then she realized that the sound of an engine was growing louder. Was it approaching her, descending? She was climbing into the cloud again and could see nothing above. She would have a word with the driver, force him to see reason. This track was in a shocking state; a wide bed of unstable stones had forced the vehicle to take to the bog in places, leaving long ruts that were over a foot deep (she measured them with her hand). With a mounting sense of disaster she knew that, half-way to the pass, she must be approaching the orchids that were her goal.

She was breathing fast now and her blood thudded in her ears, counterpoint to sudden bursts from the engine above. Puzzling over those erratic snarls, trying to reassure herself that the noise of her own blood was no more than the result of the climb, she came to a morass of exposed peat and, casting about for a way round, she saw high ground to one side—but someone else had seen it first.

She was in the cloud but it was thin, wavering to expose clear patches, and there, brave and solitary, was one pale orchid, all that was left of a tiny colony of fragile blooms now gouged and ravaged by great ruts.

Above her the engine roared like something animate and died away. The truck was stalled—mired—stationary—no matter, it was the one that had ruined the orchids; clots of peat were falling in the ruts as she watched, sick with misery.

The nausea passed and she strode straight uphill through the bogs regardless of wet feet, overwhelmed with rage. A tunnel appeared in the cloud. Above her a Land Rover was canted steeply on the point of a zigzag. She glimpsed a figure, saw the truck start to move away, and lifted her binoculars.

*   *   *

The cloud disintegrated in mid-afternoon but too late for walkers to start out for the tops, and the grey day had discouraged motorists from taking the winding lane to Borascal. At

4

five o'clock the village, now basking in sunshine, was as quiet as it had been when Miss Metcalf left, and Eleanor Salkeld decided to close her tearoom. She'd already sent her waitress home, trying not to begrudge the cash she'd had to pay Sherrel for waiting on no more than half a dozen parties; now she went out to the gate to reverse the Open sign on the discreet notice: 'Jollybeard House. Cream teas. Home Baking.'

'You're closing early,' someone said.

Eleanor's expression, already disgruntled, deepened to a glower. She saw one customer only: old, casually smart, heavy: no cream tea order, a pot of Earl Grey and one cake would be this one's preference. Despite the advanced age that weight wasn't fat but muscle. She looked after herself.

'I'm not a customer.' A reassuring smile, but Eleanor had the feeling the survey was mutual even though the eyes behind designer spectacles were shadowed by a white cotton hat. 'Not that kind,' the woman continued, and Eleanor relaxed a little, listening to the tone. 'I've taken Ashgill for a fortnight and I forgot to bring any bread. I was wondering if you could spare a small loaf.'

Eleanor started to bloom, thinking that this was a kindred spirit and there were few enough of those in the dale, old, well-educated, independent. There was Phoebe Metcalf of course, but Phoebe was rough—no, not rough but—well, aggressive, not what one might call a lady. This one, introducing herself as Melinda Pink, belonged to a past generation, soft-spoken and courteous, exclaiming with approval as she followed Eleanor indoors and saw the batch of fresh loaves on the kitchen table.

'My version of granary,' Eleanor said. 'Or there is soda bread?'

'If I took both would that be robbing you?'

Eleanor gave an angry snort and gestured towards the room they'd come through, so inviting with its linen cloths on chunky wooden tables, its ladder-back chairs. Sunlight streamed through the open door, gold on the sandstone flags. 'Six parties today,' she grated. 'And look at the weather!'

'It was a dull morning—'

'It's not that—' Eleanor stopped, swallowed, and went on, oddly defiant, as if challenging Miss Pink to contradict her: 'It's all these cheap foreign package tours . . . And our terrible weather—I mean, unpredictable. This is Lakeland. This afternoon's exceptional. And as you said, the morning was poor.'

Miss Pink nodded and Eleanor realized that the woman was, after all, very old, she'd never see seventy again; at this moment she looked rather stupid—and she hadn't turned a hair at those silly remarks about the weather. She'd find out soon enough about the salmonella but this wasn't the moment to enlighten her, not on first acquaintance.

'I shall need sandwiches,' Miss Pink said absently, accepting the loaves, 'I shall be fell-walking.'

'You'll have company then. Your neighbour, Phoebe Metcalf, she's gone over to Closewater today to photograph the orchids. There's a circular walk. You follow the old quarrymen's track'—ushering the other to the front door Eleanor pointed to the skyline—'and come back over Gowk Pass. It's only about ten miles.' Her eyes slipped sideways, reassessing Miss Pink's build. 'Phoebe's very active; she's climbed in the Alps.'

'Is hers the house with the marmalade cat? I called there to ask if she could let me have some bread.'

'So you've met her.'

'No, there was no answer.'

'Well, it's only five thirty.'

Their eyes met for a second and sheered away. 'How old is she?' Miss Pink asked.

'Seventy-eight.' Eleanor was expressionless. 'She's got the physique of a two-year-old.'

Miss Pink knew that she meant a horse, knew too that even young horses break their legs on rough ground—but she said nothing; she was only the visitor here.

Eleanor read the silence correctly. 'I'll look in on her later,' she said, adding untruthfully, 'I usually walk up that way in the evening.'

* * *

From the bedroom window which commanded a stretch of the lane Jean Blamire saw the new tenant from Ashgill pass and dismissed her, all her concentration on a few yards of tarmac. Marty's van was red, she couldn't miss it; if it weren't for the bees in the lilacs she'd hear the noise of its ragged old engine approaching. She shifted her position, sighed and rolled her neck on her spine. She should turn out the light in the oven, the roast would keep hot for ages; if it came to that she could make the gravy now, put it in the oven . . . What was he *doing*? Where was he? A striking woman with strong features, indecision made her appear grimly masculine, an expression at odds with the mane of copper hair, the skimpy frock with a cleavage she wouldn't be seen dead in outside the house despite Marty's urging her to wear it to the pub. Tall, muscular, powerful, she resembled a drag queen without make-up. What she felt like was a young bride waiting for her man, and far less concerned, if the truth were faced, with the roast drying out than with thoughts of bed. She winced, the image sneaking into her mind of the old sleeping bag in the back of his van. He'd *asked* for beef tonight, surely he hadn't forgotten, wasn't on Scafell or over in Langdale, having found someone to take him up a climb, deciding to spend the night there? Her face

8

crumpled with misery. She knew he could forget. It wouldn't be the first time.

A blackbird screamed through the lilac and she glanced down to see Phoebe's cat walking up the flagged path. I'll give him another five minutes, she thought, and then I'll change back into jeans, turn out the oven and have a Scotch. It'll while away the time. Or I could thin the lettuces, or go up and see Mum, it would serve him right to come home to an empty house. But she knew she wouldn't; she would stay and wait.

She looked up and saw the red van emerge from the sycamores. Her lips parted in delight and she was suddenly ravishing.

*　　　*　　　*

In the cramped little cottage on the bank of the beck Eleanor's waitress, Sherrel Lee, was trying to stick to her guns without getting into a slanging match with her mother. 'There's no point anyway,' she protested wearily. 'She's doing no trade, even on a Sunday. Most of the time I got nowt to do.'

'What are you moaning at?' Misella was loud and angry, the gypsy blood showing. 'Money for old rope, that's what it is. What d'you make today then: fourteen pound? You're mad to give up the job, girl.'

'Christ, Mam! All that cream! Them cream cakes!'

'You love cream c—You're not—Oh no!' Misella was standing at the kitchen window where she'd been watching the two toddlers in the garden. The latest baby was asleep on one brawny arm. 'This un's not six months, for God's sake!'

'I can't help it.' And indeed, short of spaying her, Misella thought, she didn't seem to be able to help herself. '*You* go and work for her then,' Sherrel shouted. 'See how you like it. If you're standing around doing nowt, she'll have you scrubbing out the toilet.'

'No way, not when a soul's handling food.' But Misella knew that Eleanor Salkeld hadn't much time for regulations, so maybe that extended to hygiene too. 'I always held there could have been some truth in that food poisoning,' she said.

Sherrel's eyes widened and she blundered to the door, her hand over her mouth. The little ones watched without much interest as she threw up in the lupins; they'd seen it before, when the last baby was on the way. Misella jiggled him absently on her hip, thinking that since either she or Sherrel was always available for work, there wasn't all that much difference between six kids and five—and then there was the extra benefit, another ten pounds. Not to be sneezed at—and perhaps the father . . . She pondered the identity of the father but doubted if anyone knew, even Sherrel. If our Bobby hadn't had red hair . . . And where was

Bobby? He shouldn't be playing in the beck, the water was too high. Probably up to Sleylands again but—Sunday afternoon? Maybe Swinburn was gathering and Bobby was out shepherding. He'd be back for his supper that was sure; Mabel Swinburn wasn't about to feed him.

*   *   *

Sitting outside Ashgill, the warm wall at her back, warm sun in front, a blackbird in full song, the beck a whisper in the bottom of the dale, Miss Pink sipped Tio Pepe and considered what secrets this idyllic prospect might conceal. In Lakeland walkers got lost, climbers fell down cliffs: predictable events in mountainous terrain and fitting a bleak, wild and potentially dangerous landscape. But in the dales, in cottages nestled under ancient sycamores, behind the lilac hedges, behind thick walls, who heard the screams? Time I wrote something, thought Miss Pink, who had abandoned books in favour of the lucrative market for short stories she'd established in America. Now her antennae were twitching to the ambience of Borascal. Why was Eleanor Salkeld so touchy about the dearth of customers? Why indeed were there so few on a fine Sunday afternoon in late spring?

At eight o'clock, back in the garden after her modest supper, she might have put the

11

question when Eleanor appeared, but Eleanor, obviously bewildered, forestalled her. Miss Pink's shoulders dropped; she had a premonition.

Eleanor said flatly, 'She's not home yet.' Had she not been so concerned she might have wondered at the other's immediate control of the situation.

'What time did she leave?'

'I didn't see her go but she's an early riser. Still, whatever time . . . It's only ten miles.' Eleanor's mind was leapfrogging.

They went indoors and spread a map on the parlour table. 'This is well used,' Eleanor said as it tore at a fold.

'I've been in the area before, but not to do this walk.' Miss Pink followed Eleanor's finger as she traced the route.

'See? Over the quarrymen's track to Closewater and back by way of Gowk Pass and down the zigzags to the head of the dale.'

'Passing the quarry.'

'No. Nowhere near it. And the path is so obvious: the whole way in fact. She must have been coming down in good visibility and anyway the track's at least half a mile from the quarry.'

Miss Pink left the room and returned with a magnifying glass. 'There's a path marked: from this elbow in the track, running into the quarry. If you didn't turn that corner you might continue along the quarry path.'

'Only if you were a stranger and in mist. The track's stony and cairned. That level is grassy. Certainly it runs to the quarry or appears to, but it ends smack against a high stone wall with a padlocked gate and a notice saying "Danger. Keep Out. No Trespassing." That woman's an expert; even if she weren't concentrating, she'd know immediately that she'd taken the wrong turning and retreat.'

Miss Pink straightened. 'It'll be dark soon, and there won't be a moon. Still, it looks as if it'll be a fine night.'

'You're not thinking of following her!'

'Oh no. I think you should—' Miss Pink remembered her place. 'Have you thought about calling the rescue people?'

'Actually your neighbour runs the team but . . .' Eleanor floundered. 'It would be like *reporting* it, and one would look silly if she was merely late coming down—and she'd be *furious*. And then, we're all the same age . . .' What she meant was that it seemed fitting to ask one old lady for advice concerning another, and this one had an air of authority about her.

'Would she have passed any houses?' Miss Pink asked. 'The time might be a help, and she could have spoken to someone.'

'Of course! The Swinburns! She had to pass the farmyard.'

They moved to the kitchen and while Eleanor used the phone Miss Pink produced a

13

bottle of The Macallan and tumblers. On hearing the shocked *'Nine?* Are you sure?' she poured stiff measures.

Eleanor explained her concern to the person on the line and listened to the response. 'Yes,' she said dully, 'but she knows what she's about, Jacob; she's climbed in the— what? Well, *you* do!' Heatedly.

The call ended. 'Usual bloody reaction,' she growled. ' "At her age she shouldn't be on the hill." Thinks he knows it all, thinks a compass is a toy. Hasn't walked the tops for decades, goes everywhere on wheels.'

Miss Pink proffered the whisky. 'She passed the farm at nine? It's on the track?'

'Yes to both. But even if she took in a peak or two she should be back—'

Miss Pink gaped. 'You mean she could have gone on the tops: left the track you thought she was on?'

'Phoebe wouldn't be satisfied with a ten-mile walk if the cloud lifted—as it did. Ten miles isn't much more than a half-day for her.'

'So her coming home late is nothing to worry about? It's possible she's making a long day of it.'

The marmalade cat walked in, mewing loudly, his head up, sniffing lamb chops. 'I must give him something,' Eleanor said distractedly. 'She feeds him at six. She's strict about it. I've fed him when she's away and she's adamant: it must be six. She's a believer

14

in routine. Look at him: two hours past his supper time.'

Miss Pink took the plunge. 'Tell the rescue leader. Report it, then the ball's in their court. They'll probably follow her route: it's good exercise for them if nothing else.' Her *proposed* route, she qualified to herself; there was no knowing what an active old climber might get up to, once on the tops on a nice day—or even in mist. Miss Pink had been there and knew that the spirit could be too much for aged flesh.

*   *   *

Hill farmers don't show their emotions much, all the same, Jacob Swinburn looked thoughtful, even troubled as he replaced the phone. Mabel made no move to restore the sound on the television.

'You reckon she's come to harm?'

Jacob shrugged. 'She's rising eighty, what d'you expect? Bound to happen sooner or later. And who'd try to stop her, I ask you? I'd sooner face a mad cow, that I would.'

Mabel ignored the posturing. She liked Phoebe Metcalf: a woman who had managed all her life without men. 'She could be lost. If she gets through the night she'll come down in the morning. It's not like winter time.'

Jacob shook his head. 'Her's always on the hill, and half the time in mist. Ask me, she

15

prefers mist, no one can see what she's poking her nose into, trespassing on my—'

'Now you stop that—'

'No reason she should be lost today more'n any other day.' He grinned toothily. 'More like she fell over a rock, broke summat.'

'Does Martin know?'

'She didn't say.' He looked sly. 'Be to her pal's advantage, wouldn't it, bring t'rescue team here, t'police, t'media, plenty of customers back in t'caff—providing none of 'em's scared of being poisoned.'

'Dad! That were a stunt and you know it. Eleanor's baking's better'n mine!'

'Better watch meself then, hadn't I, make sure I eat same vittles as yourself.' He was good-humoured, it was a joke.

CHAPTER TWO

The rescue team didn't make a big thing of it; Phoebe Metcalf had been a tiger well into middle age and she'd earned respect among mountaineers. Moreover it was a fine night, no one wanted to alert the media at this stage and humiliate an indomitable old girl crawling home with a sprained ankle. The full team did not go out, only Blamire, the leader, with another man walked from Borascal to Closewater while three members traversed

16

Gowk Pass, but between them they covered all of Phoebe's proposed route and found no sign of her.

By first light next morning the search proper began, concentrating on the second half of the route: over and above Gowk Pass. It was thought that, with the cloud having lifted yesterday afternoon, she must have diverged to climb fells above the pass.

Miss Pink didn't offer her services to the team; old, stiff and heavy she knew she couldn't keep up and would be viewed as an encumbrance. She went out alone and she started from scratch, at the farm called Sleylands.

A tractor was idling in the yard, a small boy fiddling with the controls. Unwilling to approach a tractor with a child in the driving seat, Miss Pink paused, undecided, and at that moment a burst of rock music drowned the sound of the engine. The volume was turned down immediately and a craggy fellow in a cloth cap and wellies erupted from a barn, shouting. The boy protested shrilly and moved over as the man climbed up, noticing Miss Pink as he reversed but not acknowledging her. Sunshine lit the little boy's hair which gleamed like polished mahogany. It was cut in a thick pudding basin thatch over a shorn base.

The tractor left the yard and started across the fields. Miss Pink transferred her attention to the house. She was seeing only the rear, but a neat and pleasing rear, the flagged roof sweeping down to the top of what would be kitchen windows, many-paned and sparkling clean, petunias vivid splashes of colour in baskets under the eaves. A large woman in a print overall emerged from the back door, carrying a bucket and chirruping. Hens came running over the cobbles. Miss Pink advanced to negotiate for eggs, and to confirm the last sighting of the missing woman. She winced at the thought. Last?

Mabel Swinburn said it was her husband who had seen Phoebe walk past the yard at nine o'clock. She'd waved but she hadn't stopped. 'It's a rocky old track,' she told Miss Pink, signalling disapproval of another old lady proposing to follow the same route. 'Always clarty on top,' she warned. 'Easy enough to sprain an ankle.'

'But there's plenty of people about today,' Miss Pink pointed out. 'And I shall have perfect visibility. Besides, another pair of eyes on the search . . . One hates to think of a poor soul alone up there, injured, hoping desperately to be found.' She was laying it on thick but the more one talked the more other people responded. What was 'clarty'?

Mabel smiled tightly. 'Hardly a poor soul.' She looked beyond the visitor to the track. 'She's at home on the hill, she's not afraid of anything, that one.' The smile broadened. 'People neither. She's crossed swords with

Swinburn a few times, I can tell you, and he's not the only one. If Phoebe Metcalf sees someone doing owt she don't approve of, she's down on 'em like a ton of bricks.'

'Really? A person with strong views.'

'You can say that again.' Mabel flushed and looked shifty. A plain, stolid countrywoman, she was disconcerted. 'Like—speeding,' she announced loudly. 'And young Bobby there: on the tractor.' She gathered herself, seemingly on firmer ground: ' 'Course, I'm one with Phoebe there: he should never be allowed to drive t'tractor at his age. Swinburn thinks I don't know but I've seen 'em. Why, he can't even reach the controls! There are some terrible accidents on farms, specially in hill country.'

'Fathers do tend to spoil sons,' Miss Pink murmured, blandly flattering. Mabel was pushing sixty so she would have to be the grandmother—but Mabel was suddenly furious.

'He's nowt to do wi' me! He—comes over like, to play . . . he's good with animals, helps out. He needs to get away from all his brothers and sisters down there.' Miss Pink said nothing. 'He's from Sunder,' Mabel added weakly; someone had to fill the silence. 'Yon damp old place on t'beck.'

'I only arrived yesterday.' Miss Pink was soothing, 'I haven't had time to meet people. But I'm keeping you. I'll come up for the eggs

19

this evening.'

'That way I'll know you've returned safe.' The tone was harsh.

'Miss Salkeld knows my route.'

'I'm surprised she didn't come with you. She's something of a walker herself.'

'She's expecting a lot of customers, with the searchers, and no doubt the media arriving, not that it's been publicized that anyone's missing.'

'Someone will have rung the papers, get a few pounds for the tip-off. We can do without the media: blocking the lane with their traffic. Still, Eleanor will be glad of the trade, the tearoom's been dead since the salmonella scare. A wicked thing, that was.'

There was a pause. 'She didn't tell me,' Miss Pink said.

Mabel looked at her sharply, considered the proprieties, and took the plunge. 'She wouldn't, but then you'd have heard soon enough from someone. Gossip runs through this dale like a moor fire. A letter went round from some government office telling folk they were about to be interviewed by food inspectors if they'd had any truck with Jollybeard because of people going down with salmonella poisoning after they'd eaten there. It were published in local paper. And there weren't a word of truth in it!'

Miss Pink was shocked. 'You're saying it was a hoax?'

'From start to finish. 'Course Eleanor, she went storming into town, made the editor print a long piece t'following week saying it were a lie, but damage were done by then. Folk would be saying there's no smoke without fire. That were Easter time and her trade's not recovered since. I feel sorry for Eleanor, that I do.'

'Had she upset someone?'

'No.' Evidently Mabel felt that was too abrupt. 'Not to my knowledge,' she amended. Her mouth twisted. 'Now, if it had been Phoebe . . . even himself . . . Farmers and tourists are always at each other's throats. He were driving cattle up lane last back-end and a car come down and tried to push through. One old cow felt herself being crowded and she jumped up and come down on t'car bonnet.' Mabel chuckled. 'New car too. You can imagine the language on both sides.'

'But elderly spinsters don't have confrontations with their customers.'

'You're right. Eleanor wouldn't. Now if it had been Phoebe . . .'

*   *   *

Toiling up the quarrymen's track on automatic pilot Miss Pink thought what a nasty trick it had been, and how clever to send out letters purporting to come from a local government department, and how devastating the result for the victim. It implied forgery and theft, and action by a civil servant or by someone who had access to official letterheads. This was more than a practical joke, here was a vicious mind at work. The somewhat shabby condition of Eleanor's house suggested that there wasn't much money to spare at Jollybeard. What could she have done to be targeted so ruthlessly? The more intricate the plot, the more disturbed the plotter. Disturbed, deranged? Dark thoughts for an idyllic morning.

She came to the fell gate and the open moor and suddenly all the larks were trilling as they climbed towards a cerulean sky. Curlews wailed and bubbled, the sun was hot on her back, the stony ground gave way to a peaty path and everywhere there were yellow stars of tormentil. That reminded her of Phoebe's goal which had been the orchids below Gowk Pass but this too was orchid territory and the woman could well have strayed from the path to investigate a wet flush. However, a few steps to one side put paid to that theory; the path was the only dry route through bogs, and 'dry' was relative up here. Obviously 'clarty' meant mud. How far had Phoebe gone before she diverged from the route? She was a small woman, according to Eleanor, so she'd have taken a small boot size. That was a help because the two rescuers who had come this way last night had large feet; their prints were plain in the peat and it was there that, not always overlaid, a boot—probably a size 5—had left its mark. Useful. It seemed likely that Phoebe had reached Closewater.

Miss Pink lingered at the top of the escarpment above the lake, regarding the nearby beck with suspicion. In places the cascades would be close to the line of descent: slippery crags, deep pools under waterfalls. Had Phoebe approached the water looking for spring flowers, taking photographs?

As she hesitated she became aware of spots of colour in shadowed depths below. People were moving up the bed of the stream. The rescue team, or some members of it, had had the same idea. She relinquished the hazards of steep wet rock to people better equipped to cope with them and she continued to the lake.

Police, rescue vehicles and a number of unmarked cars were parked at the head of Closewater but she could see no people in the vicinity. Several paths took off from here but she dismissed the one running down the far shore of the lake, and another heading due north into the central mountains. It was the southern route, between here and Borascal, that must be eliminated first. There was a possible alternative, a path going due east to a ridge. Had Phoebe taken it, she would—could—have turned south to a hill called Blaze Fell and dropped down to Gowk, thus extending her walk by doing three sides of a square instead of one. And then Miss Pink remembered the orchids. Phoebe would have gone straight to Gowk and then climbed a peak. That is, if she had climbed any peak.

She passed a notice requesting off-road vehicles not to use the track when it was wet— 'clarty' she thought, pleased with the new word, and was immediately disheartened when she realized that the rescue team considered itself an exception. Several vehicles had gone ahead of her; their ruts gouging the peat.

She found the orchids, or rather what was left of them, and was horrified to find all but one or two squashed out of existence, the colony annihilated by a morass of ruts. She climbed the last few hundred feet to the pass mentally composing a scathing letter with copies to the National Park, the local Environmental Agency, the British Mountaineering Council . . . A Land Rover was parked on top, a rescue vehicle. Still fuming, she glared up the slope of Blaze Fell and, thinking that the rescuers would be there, she turned in the opposite direction. At this moment she had no wish to meet any rescuers.

Morosely she tramped through thick heather making for an outlying hill called Scoat Pike. She came on a small tarn where a sandpiper took off piping frantically and a fox had left its prints in white sand. She looked for the mark of a size 5 boot, but if Phoebe had been here yesterday she hadn't touched the sand.

From the summit of Scoat Pike and with the aid of binoculars she could see people on Blaze. They seemed to be wandering at random among peat hags which showed deep and ragged across the southern slope: bone-breaking traps for the unwary in mist. But the old climber and wilderness traveller described by Eleanor wasn't unwary; she'd be less likely to fall over a peat bank than would Miss Pink. She sighed, she was no nearer discovering the woman's whereabouts than she had been when she started. She looked glumly at Blaze, knowing that the scattered nature of the figures meant that they'd been equally unsuccessful. Why didn't they mount a sweep search? The answer was obvious: because they had no idea where to sweep. Once something were found—a rucksack, a hat—then the search would concentrate on the immediate area.

She looked towards Gowk and thought that if she reversed her steps towards the sandpiper tarn she might descend diagonally to intercept the Borascal path without having to retrace her steps. And she was right; there was a pleasant grassy ridge which she dropped down without trouble until, at an intrusion of mossy bedrock, she turned aside to avoid it and, glancing rightwards, pulled up in astonishment. A short distance below was a titanic chasm: rock walls dropping for what looked like a hundred feet:

vertical, even overhanging. Through the shadowed cleft there was a glimpse of sunlit pastures in the dale above Borascal.

Her first thought was that she had found Phoebe, or rather, the spot where she'd come to grief, but her second was that no mountaineer would go near this place even if, like Miss Pink, they had forgotten that a quarry was marked on the map.

She continued to descend with a wary eye on more canyons and cavernous slopes coming into view, now seeing with relief that she was approaching a high wall, beautifully built, and the stones so carefully aligned that even a young climber would have had difficulty surmounting it. If Phoebe had come down here she would have turned and followed the boundary, not crossed it.

The wall came to a beck, stopped, and started again on the far bank. The gap was closed by a robust watergate of poles and vertical slats which would allow nothing but water to pass. The carcass of a small sheep was pressed against the slats, prompting speculation on the source of Borascal's water supply.

The beck was high after the recent rain and she was forced to wade. After the water and the rough ground outside the wall she was relieved to see a level green path ahead, leading almost certainly to the Borascal track—and then she recalled the map. And here was the padlocked gate in the wall and a notice, red on white, saying 'Danger. Keep Out. No Trespassing.'

A man was striding along the green level, a collie at his heels. He had long, reddish hair—a foxy colour—and in the moment that Miss Pink thought the hair was rather too stylish for a man she saw that this was a tall woman.

'The quarry's been searched,' she said as she came up.

Miss Pink considered the full pack, the boots, the gaiters peat-stained to the knees. 'You're with the rescue team.'

The other nodded. 'You weren't thinking of going into the quarry? I mean, it's full of pitfalls for—' She stopped, disconcerted. Miss Pink's advanced age and bland stare could have that effect on people.

'I'm keeping an eye open,' she said pleasantly. 'I haven't found anything. My name is Pink, and I'm staying in Borascal.'

'I know. I live at Elfhow, next door to Ashgill. I'm Jean Blamire.'

Miss Pink extended a hand, amused by the formality in this place. 'There's no sign of her?' She nodded to the slope of Blaze Fell.

'No.' The woman looked distressed. 'I'm fond of Phoebe, I can't understand it. I mean,' she rushed on, 'I *know* her. This isn't like her at all'—she gestured wildly—'getting lost.' She looked past Miss Pink. 'They searched the quarry,' she repeated. 'Anyway, she'd never climb the wall. She's not there.'

'Then where is she?' Miss Pink fondled the collie distractedly. The woman's vagueness was infectious.

'My husband reckons she went down the wrong side of Blaze—or even Scoat. You were on Scoat. You didn't see any tracks? She has a small foot, she's a tiny woman.'

'There were no human prints on Scoat,' Miss Pink murmured, realizing that the team had been watching her, which was only to be expected: a solitary walker. After all, that was what they were looking for, except that— would Phoebe be walking by now?

Jean Blamire sighed and the strong features set in ugly lines. 'She's nearly eighty, but then it's how old mountaineers prefer to go. My husband says it's how he wants to end— eventually.' She shuddered.

'Your husband is the team leader?'

'Oh yes.' The pride was unmistakable. The expression softened as she turned to stare up the slope. 'He's coming down now. Why's that? Have they found something?'

'Presumably he's coming down for the Land Rover.' Miss Pink was tart but the tone was lost on the younger woman.

'That'll be it. He'll have sent the others over the hill and someone has to pick them up on the far side.'

Anyone could have done that, Miss Pink thought, but men were possessive about their vehicles, particularly when the terrain was as rough as that over Gowk Pass. As if she were telepathic the woman said, 'They don't need him. Blaze is an easy fell to search and visibility is perfect. If she's there they'll find her. It's not like a cliff rescue when Martin has to be at the sharp end.'

'Where are the cliffs in this area?'

'He goes into the central fells to help out when necessary. He's an expert guide.'

'Martin Blamire?' Miss Pink murmured.

'You must have heard of him, he's always in the papers and on TV.'

Miss Pink made no response, nor was it necessary; Jean Blamire was watching her husband' s approach with the rapt attention of a lover. He was certainly a pleasure to watch; neat, fast and flexible, he dropped down the steep grass as if he had shock absorbers in his joints. The collie ran to meet him. Behind him, high on the hill, two figures were stationary on the skyline.

He jumped down to the grassy level and faced them, scarcely out of breath: a good-looking fellow but showing signs of wear. The narrow eyes were too deep in their sockets and there were lines from the nostrils to the corners of the somewhat prim mouth. A fringe of beard followed the outline of a large chin. He wore no hat and his hair, although wet with sweat, was short, with blond streaks. This was a man who took care of his appearance. He smiled and was suddenly engaging.

'You found something?' he asked of Miss Pink.

She was surprised. 'Nothing. You didn't come down thinking that I had?'

'No. I came down for my truck.' His eyes slid past her. 'We searched there.'

'I told her,' his wife said quickly. 'We were just chatting.' She sounded apologetic.

'You can bring a vehicle across the pass?' Miss Pink sounded curious. 'I suppose an exception has to be made in the case of Mountain Rescue.'

He blinked and stared, then nodded slowly. 'For farmers too. You saw the orchids? What we ought to do is transplant them to some place where they won't come to any harm.'

'What orchids?' Jean looked bewildered

'Wild ones on Gowk.' He was offhand, turning to Miss Pink. 'I can give you a lift. I'm going down the dale.'

'I'll walk, thank you. I'm staying in Borascal.'

'This is Miss Pink,' Jean said. 'She's at Ashgill.'

'Oh. Brilliant.' Miss Pink frowned. 'Nice time of year,' he added vaguely. 'It's a great centre for walking. You coming, Jeannie?'

He started diagonally up the slope. His wife threw a quick glance at Miss Pink, raised a hand and followed at the same speed but keeping a few paces in the rear.

Miss Pink dawdled along the level, glancing into the quarry as more walls and chasms were revealed, thinking that it couldn't have been exhaustively searched, there hadn't been enough time—but then there was that wall. Phoebe would never have climbed it.

Actually the wall was breached in a second place, a third if one included the watergate at the top. A bird's-eye view of the quarry would show a long oval comprising the lower reaches of the beck and one or two feeder streams. The base of the oval was on the floor of the dale where there was a turning circle and the end of a tarred road, narrow and weed-grown now that the quarry was no longer in operation. The Gowk path came down to the turning circle but Miss Pink's interest was in the main access to the quarry, marked by another padlocked gate and another Danger notice. The curious thing was that here there was a stile in the wall: a stone step-stile formed by projecting slabs of rock. So there was an acceptable way into the quarry, but why had the owners placed a Danger notice in this place? Presumably to cover themselves in the event of an accident.

She climbed to the top of the stile and studied a patch of mud on the far side. It was unmarked. No one had entered the quarry at this point since the rain of several days ago.

*   *   *

'I'll drop you at home,' Blamire said. 'And you can find me some dry socks. I'll meet you at the Lamb.'

Jean's nostrils flared. 'What will you be doing?'

'I have to go to Lambert's. Tomorrow I'm going to need everyone I can get if we don't find her today.'

'Make sure you leave him a written message then. Isa's bound to forget. That woman's as thick as two planks. And why didn't you take Walter today?'

'Because I thought we'd find her soon enough. I can't do with novices on a search; they're a liability.'

'So why take him tomorrow?'

'For God's sake, woman! Don't I have enough on my plate without you nagging at me all the time?'

'Marty!'

'I'm sorry, I'm sorry.' He thrust out a hand to her as the Land Rover jolted down the stony track. 'Look,' he said softly, 'I've got a missing woman to find and I haven't a fucking idea where she went, and down there'— nodding ahead to the dale—'the media's waiting for me. How long will they hold me up?'

'I'll give Isa the message—'

'It's quicker for me to see her. You get me some dry socks, we'll meet at the Lamb, right?'

It was an order.

CHAPTER THREE

In the Fat Lamb Dorcas Honeyman lined up
three measures of Famous Grouse on the bar
and thought that the profits from this day were
well worth the pain of her aching feet. There'd
be a brief respite shortly because she'd insisted
that Ralph close the bar at three o'clock but
they'd be open again at six. She'd need to
bring Misella in to help. If the search hadn't
been successful they'd do a roaring trade this
evening and tomorrow. She rang up the sale,
proffered change, and two pounds were left on
the bar. She pocketed the coins without
expression; there were advantages to being
seventy years old, dumpy and dull and wearing
an apron; strangers took her for the help
rather than the licensee's mother.

The low-ceilinged bar was crowded with
reporters and tourists. 'It's three o'clock,'
Dorcas told Ralph. He knew if he didn't call
time she would.

'They'll be away now,' he assured her.
'Martin's come down. I saw him turn up t'lane.
You missed un.' Ralph grinned. It wasn't often
his mother missed anything.

'Tell them he's back.' She indicated the
customers. 'They'll be after un like flies on

meat.'

'No need. Here he comes now.' He raised his voice. 'Here's Blamire,' he told the nearest group. 'Maybe they've found the lady.'

Eyes switched to the windows and the open door. The bar emptied of reporters, the tourists longing to follow but most restrained by their wives. 'Three o'clock,' Dorcas announced in a no-nonsense voice. 'Last orders, please.'

As if discharged the remaining customers drank up and crowded outside to hover on the fringe of the group clustered about the Rescue Land Rover.

'Lock the door,' Dorcas ordered, drawing herself a brandy.

Ralph turned the key softly, uncapped a bottle of German beer and lumbered after his mother, ignoring the glasses cluttering the bar.

They sat at the big scrubbed table in the kitchen, mother and son easing their feet, Dorcas feeling her age, Ralph his weight. He was the wrong side of fifty and although his legs were like tree trunks they were out of all proportion to the amount of flesh that they had to support. He didn't look a healthy man: balding, with small eyes above plump cheeks, a tight mouth: it was as if the features were being compressed by increasing deposits of fat.

Dorcas sipped her Martell thoughtfully. 'She wasn't daft,' she said.

Ralph blinked. 'Who?'

'Phoebe o' course. Who else?'

'She were gey careless.'

'How d'you make that out?'

'She'd tackle anyone: Swinburn for not burying sheep, Dwayne Paxton for cheating on—'

'For taking cash just.'

'So? You paid, didn't you? And she laid into Sherrel for being on benefit.'

'Benefit's legal—mostly. What Phoebe took exception to was Sherrel having all them kids.'

'Having kids is illegal?'

'And who's t'father of this on?'

'Eh? Sherrel? Again?'

Dorcas stared at him. He swallowed and fidgeted. 'Could be anyone,' he muttered.

'And that's just as well.' The tone was loaded.

'What's Sherrel got to do with Phoebe going missing?'

'It was you who said she was careless.'

'Who? Phoebe or Sherrel?'

Dorcas's dry brown cheeks cracked in a reptilian grin. 'Both of 'em, but what I meant was Phoebe put folks' backs up. Snake in the grass. Plenty'll be glad to see t'back of that one.'

*   *   *

Isa Lambert didn't hear her husband come home but it would have made no difference if she had. She was sprawled on the sofa in their living room watching *Neighbours* and drinking Cranberry Pressé. With her long blonde hair sleeked to her scalp, framing high cheekbones and a swan neck, with the big grey eyes and sulky mouth, she had the look of a bored adolescent, which was near enough the truth. Married for only two years to a local government employee ten years her senior, now she watched happy people frolicking in a pool in Australia and thought she would go mad with despair, stuck with Walter and his cranky sister in a dead-end dale where nothing ever happened. Well, nothing unless you made it happen yourself.

He came in the door then, carrying his briefcase and a stack of files. Dropping them on the table he came over and kissed the top of her head.

'All right, love? You smell nice.'

She stood up slowly. 'This heat's killing me. We ought to have a pool.'

She drifted to the kitchen to find something for his tea. He had a cooked meal in town at lunch time, and for that she was devoutly thankful. She liked the idea of dinner at night but not the chore of preparing it.

Walter watched her dithering at the fridge, mystified by her boredom, by his own inability to alleviate it. Although dales born and bred, he didn't look it: pale-faced, pale-eyed, with bloodless lips and lank hair poorly cut, he was tall but gangling with large hands and feet. He was a homely fellow, a keen gardener but otherwise with a leaning towards desk work rather than physical activity.

'Where's Gemma?' he asked from the kitchen doorway.

'She didn't tell me where she was going.' A tea bag fell on the floor. Isa retrieved it and dropped it in a mug.

'I wish she would tell you. She's only fifteen.'

'She can't come to much harm in the village.'

'Dwayne Paxton is twenty-one,' he said heavily. 'And he's the last person to be bothered that she's under age.'

'You're saying I should speak to her?'

'She won't take it from me, Isa. You're close to her age—'

'She's your sister—'

'Half-sister—'

'It's the same thing. All right then, speak to Dwayne.' She was suddenly casual, thinking that he'd never dare approach a hunk like Dwayne Paxton, then wondering if he might at that. He could sometimes be quite stern. 'You could threaten him,' she suggested. 'You work for the Council, tell him what the penalties are for sex with minors.'

'Oh no!' He was aghast. 'You don't think they're having—that they have a relationship!'

'Come on, Walter! You think they sit in his

37

truck and talk about the telly? It was you said she was under age. Under age for what? You know what's going on; you're blocking it out.'

'I only heard last week. I wouldn't have known then if you hadn't told me. And all you said was they'd been seen together in his Land Rover.'

'That was Phoebe Metcalf; she told me.' She grinned slyly. 'Now there's one who wouldn't be bothered about speaking to Dwayne—'

'Good Lord! Phoebe! I'd forgotten—Is there any news?'

'If they don't find her before dark they're going to need as many men as they can get tomorrow.'

He frowned, pondering. 'I've got a meeting in Carlisle in the morning. In any case I can't keep up with the team, Martin knows that.'

'That's what I told them—that you had a meeting tomorrow.'

He wandered out to the garden. On this warm evening the cottage walls were giving up their stored heat of the day. There was no breeze, he could hear Sherrel's kids playing in the beck. Too young for the beck, he thought—and try telling Sherrel that, it would be as effective as telling Gemma she was too young for boys—for men, rather. And there was Phoebe lost on the fells; young and old, suddenly everyone in Borascal seemed to be at risk. Behind him Isa shouted that his tea was ready.

It was pizza. He eyed the hot pepperoni and melting cheese without enthusiasm. Her expression hardened.

'I did wrong. Again.'

'It's just that, on a warm day . . . A salad might have been a better idea.'

'Right!' She snatched up the pizza, stalked to the kitchen and the lid of the pedal bin crashed back against the wall. He smothered a sigh, crossed to the ornate bread cupboard that took up one side of the living room and reached for the bottle of Glenlivet. At the sink, adding a few drops of water to his modest measure of malt, he saw that she was trying to slice a tomato with a blunt knife. There were wilted lettuce leaves on a plate, obviously unwashed. He went back to the bread cupboard and topped up his drink, trusting that a stiff measure would neutralize the bacteria in unwashed lettuce. And suddenly, unbidden and unwelcome, the memory of a recent television drama surfaced: the wife adding aconite to horseradish sauce to accompany the beef for her husband's dinner. He shook his head; he was watching the wrong kind of television.

'When did the team come down?' he asked as she slammed a plate on the table.

'I don't know. Did they?'

'Well, how did they tell you I might be needed?'

'They've got mobiles!' There was a pause. 'Actually Martin called.'

'Called here? Then why did he come down?'

'I don't know how Mountain Rescue works! All I know is he came here and said they needed more people tomorrow. You don't have to go if you can't keep up.'

'Martin said that!'

'No—well—I mean, it didn't sound all that urgent.' She knew she had gone too far.

He studied her, savouring the whisky, conscious of the brilliance of the evening, the heady scent of wisteria, all heightened perceptions . . . 'He didn't come for that,' he said.

She swallowed. 'So what did he come for?'

He thought how pretty she was when she showed emotion, even fear. He sighed. 'It doesn't matter.'

'Doesn't matter?' she shrilled. 'What are you insinuating?'

'I'm not insinuating anything. I'm wondering what brought him down from the hill. Where's the rest of the team?'

She was confused. 'Still out,' she said weakly. 'He left them on Blaze Fell.' Her tone quickened: 'He had to drive the Land Rover round to meet them on the other side.'

She eyed him hopefully. 'That's why he came down. He called here just as an afterthought—to tell me you were needed.'

He smiled, not unkindly. 'You're not an afterthought, love. Not to anyone.'

*   *   *

The property called Blind Keld had been bought by incomers who planned to use the house as a holiday home and to let the land for grazing. Local firms were doing the renovating and Dwayne Paxton was employed on the less specialized work. At the moment he was rebuilding the garden wall; that was when Gemma didn't arrive and they retired to the master bedroom, a bare place smelling of plaster and new wood, empty except for Dwayne's sleeping bag on the parquet floor.

At twenty-one the local Don Juan had the kind of chiselled features and cool green eyes that could have been used to sell any upmarket product and, as if that weren't enough, he had the body of a young Stallone but, alas, the intelligence of an ape, and Gemma was growing tired of him. This evening at Blind Keld she sat up, ran her fingers through her hair and contemplated the valley, or as much of it as she could see through the fancy iron railings outside the french windows. She had violet eyes, hair like blonde chrysanthemum petals, and purple nails. She wore a necklace of moonstones and lapis lazuli and nothing else.

'You got a back like a boy,' he said lazily,

propped on one elbow on the sleeping bag.

Her mind was elsewhere. 'She's not going to stay much longer.'

'Who?'

'Isa. She hates him.' After a moment she added, 'Hates me too.'

'Why'd she marry him?'

Gemma shrugged. 'Walter's got a white collar job and she'd have thought he'd have cash. Her brothers are lorry drivers.'

'What's wrong with that?'

'Nothing's wrong with it, but our house is a step up from a back street in Carlisle.'

'Nothing happens here though. She wants to party, right?'

'Of course she does, she's a townie. And Walter's not what you'd call sexy. I can't imagine anyone wanting to go to bed with him.'

'Where's she getting it then?'

'Who knows? You maybe?'

'Don't be daft, woman. I've got you.'

'Dream on, Dwayne Paxton; I'm my own woman, not yours, nor anyone else's. I'm hungry, I'm going home.'

She stood up, pulling on her jeans and T-shirt, not in any particular hurry, merely finished with him for this evening, and needing to eat.

CHAPTER FOUR

'Bless you,' Eleanor exclaimed as Miss Pink poured the whisky. 'I'm dead on my feet. By three o'clock I had to start baking again and they were eating the scones straight out of the oven. By six there was only tea but by then everyone left because the Lamb was open.'

They were in Jollybeard's kitchen, pint mugs of tea before them and an almost empty bottle of The Macallan. A thrush was singing full throttle in the garden, watched intently from the windowsill by Cooper, the marmalade cat.

'How did you manage with only one waitress?' Miss Pink asked.

'Don't ask. Sherrel was sick and her mother came. I don't make a habit of employing Misella but today was exceptional. Anyway the press and the tourists were too excited to notice who was waiting on them.'

'Something wrong with her?'

Eleanor looked uncomfortable. 'Not really. It's just that she's not exactly tearoom material. Doesn't change to come up here and she smells of babies—and—well, they're—they were travelling people, you know?'

'Travelling—?'

'Gypsy types. Look, I'm not prejudiced; I employ Sherrel, for heaven's sake, but

43

Misella—I mean—handling food and so on
. . .' She snatched at her whisky and drank
rather than sipped.

'This must be the family in the cottage on
the beck,' Miss Pink observed. 'I can hear
children playing down there. How did they
come to settle in Borascal?'

Eleanor got up to move the kettle off the
hotplate. With her back to the visitor she
started to fidget with a tea towel. She turned
and said quickly, 'With all those children it was
better to settle. They do that: the travellers.
The children can go to school.' There was an
air of defiance about her.

'And the father continues to travel,' Miss
Pink said politely.

'There's no father.' Eleanor's shoulders
dropped. 'Different fathers,' she added, 'which
makes it worse. They survive on benefit.'

'You contribute. The mother—grandmother—would have done well for tips today.'

'It wouldn't make up for the weeks of lost
custom—' Eleanor stopped suddenly.

'I know about the salmonella.' Miss Pink
was full of sympathy. 'That was a shocking
thing to happen. Have you any idea who was
responsible?'

Eleanor's face crumpled. 'No one. I've gone
over and over it in my mind. Personally I think
it was a joke.'

'It wasn't funny.' Miss Pink thought about it.
'Perhaps you're right. There's a certain kind of

44

twisted mind that derives amusement from inflicting cruelty. Perhaps he—or she—would get relief that way. Relief from what? Unbearable pressure? It could be.'

'That doesn't sound like anyone in Borascal. We're a pretty stolid lot.'

Miss Pink's eyebrows rose a fraction. Cooper stood up, stretched luxuriously and jumped down into the garden.

'He's gone to see if she's come home.' Eleanor looked forlorn. 'And there's still no sign of her anywhere.'

'If mountaineers refuse to stop going on the hill, at some point this is bound to happen.'

'But there's nothing wrong with her! Well, apart from her eyes and a touch of arthritis, but we all—'

'What about her eyes?'

'She has cataracts. She wears those reactive glasses but she can see perfectly well. She still drives.'

Miss Pink was thoughtful. 'Even then,' she murmured, 'and with stiff joints, even if she had fallen, they'd have found her. On the other hand I'm sure they didn't have time to search properly. Suppose there had been a rock fall?'

'Melinda! There are no cliffs around here. And she didn't go into the central fells because she had to be back to feed Cooper. I tell you there are no cliffs except in that gully above Closewater, and you said they were searching

45

there.'

'There are cliffs in the quarry.'

'But you said the team went there too. Anyway, why should she go in the quarry?'

'To look for a rare flower, or a fern . . . suppose she'd seen a peregrine's nest? She had a camera because she was going to photograph—Eleanor, the orchids are finished; vehicles have crushed them into the peat. They'll never recover.'

'Oh, that's a disaster! Can't any of them be saved?'

'One or two perhaps. Blamire suggested they might be transplanted to a safe site.'

'It's an idea but I doubt that they'd take. That track has become far too popular for off-road vehicles. It should be banned to all traffic; even horses can damage fragile ecosystems. Yes, we should try to save the remaining orchids. And you met Martin; he's a good chap, something of a local hero.' She was beaming.

'So his wife gave me to understand. Role models.' In the face of the other's surprise Miss Pink elaborated: 'For the local youth. One rescuer put it to me that becoming a member of a rescue team is an alternative to joining a gang. Glamorous too, and by the time new recruits discover that bringing a casualty down on a stormy winter's night is sheer hard labour they're caught up in the camaraderie. Not so different from a gang actually. And, of

46

course, the team leader is a god. Blamire's wife seems to think so. A very tough girl, I imagine.'

Eleanor nodded. 'She adores him. They make a fine couple, don't you think? It's amusing in these times to find a powerful woman: the epitome of a feminist, you'd say, in thrall to her man.'

Miss Pink's jaw dropped. 'In thrall?'

Eleanor blushed. ' "La belle dame sans merci"? "Has me in thrall"?'

'You have it the wrong way round; it's Jean Blamire who's in thrall, not her husband.'

'No matter. It's the "thrall" bit I like. What does it mean?'

'Shackled.'

A faint rumble seemed to permeate the thick walls. 'Plane?' Eleanor hazarded.

'Thunder. It was too hot this afternoon, you could feel something brewing. It's only a summer storm: soon over.' But Miss Pink was thinking that if Phoebe were alive and injured, a drenching could prove the last straw.

'I do wish Misella wouldn't let the little ones play in the beck,' Eleanor said. 'The water rises too quickly in a storm.'

'It's quite high at the moment. I had to wade the stream above the quarry. There's a drowned sheep plastered against the watergate. Where does Borascal get its water?'

'Not that side, fortunately. There's a reservoir across the dale that supplies our water. Jacob grazes the ground above the quarry. He'll have to move that sheep; it's disgusting, actually *in* the beck, you say? Phoebe will go mad. It's one of her *bêtes noires*: Jacob leaving sheep out to rot. It's all right on the tops where the eagles can get at them but in water? Never.'

'Mabel said something about her husband having confrontations with Phoebe.'

'Oh yes. Where most of us would write to the Council about abuses, even make anonymous phone calls, Phoebe wades straight in: unburied animals, drums of sheep dip in his tip—I tell you, if Martin Blamire's the local hero, Phoebe's our resident fury: goes marching in like a dragon breathing fire. She's afraid of no one.'

'And of nothing?' Miss Pink muttered. Their eyes met across the table. 'Is she a keen photographer?'

'Why? She's a very good one. Come, I'll show you.'

Miss Pink followed her into the tearoom where subtle Lakeland watercolours were foils to one black and white print. The viewer looked down through the shadowed walls of a chasm to the sunlit floor of a dale.

'That's the quarry!' Miss Pink exclaimed. 'I love the contrast in the lighting.'

'I said she's good.'

Miss Pink continued to stare at the print. 'I'm going up there.'

48

'But they searched—'

'They didn't have the time to make a proper job of it. And look at that'—indicating the picture—'good photographers are always going back to sensational subjects. With the mist evaporating yesterday afternoon the lighting effects would have been thrilling. I think she could have gone into the quarry.'

'Well, maybe, but you can't go up there on your own, and I can't come with you tomorrow; we'll be crowded out as the word spreads.'

'I'll be careful. I'm not about to do any climbing—and you'll know where I've gone.' She was walking to the door as she spoke and suddenly she pulled up short. 'Damn! Look at that!'

Great cumulus clouds were boiling up the sky, showing over the tops of the sycamores, expanding as they watched. Thunder muttered among the western fells. Eleanor inhaled sharply.

'Oh, poor Phoebe! This could finish her. Is there nothing we can do?'

'We can go to the quarry. Now.'

*   *   *

They were forestalled. When they reached the turning circle at the head of the dale they found two Mountain Rescue vehicles and a police car parked there. As they stood beside

49

Miss Pink's Peugeot, sniffing the stagnant air, speculating on which way the searchers had gone, men approached the quarry gate from the far side, walking without haste. Obviously they had found nothing. They were a second team that had been called in to assist the local men. Not unkindly, having sized up Miss Pink's workmanlike gear, they said that they had searched the quarry meticulously; definitely Phoebe wasn't there. The consensus now was that she'd gone north from Closewater.

One of the police officers was a woman wearing an anorak and trainers. Seeing Miss Pink's expression when it was suggested that a walker could deviate so far from her proposed route she mistook scepticism for concern. 'She could be in a barn,' she said reassuringly. 'If she broke her ankle, say, she might have taken shelter and be waiting for rescue.'

Eleanor stirred, started to protest and stopped. Miss Pink tried to visualize a feisty little mountaineer in a barn with an injured ankle waiting for rescue.

'Nothing more we can do tonight,' the team leader said. 'Blamire's covered the far side of Blaze and the eastern fells. Tomorrow we'll concentrate on the ground north of Closewater.'

'She'd have crawled down!' Eleanor exclaimed as they settled themselves in the Peugeot for the return. 'No way would she have holed up in a barn. And there aren't any barns between here and Gowk. And she didn't go into the central fells, she had to be back at six for Cooper.'

* * *

The storm struck at ten o'clock. The wind came first, roaring up the dale like an approaching train, lashing the trees and beating down tall garden plants, stakes and all. The air was full of flying leaves and twigs. Lightning slashed the gloom and in Phoebe's woodshed Cooper's nerve broke and he made a dash for the nearest house, Ashgill, where Miss Pink dried him with a towel, crooning reassurance, and allowed him to sleep on her bed.

The morning was a sweet contrast: noisy with birds—those that weren't more concerned with grooming and warming their backs in the sun; trees dripped like rain but already the lawns were steaming, people waiting a while before going out to salvage what they could of beaten lupins and columbine. Down in the bottom the Rutting Beck rushed between its banks, coloured amber from the peat.

At Sunder Misella tied a clean apron over her rusty black frock and made for the door. 'And don't you let none of 'em near that water,' she flung at Sherrel who was feeding

51

the baby. 'Not Bobby neither. Send him up to Sleylands where he can't come to no harm.'

Curled on the sofa, his mouth full of peanut butter sandwich, Bobby nodded quick agreement without taking his eyes off the television screen. But unlike his siblings he wasn't watching Kilroy, he was avoiding eye contact with his grandmother. Bobby was dyslexic but as if to compensate he had a vivid imagination. He knew that if he were to meet Misella's eye she'd see that he was thinking that it was market day and Jacob would be in town. Giving her time to get out of sight, and waiting until his mother had gone into the kitchen, he slipped out of the door and through the front gate, closing it silently behind him.

The lane was empty, gleaming with long puddles and stretches of silt marked only by a squirrel's prints and Misella's shoes. Halfway to the road there was a gap low in the hedge; it had been made by a badger and enlarged by Bobby and it was one of his private runs. He dropped down, nimble as a weasel, and squeezed through to the bank of the beck. He stopped, his eyes alight.

Misella wasn't being over-cautious when she stressed the dangers of high water but Bobby was one of those rare children: traveller's child, country boy; who, if not old enough to think laterally, had an animal's instinctive fear of elemental power. So his initial delight in the flood was followed by boredom and he wandered a short distance upstream scowling, trying to think what options were left if playing in the beck was impossible, and there was no one at Sleylands. He didn't count Mabel.

The water was going down but slowly; it had been high overnight. He kicked through the litter of dead rushes that marked the limit of the flood, looking for treasures in a desultory fashion and finding nothing, but then he was on the outside of a bend. On the opposite side the bank was higher, undercut, and there was a bay and a heap of wrack that looked promising.

He didn't consider trying to cross at this point; he ran down the near bank following a vestigial trail—a quick glance round as he came to the footbridge below the Fat Lamb— and he was across and trotting up the far bank. Now he was on a proper footpath and saw that there was someone ahead, the mud marked by a cleated boot.

He came to the bay and slithered down the broken bank. His face fell as he surveyed the pile of plant debris which he saw now was caught about a plastic feed sack. Jacob threw rubbish in the beck when he didn't tip in the woods. Bobby kicked the pile apart and, finding nothing more than a broken styrofoam beaker, he threw the empty sack in the water and turned to climb the bank. A pale object caught his eye: the brim of a cap.

It was soaked of course but, turning it in his hands, he was enthralled. Even dark and wet he could see that it wasn't old: a blue denim cap with a pale brim—different from the cheap caps his mates wore. The picture (as he thought of it) was extraordinary, even to an eight-year-old. There were mountains and little trees and a big bird; there was a bear and a wolf: all minuscule but distinct. There were some letters too but he ignored those, he couldn't read. Under the pale brim there was the other kind of writing (he could recognize a difference between letters and figures) and this had a vaguely familiar look to it . . .

'Bobby Lee?' a voice said.

He whipped the cap behind his back and gaped at a large old lady on top of the bank. He nodded dumbly. How long had she been watching? Had she seen him throw the sack in the beck? That was littering, they said so at school.

'I am Miss Pink,' she announced chattily. 'You're from Sunder. What have you got there?'

'Me 'at.' He gulped. 'I dropped un in t'beck.' Mouth pursed in defiance he slammed it on his head, the wrong way round.

'No school?' Miss Pink asked.

'It's half-term, miss.' He could have kicked himself, thinking she was a teacher. She couldn't be; a teacher would have known it was half-term.

She nodded. 'Of course. You were driving Mr Swinburn's tractor yesterday.'

'Not driving.' He was quick. 'Just sitting on it like.' His confidence returning, he added loftily, 'I help out when un needs an extra hand.'

Miss Pink didn't pursue the matter of the tractor. She frowned at the beck. 'Where did you cross?'

He gestured downstream. 'There's a bridge.'

'That's right.' She regarded him thoughtfully. Too thoughtfully. She was wondering what he was doing on this side of the beck.

He shifted his feet. 'There's me mam! I gotta go now.'

He clawed his way up the bank trying to keep as much distance as possible between them, and set off down the path—too fast—slipping a little in his trainers. She followed slowly. Her hearing was good and she knew that no one had called him. What was making him so nervous? Was it that reference to driving the tractor, or was it that he shouldn't have been playing on this side of the beck? Or was it merely because he'd dropped his good hat in the water?

*　　　*　　　*

The plastic feed sack floated down the Rutting Beck provoking rage in Tom

Howe, resignation in his wife. Ardent conservationists, the Howes carried bin bags and collected litter on their walks. Tom, thin and volatile, whose tendency to ulcers had prompted early retirement from the violence of inner-city classrooms, was feeling particularly frustrated. They hadn't long moved into their cottage below Borascal and had planned to watch kingfishers this morning, but the storm had put paid to that. No bird could feed in this opaque water, even the dippers were sitting tight until it cleared. Then the feed sack came by and Tom erupted.

'It doesn't have to be Jacob,' Patsy said comfortably; she had a soft spot for Mabel and her free range eggs. 'They all throw rubbish in the beck,' she went on—which wasn't true but it was second nature to remain calm in the face of her husband's tirades, so bad for his stomach. 'Is that a buzzard?' she asked quickly, aiming for distraction.

'Sounds like one.' He was grudging. Now that they were retired and looked upon themselves as genuine country folk instead of city types who owned a holiday cottage, they were taking up Nature seriously. He couldn't ignore a buzzard.

'There it goes,' Patsy whispered as a large shape crossed the line of the beck, oddly sinister glimpsed through the leaf canopy.

Downstream from Borascal the water ran through straggling woodland: alders on the

56

banks, ashes and oaks on drained slopes above. The alders had been deep in the water and when the level dropped, all the scourings of the dale were left tangled in low branches: mats of dead vegetation, old posts and planks, more plastic.

'He's landed,' Patsy said, nudging Tom's arm. 'There should be a nest. They'll be feeding young, won't they?' A motherly soul, she treated him as she'd treated the children, and it worked.

'It's still calling.' He transferred his attention from the storm debris to the sky. A shape glided clean of the foliage. 'That's no buzzard!' His voice rose. 'Look, see its tail? It's forked.'

'It's the kite!' Patsy gasped. Some distraction this.

'Oh, my God!' His eyes were shining. She hesitated, blinking, biting her lip. Should she try to put the brake on? But this was pleasure, not a negative emotion. In any event, he was rushing along the bank.

'You're making too much noise!' She tried to call softly, he was going to drive the birds away.

He did. One took off, then the other, but at this point the trees on the opposite bank had been felled. A field of oats came right to the beck and the watchers had a clear view of two birds like large buzzards but with the unmistakable cleft tail. They floated across the oats to land on a dead elm. Two pairs of binoculars rose simultaneously.

After a while Patsy said, 'They're *waiting*. They have to be nesting here. They want to come back.' He said nothing. She tried again. 'The young birds will be getting cold.'

'Rubbish. It's the end of May. They'll be fully feathered.'

Patsy started to stroll upstream, trying to remember where kites nested: rock faces or trees?

A crow flapped across the beck cawing angrily. Crows' nests, that was it; big raptors used unoccupied crows' nests. So this crow was trying to regain its old nest? Or the kites wanted to raise a second brood and they were after an occupied crows' nest? There was indeed something big in an alder ahead but it was too low for a nest; it could have been around high water mark last night. Which was how debris came to be snagged there—and that explained the kites and a carrion crow: all scavengers. A drowned sheep hung in the branches, hindquarters dangling, something large but curiously familiar at the end of the legs.

Fascinated, mesmerized by such a common object in so alien a position, too disorientated to call to Tom, she advanced step by cautious step and stopped, quite close, close enough for her brain finally to name the object on the hoofs that her eyes refused to identify—or wouldn't. It was a boot.

No sheep. Coldly and carefully she traced the upward line of a gaitered leg, then came a litter of dead rushes but a shape showing through, little larger than a sheep. No head was visible or at least she couldn't make one out, and thinking that there might not be one, she retreated thoughtfully, wondering how she was going to distract Tom in this situation.

CHAPTER FIVE

At eleven thirty Isa Lambert was in the Lamb, Honeyman having trawled the village in an effort to find someone, anyone, to help out in view of the expected influx of customers on the second day of the search. Sure enough, half an hour after opening the bar was overflowing, people not only sitting outside at the tables but lining the wall on the far side of the road. Drifting across the tarmac they gave the scene the air of a French *place* rather than a thoroughfare. Honeyman was beaming and even Dorcas looked smug. As for Isa, carefully groomed but becomingly flushed, wearing a blue frock with bootlace straps and gold sandals, she pranced between tables and the bar, happily aware of speculative glances and the way the frock clung to her skin in the heat. Absorbed in the bustle of a mainly masculine atmosphere she ignored the women and didn't even notice that one was so old she couldn't possibly be a reporter despite the fact that she was sitting with three of them.

Miss Pink, who had no aversion to sharing a picnic table, sipped her vermouth on the rocks and listened to the gossip. This was an idle moment but unlooked for. She could formulate no plan of action. With so many young fit searchers on the hill she would be redundant; on the other hand to walk, as she had done earlier this morning, seemed heartless in the circumstances. Like the reporters she was waiting for something to happen.

More holidaymakers arrived: bursting with the news that there were divers in the beck not a mile below the village. The Lamb emptied, leaving only Miss Pink, the Honeymans, Isa and the new arrivals: two smart young fellows who went in the bar. Miss Pink drifted after them.

'But why divers?' Isa was asking.

'Apparently the body's caught up,' one of the strangers told her with relish.

'She'll have been washed down in t'flood,' Dorcas said, as if it was an everyday occurrence.

Isa shook her head in disbelief. 'How could she?'

'You know her?' Miss Pink asked. The girl turned blank eyes on her. 'Phoebe Metcalf?'

Miss Pink's tone was soft, too soft; the girl's eyes rolled and she crumpled, one of the young men having just time enough to catch her head before it struck the stone floor.

'Now look what you done,' Honeyman told Miss Pink, evidently amused.

'Put her on t'settle,' Dorcas ordered, emerging from the bar to push Isa's head to her knees.

The girl recovered quickly but she stared blankly through rather than at them, pushing away the brandy offered by Honeyman. After a while she said weakly, 'I never knew anyone who died before.'

'I have to go and tell Miss Salkeld,' Miss Pink said.

'You know her too?' Honeyman was astonished.

'Aren't you a reporter?' Isa said. 'No, of course not.'

'I'm staying at Ashgill.' Miss Pink frowned. 'Why do you assume it's Phoebe? We don't know that it's her.'

'No one else is missing,' Dorcas said. 'We'll know soon enough.'

After a while a few people drifted back. The body hadn't been identified but it was that of a little woman, very old, dressed like a walker, except that she'd lost a boot. No one had any doubt that it was Phoebe.

*   *   *

61

Mabel Swinburn was washing eggs when the newsflash came through on the local radio: not that it was Phoebe but that the search was being called off, the body of en elderly woman having been found drowned in a flooded beck. Mabel's hands were still as she stared through the open window to the Closewater track where Phoebe had passed two days ago and waved to Jacob but didn't speak. And Jacob and young Bobby had gone off in the opposite direction . . .

Her son-in-law's old van appeared in the yard gateway and rattled over the cobbles. Time they had a decent car, she thought distractedly as her daughter emerged, waved, and strode to the back door.

'You heard t'news?' Mabel was tense.

'No. What?'

'Phoebe. They found her in t'beck.'

'Oh, Mum! Drowned, you mean? That's horrible. How did it happen? That poor little lady. You'd never expect it, would you? She was so nimble.'

Mabel shrugged and picked up an egg. 'It would have been nice if one of us could have said goodbye.'

Jean gaped. 'Well—yes, but she wasn't a relative. You mean she died all alone.' There was a momentary silence. 'Dad saw her. Didn't she say *anything*—call out to him?'

Mabel was studying the egg as if it had been

laid by something alien. 'Him and Bobby went in the wrong direction,' she said dreamily, seeing the image in her mind. 'She waved just.'

'Bobby was up here on Sunday?'

Her mother looked up, frowning. 'No—yesterday.' She gasped. 'I'm going senile. It was Sunday Phoebe went by, of course. It were Miss Pink as called yesterday. Twice. She came up in the evening for eggs. A very gossipy lady.'

'No, Mum, you gossip. I met her. Martin has no time for her: another accident waiting to happen, he says.'

Mabel wasn't listening. 'I wonder if your dad knows. Someone at market must have picked it up.'

*　　　*　　　*

Jacob, who had nothing to sell today and had come to town merely to have a pint and a crack with his cronies from other dales, was considering a pen of Swaledales when someone told him the missing woman had been found in the Rutting Beck.

'You were one of t'last to see her, weren't you?' observed Ben Thornthwaite who grazed land north of Closewater.

'On Borascal side,' Jacob grunted. 'More folk coulda seen her your way.' He thought about that. 'Depends on where she fell in,' he added.

63

'Her had to go in your side if her's in Rutting Beck,' Ben's lad put in aggressively; as if his father had been accused of something. Young Sammy was like that; Jacob thought the hostility must be in order to counter the effect of the gold ear-rings and the long hair.

'It don't make no odds,' Jacob said. 'Wherever she went in she were too old to be on t'fell. Eighty! Asking for trouble.'

'She got it.' Bored, young Sammy slouched away to the Saracen's Head. His father turned with slow deliberation to the sheep. 'Poor lot here,' he said dismissively and they moved on to the next pen.

*　　　*　　　*

Martin Blamire was searching a dale north of Closewater, heading towards the central fells. The call came through at midday—to the relief of the team who had been expecting it in view of Phoebe's age, although the manner of it was somewhat surprising. However, it wasn't a rare occurrence; people might cross a beck in the morning, then there'd be a storm and a few hours later the stream would be impassable but folk still tried to wade it.

'Where did she have to cross a beck on the way down from Gowk?' someone asked.

'She went over Blaze,' a voice said firmly. 'Then she'd have to keep crossing becks on the way down as she looked for drier ground on

64

t'other side or came to side streams.'

'Storm didn't break till ten,' someone said.

They started to return to the vehicles, speculating as they went, Martin coming last with his deputy, Strickland.

'Not a bad way to go,' Stricky said. 'Hopefully she hit her head first.'

Martin was startled. 'What makes you say that?'

'So she didn't know she was drowning, man! But then the cold water might bring her round.'

'It's the way she'd want to go,' Martin said, ignoring the last words. 'These old climbers: they're all the same, determined not to die in bed. You have to admire them.'

*   *   *

'I've got to keep going,' Eleanor protested. 'If I sit still I shall think.'

Miss Pink had just made a fresh pot of tea. 'At least sit down to drink this,' she pleaded. 'Misella! Come and have some tea.'

Misella came in from the empty tearoom with a loaded tray. All the customers had left for the Lamb or the scene of the recovery operation lower down the dale. Deft and powerful, she balanced the heavy tray on the edge of the sink and unloaded the used crockery. She sat down at the table and waited expectantly for Miss Pink to pass the brandy

65

bottle. Sugar was spooned into mugs. They all knew about sugar for shock. Hot alcohol fumes filled the kitchen. Outside a woodpecker laughed crazily.

Misella said, 'The body had to go by our place.' She looked at Miss Pink. 'What time would that be?'

'You should go home to Sherrel,' Miss Pink said. 'She has to be told and it's better coming from you. Isn't that so, Miss Salkeld?'

Eleanor's face was drawn with misery. She said emptily, 'There's nothing to do here. Go home, Misella. I'll send for you when things get back to normal.' She shuddered.

'She were very old,' Misella said. 'She'd had a long life.'

'It's still a shock,' Miss Pink reminded her, staring pointedly at the woman's mug, willing her to drink up and leave.

'Shall I close the door?' Misella asked, indicating the front room. 'Mark of respect like,' and then, abruptly: 'Here, we got a customer. It's the police, mum!' It was a whispered hiss and carried a strong note of concern, even fear. Bobby, her grandson: he had been nervous too, on the beckside.

The policewoman they'd met yesterday appeared in the doorway, in uniform now, although in shirt-sleeves. Calm eyes observed them—and the brandy bottle—but there was no lack of sympathy in her tone.

'Good afternoon, ladies'—afternoon?

66

thought Miss Pink, what happened to the morning?—'I think you've heard the bad news.'

Misella had stood up; the others remained seated, Eleanor withdrawn in the face of this unwonted interruption, Miss Pink resigned. 'Is it Phoebe?' she asked.

'That's what I've come about.' The woman looked at the teapot suggestively.

Eleanor made no move. 'Sit down,' Miss Pink ordered. 'Misella, get the officer a mug and then . . .' She left it hanging.

'You'll be Miss Salkeld,' the woman said pleasantly.

'No, I'm Melinda Pink. This is Miss Salkeld. We've all had a nasty shock.'

The hint worked. 'I'm sorry!' Eleanor exclaimed, coming to life. 'What must you be thinking of me? Thank you, Misella'—as the woman poured tea for the visitor. 'Please help yourself to brandy if you're allowed . . .'

'I'm Sergeant Winder, from Bailrigg.' She smiled and declined the brandy. Behind her back Misella slipped out of the kitchen, quiet despite her size, Miss Pink observing her departure without expression.

'We need identification,' Winder said. 'Are there relatives, d'you know?'

Eleanor was bewildered. 'Cousins,' she ventured. 'She came from East Anglia originally: Norwich way. She was an only child so there'd be no nieces or nephews, and

67

cousins could be old; probably there are only distant ones left.'

'Then'—the sergeant looked from her to Miss Pink and back—'would you be willing . . . one of you?'

'I never met her,' Miss Pink admitted. 'I'm on holiday here. I only arrived on Saturday.' She frowned fiercely, trying to think who else might have known Phoebe well enough . . .

'I'll do it,' Eleanor said. 'Someone has to, and there's no one else.'

'I'll drive you.' Miss Pink was firm.

'I have a car outside.' Winder smiled, equally firm.

'We'll take my car.' Miss Pink stood up. 'We have things to do.'

The sergeant wondered what this formidable old bat had been in her working life: hospital matron, prison governor, police?

*   *   *

Miss Pink had lied; they had nothing to do in Bailrigg town other than view the body where it had been placed in the mortuary attached to the hospital. It was, of course, Phoebe; they had been prepared for that but unprepared for the cleanliness of everything: not the surroundings so much as the body which looked as if it had been carefully washed. In a sense it had been: by the beck. Phoebe looked like a shrunken wax witch.

'She *had* shrunk,' Eleanor acknowledged on the drive home. 'She said that the vertebrae impact with age. She had back trouble. She didn't rock climb any longer.'

'Poor balance?' murmured Miss Pink, her eyes on the road.

'Could be. Maybe she missed her footing as she tried to jump across the beck.'

'Which beck?'

Eleanor made no response and there was silence in the car until Miss Pink, seeking a fresh topic, said with casual amusement, 'The Lee family don't hang around when Authority appears.'

Eleanor blinked as she sought to change mental gear.

'The Lee family?'

'I met Bobby by the beck this morning. He would see me as Authority no doubt. He was nervous as a wildcat. And Misella wasn't slow in leaving when the police arrived.'

'Oh, Bobby's always up to some mischief.' Eleanor shifted in her seat. 'We've all got something to hide.'

Miss Pink suppressed astonishment, then thought better of it. 'You have?' she asked in wonder.

'Not me, no. Nor you, of course. I mean, people like the Lees.'

'Meaning one-parent families. Because Bobby has no father to keep him in order.'

'Oh, Bobby has—' There was an audible

69

gasp.

'Has what?' Miss Pink asked brightly.

'He's got Misella. She keeps them all in order, including Sherrel. A matriarch, you know?'

That wasn't what she had been going to say. Bobby had—what? And what secrets did Misella the matriarch have? This wasn't the moment to push Eleanor in a direction she was loath to go. Miss Pink changed the subject again and wondered if they might take an excursion tomorrow, Eleanor wouldn't want to open the tearoom. They might visit a stately home, gardens; what would she like to do?

'Sleep,' she said. 'Get drunk and go to bed.' Apparently she could see no further than the immediate future.

And so it happened that at five o'clock, taking a last look round the kitchen, having seen her friend to bed—not drunk but exhausted—Miss Pink was alone downstairs at Jollybeard when Sergeant Winder returned with the request for a statement relating to Eleanor's knowledge of Phoebe Metcalf.

No, Miss Pink said, not inviting the woman to sit down, Miss Salkeld was deeply asleep after taking a couple of tablets; the statement would have to wait until tomorrow, there was no urgency. She ended on a subtle note of inquiry.

'Not urgency exactly,' Winder admitted. 'It's just that we'd like to know more about the deceased's state of health, who her doctor was and so on.'

Immediately Miss Pink was on the defensive, sensing ageism, defending the dead woman. 'There was nothing wrong with her health,' she said angrily, dismissing the thought of cataracts, arthritis, a bad back. 'Anyone could make a mistake in judgement when crossing a flooded stream. Why, even fit young men drown—' She stopped, aware of stridency.

'She may not have drowned,' Winder said quickly, daunted by such vehemence, seeing she'd touched a nerve.

'But she was—' Miss Pink checked and was suddenly tense. 'How *did* she die?'

Winder bit her lip and tried for damage limitation. 'We won't know until they've done the autopsy but you see, at her age she could have fallen in the beck.'

'Or fallen over when she was wading. That's obvious, but she didn't mean to . . .' Miss Pink tailed off. Mean to what? 'Why ask about her state of health? Something's been discovered— during a preliminary examination?'

'The skull is fractured.' Miss Pink's eyes widened.

Winder swallowed. 'And that's all I know. She fell—could have fallen—from a height. A stroke maybe. If so they'll find out—'

'Her arteries must have been as sound as yours.'

71

'Oh, you did know her.'

'I know what she *did.* I never met her. You're saying she died, then fell in the beck?'

Winder's eyes narrowed. 'What are *you* saying?' She hesitated, choosing her words now. 'Miss Salkeld said there was no one else who could identify her, meaning she had no friends here?' The slightest emphasis. 'You say you know what she did; you mean climbing mountains, but do you know what she did in the village: how she got on with her neighbours?'

She was a bloody-minded little termagent, Miss Pink thought, and what this woman wanted to know was: did Phoebe have any enemies? 'She kept herself to herself,' she said with the doltish air of a villager closing the door on gossip.

* * *

Gemma was with Dwayne at Blind Keld moodily watching him at work on the garden wall. A transistor played at full volume so when the newsflash interrupted the music there was no question of their missing it.

At the announcement that the body of an elderly woman had been found Dwayne froze with a large rock still in his hands. They stared at each other, their expressions identical and vulnerable.

Gemma recovered first, closing her eyes

72

slowly, opening them, cool again, studying his face. He dropped the stone with a crack.

'So?' she prompted.

'She won't trouble us no longer.'

She scowled. 'She never did trouble me. Oh!' She forced a laugh. 'You never said. Don't tell me she got on to you about me! She threatened you? Or did she try blackmail?'

'Don't talk daft.'

'What was it then? Dwayne Paxton, you've been up to something. You can tell me, 'fact, I'm the only one you can tell. Come on, you know you're going to sometime.'

He shrugged. 'It were nothing. I mean that!'—seeing her scepticism. 'Everyone does it: takes cash for a job. Who's going to bank a cheque? Leaves a trail, don't it?'

'I don't believe this. You're saying she threatened you because of some bit of income tax fraud?'

'Take off! Here's Birkett; there'll be hell to pay if he sees you.' A van turned in from the road and started up the drive.

'He's not going to sack you, I just brought you your dinner, didn't I?' All the same she slipped round the side of the house and through the buildings. She could have stayed, defying both him and his boss, but her heart wasn't in it. Phoebe had died and Dwayne was rattled, enough that she was uncertain where she might stand herself, being associated with him. She started to work her way across the

73

pastures to the village, feeling that it would be comforting to talk to someone older, someone adult. Dwayne was still wet behind the ears.

* * *

Miss Pink was working on a bed of oriental poppies, staking the least damaged, salvaging what she could after the storm, feeling guilty that she hadn't done it before but then, with Phoebe missing . . . It seemed strange to return to everyday life: staking poppies in the company of a sleepy cat. Cooper was lounging on the drystone wall that divided her property from that of the Blamires. He seemed quite contented at the moment although she guessed that he returned often to his home to see if Phoebe had come back. She wondered what would happen to that cottage. Of course there would be a will . . .

There was a sudden rush like a foot charge and Cooper was up on his toes, every hair on end and spitting like a cobra at something on the Blamires' side.

'Whisk! For God's sake!'

Jean Blamire's face appeared, looking to see whether she should be apologetic or amused. She was half-stooped, holding the collie.

Miss Pink had straightened. 'No harm done,' she said comfortably. 'Cooper looks as if he can take care of himself.'

74

'I know he can. Whisk was bluffing. He's scared stiff of Cooper.' Jean pushed back her mass of chestnut hair and looked contrite. 'You're looking after him? That's sweet of you.'

'He's been commuting since Sunday.' Miss Pink couldn't take her eyes off that hair. 'Eleanor's gone to bed, d'you see, and I've locked up at Jollybeard so he had to come here.'

'Eleanor's ill?' It was early evening, an odd time for bed.

Miss Pink realized that Jean hadn't heard of the latest developments. She said kindly, 'Someone had to identify the body; not a pleasant experience for anyone, let alone a friend.'

'How ghastly. Eleanor did that on her own?'

'No, I was with her.'

Jean shook her head in wonder. 'You weren't fazed by any of that?'

'No.' It wasn't the moment to reveal that she'd seen a lot of bodies, and many of those in a worse state than Phoebe's. One was enough on this gentle evening.

'This is ridiculous,' Jean exclaimed, 'talking over the garden wall. Why don't you come round and have a drink? I'm on my own.'

Was that reassurance or a plea? Meaning my husband can't object because he isn't here, or I'm in need of company?

Miss   Pink's   cottage   was   furnished

impeccably from Heal's but the Blamire place was in keeping with rural Cumbria. It was a mixture of old and not particularly good oak furniture, and the kind of post-war pieces that were once produced as 'utility' and which had worn badly over the decades. Seated in a shabby armchair Miss Pink accepted a glass of red wine and beamed at the huge empty fireplace with its heap of wood ash. The collie nosed at her free hand.

'Whisk isn't a rescue dog then,' she observed. 'If he was he'd be on the hill with your husband.'

'He's an idiot—Whisk, I mean. I've tried to train him but it's difficult when there are two people. Different methods.'

'The search has been called off anyway,' Miss Pink pointed out, as if that had anything to do with the dog. 'I suppose there are things to do—what's it called? Debriefing?'

'He'll be late tonight. The base is in Bailrigg and he has to sort out all the equipment so that they can be ready for the next call-out—which could come at any time, you never know. As the leader he's always on call.'

'Really. He must have a very sympathetic employer.'

'Oh no. He's self-employed.'

Miss Pink found the adulation excessive but she played along. 'He's a mountain guide?'

'Of course. But mainly he's an author. He's written a book on the south-east Lakes, and now he's doing the south-west quadrant. And he does features for newspapers and magazines and he reviews books; you name it and Martin's in there beavering away.' She drew breath, her eyes shining. 'And he has his sights set on an outdoor activity centre staffed by some of his mates in the team.'

Privately Miss Pink thought that another outdoor activity centre was as superfluous as another book on Lakeland but all she said was that premises might prove hard to find, and expensive.

Jean shook her head. 'We're lucky. My dad has to retire sometime and him and Martin have seen a way to turn things round. I mean, what with BSE and market prices there's no point in farming any longer: not hill farming anyway. You have to diversify. We've started negotiating for the Change of Use for the farm. It's no secret.' Miss Pink was looking blank. 'My dad's Jacob Swinburn,' Jean went on. 'You get eggs from my mum.'

'Ah. You mean that Sleylands would become your outdoor centre.'

Jean grinned engagingly. 'Of course there's no money—yet—but bits can be sold off: houses, barns; Dad owns a raft of property. This house is his, and Sunder, but apart from land and buildings he doesn't have a bean. However, I'm an only child.' She said it with an odd air of defiance.

'Should you be telling me this?'

'Why not? Everyone knows. No one's got any secrets in Borascal. We've all grown up together—' She stopped and her eyelids drooped. 'We soon find out about incomers!'

The words passed Miss Pink by. Sunshine caught the woman's hair so that it shone like chestnuts—like Bobby's hair in fact. And both of them were involved with Sleylands, with Jacob. When Jean said she was the only child did she mean the only legitimate one? Was Bobby her half-brother? Miss Pink pondered. No secrets in Borascal?

'You haven't told me what you do,' Jean said, which was quite startling because until now she'd conveyed the impression of a rather silly woman subservient even in her own mind to her husband, and yet here she was taking the initiative.

'I write,' Miss Pink admitted. 'Short stories mostly.'

'Really? Have you sold any?'

Wrong question. 'A few,' Miss Pink said, adding smoothly, 'I live in Cornwall and I travel. I'm fond of America.'

The other hesitated then, 'What brought you to Borascal?'

'An advertisement in *The Lady*.' Miss Pink was bland.

The collie, who had been dozing on the hearth rug, scrambled to his feet as a shadow darkened the doorway. A young girl stepped into the room: pretty, blonde, vital.

78

'Hi! There's no one about and this place is dead.'

She dropped into an armchair and bent her head to the dog's. 'How's my old Whisk? You can't go out 'cause that Cooper's patrolling the lane and he'll kill you.'

Pointedly ignored, Miss Pink waited for the introduction. Jean said indulgently, 'This is Gemma, our neighbour. Gemma, this is Miss Pink from Ashgill.'

'Hi.' She made no move to get up. 'You're Eleanor's friend. She's closed the tearoom, Jean.'

'She's not feeling too good.'

Gemma shrugged. 'Who is? Can I have some wine?'

'Certainly not. There's Coke in the fridge. She's fifteen,' she mouthed as the girl went to the kitchen. 'What have you been doing with yourself today?' she asked lightly when the visitor returned to slump in the chair again, spilling her drink. Behind the patronizing tone there was a sense of tension which Miss Pink thought had less to do with her own presence than the relationship between these two. They weren't easy with each other.

'I've been helping Dwayne build a wall at Blind Keld. I'm his mate as you might say,' Jean threw a glance at Miss Pink. 'He's my friend,' Gemma added with studied emphasis.

Jean appeared to be at a loss. Miss Pink said vaguely, 'We've all had something of a shock.'

Gemma was puzzled, then sulky. 'I didn't really know her.' She caught Jean's eye. 'It was Dwayne she laid into, not me, and it wasn't—'

'I don't think we want to—' Jean began.

'She got on everyone's wick!'

'Gemma!'

'I mean, what's it got to do with her? Interfering old bat. Dwayne said what she needed was—'

'Stop right there!' Jean was on her feet, signalling wildly to Miss Pink, making for the door. She paused. 'You can be as rude as you like in your own house but not this one—and in front of a guest! And I don't give a damn what Phoebe said to anyone; she was a neighbour and she drowned and you're a callous little—' She didn't finish for Miss Pink was crowding her out of the door and now they were in the garden making for the gate.

Jean was shaking as she lifted the latch. 'I'll walk you to your place,' she muttered. 'Oh, my God, why did I have to fly off the handle? She's an orphan—but she's impossible. This Dwayne: he's twenty-one, and look at her: no discipline at all.'

'Who does she live with?'

'Her brother. He's a wimp—well, not really, that's what Martin says; I quite like him actually, but he can't cope with Gemma. And her sister-in-law's not much older than the girl. What could Walter do: lock her in her room? What can anyone do? I suppose Phoebe told

Dwayne what happens to men who go with under-age girls. And Gemma, she flaunts it! But then of course she wouldn't be for the high jump, would she? It would be Dwayne.'

'She came here for a reason.'

'Pardon? Oh, you think I should go back, apologize?'

'She needs to talk. She could be more shocked by Phoebe's death than it appears.'

*   *   *

Walter Lambert had had a long day: a meeting in Carlisle in the morning, a sandwich bolted as he drove back to the office, and a hold-up on the motorway after an accident. As if that wasn't enough on a hot day at the end of it he was trapped in a tailback at roadworks ten miles from home, and that in close proximity to a pub. A number of cars left the queue but Walter didn't drink and drive. All the same he agonized over the thought of a pint of cold lemonade, even a can of Sprite, but the car in front was moving, the one behind hooted, and not gently; intimidated, he edged forward. The desert must be like this, but not so bad, there were no fumes in the desert. By the time he turned off the highway he was dehydrated. He put his foot down, remembered that most accidents happened close to home, the obvious hazards over, and dropped his speed. He was aware of the hot breeze, of crusted lips and a

81

dry throat. He thought of cold lager, and there was none in the house. Well, if a pint of lager on an empty stomach made him incapable he'd leave the car and walk home.

The Lamb was dark and cool; it was early and the only customers were a couple from one of the holiday cottages whom he knew by sight. They greeted him affably.

'Hard day?' Honeyman inquired, eyeing the loosened tie, uncapping a bottle of Stella Artois.

Walter nodded, pulling out his wallet, reaching for a note. He drank with inordinate relief and felt his body swell like dry earth in rain. He wondered if he'd caught a touch of the sun.

Honeyman said, 'Tell Isa I'll not be needing her tomorrow. Now the body's found the media's lost interest and we're back to normal.' He was expressionless but there was a hint of contempt in the tone.

Walter blinked. 'Isa?'

Honeyman saw that the man didn't know— but then he'd been at work all day. 'She come down and give us a hand,' he explained. 'Great help, she were; we was run off our feet—or we would have been but for her: right little waitress she is—no, wrong word, more like a hostess? Ornamental, as you might say.' Honeyman loved to stir it.

Walter was bewildered. 'She was serving behind the bar?'

'No, no. Me and Mother was here. Isa was waiting tables. We were overflowing into t'road. Traffic had to slow down. This was before they found the body o' course.'

'Waiting tables? You don't do food.'

'Do a bit with the microwave. But there were drinks to take out, empty glasses to collect afore they broke—a right party it were—tables to wipe—'

'A pot boy. She was working as a pot boy.'

'Oh no, I wouldn't call her that. Hey, you didn't pick up your change. Walter! Be sure to tell her I don't want her tomorrow—'

CHAPTER SIX

'Enemies?' Eleanor was astounded. 'The police are asking if Phoebe has enemies?' She had risen late and now it was eleven o'clock and Miss Pink had arrived for coffee, trailed by Cooper.

'The sergeant wasn't specific but the implication was obvious,' Miss Pink said. 'The skull is fractured. I've been looking at the map, reminding myself of the descent from Gowk Pass. She wouldn't have to cross any beck with enough water in it to sweep her away . . . But if she climbed Blaze and came down the dale she'd be following the Rutting Beck for a mile or so. Does that path go close to the beck?'

'You don't have to cross it, only side streams, and they're no more than trickles. I don't believe Phoebe fell in any beck.'

'So how was it she came to be found in one?'

'I think she was pushed.'

'By whom?' Miss Pink hadn't turned a hair.

'As the police implied: by an enemy.'

'In Borascal?'

'There's no lack of them.'

'Tell me about it.'

Eleanor stared through Miss Pink for a moment before starting to enumerate: 'Dwayne Paxton for one. He does odd jobs and charges VAT, which is illegal because he's not registered for VAT. Then he insists on cash payments and he doesn't give receipts so he's defrauding not only Customs and Excise but the Inland Revenue as well. Having said that, I think Dwayne could be more concerned with the possibility of Phoebe informing on him because of his friendship with Gemma.'

'Did Phoebe know about that?'

'She'd seen them together and she told me she'd spoken to him, said that he could get ten years. He's thick and he could have seen that as a threat rather than a warning.'

'Could he have retaliated?'

'You asked me who were her enemies, not who could have killed her.'

'It could be the same thing. Who are the other candidates?'

'Swinburn.' Eleanor stopped on that, thought about it and shook her head. 'Trivial?' she asked of herself. 'But no less than defrauding the taxman. And people hold grudges . . . Then grudges are exacerbated, and goodness knows, Phoebe was always catching him out. She said the chemical from his sheep dip fed into the Rutting Beck. He has a tip in a little quarry lower down the dale: old fence wire, broken machinery; oil drums, drums that have contained heaven knows what kind of toxic compounds, dead sheep—that's when he troubles to remove a carcass from the fields.'

'What about Bobby Lee?'

Eleanor's jaw dropped. 'Who told you?' Miss Pink sketched a smile which the other accepted for more than it was worth. 'It's no secret,' she admitted. 'And Phoebe would never condemn Jacob for that. After all, he's done the right thing; the family lives rent-free at Sunder despite Bobby being the only—well, the little ones aren't in the least like Jacob. And since he contributes to Bobby's upkeep but not to the others . . .'

'Swinburn helps out with Bobby?'

'Regular as clockwork: a tenner every Friday evening, over the garden gate.'

'No! How humiliating!'

'I doubt if he sees it that way. Certainly Sherrel doesn't. She'll take all the hand-outs she can get. The Lees do very well with child benefits and income support and help with the council tax, and then of course either Sherrel or Misella is working at any one time. Mind you, I don't *know* that they're claiming more than they have a right to, and I understand you can earn up to a certain figure even if you're on benefit . . .' She trailed off, blushing.

Miss Pink sighed, aware that this form of connivance was by no means confined to one Lakeland dale. 'Would Phoebe have been incensed at benefit fraud? Would she view it as living off the gullibility of the taxpayer?' There was the slightest edge in her tone.

'She never said anything.' Eleanor was stiff. She said defiantly, trying a clumsy distraction: 'She had no problem with illegitimacy. What countrywoman has?'

'Who else in Borascal might have taken exception to her—er—forthright opinions?'

Eleanor blinked, marshalling her thoughts. 'Who else is there excluding the holiday people, because we're only considering locals here, residents? It couldn't be anyone else, could it?' Miss Pink said nothing and Eleanor moistened her lips. 'The Blamires?' she suggested brightly. 'Never. Phoebe admired Martin. She was a simple soul, thought Mountain Rescue was an admirable institution, one of the emergency services. She didn't have much time for Jean: no backbone she said.' Eleanor grimaced, as if apologizing for her friend. 'Come to that, she had no time for Isa Lambert either but then Isa doesn't trouble to hide her contempt for our lifestyle; no social life here, she says, but then they don't entertain—couldn't—she can't cook. And she doesn't know how to behave when they go to other people's houses. I doubt if she ever sat at a table to eat before she married. The girl's lazy and ambitious; she married up and now she's got one foot on the ladder, her sights are on the next rung. I wouldn't be surprised if she finds herself a job in Carlisle once she's passed her driving test; the excitement in the Lamb yesterday will have spoiled her for staying at home and looking after her house, as if she ever did.'

The venom was scathing but all Miss Pink said was, 'Waiting at the pub was a temporary measure then?'

'Yes, Walter wouldn't have allowed it had he known, although if he can't cope with his sister he's unlikely to have any influence with his wife.'

'I met Gemma but I've yet to meet the brother.'

'He's a pleasant enough chap but a bit inadequate although, give him his due, he has made himself responsible for Gemma. She's his half-sister, hence the age gap—he's in his thirties. His mother died, his father married again, had Gemma by the second marriage and then both of them died on holiday: an earthquake in El Salvador. So Walter and

Gemma have known a lot of tragedy and I shouldn't call him inadequate, he's probably competent in his job but there you are: he's a desk-wallah, not an action man. No wonder Isa was enjoying herself at the Lamb . . . Now *there's* a deadbeat: Ralph Honeyman. Poor fellow, it has to be glandular; with such a gross body how can he be anything but ineffectual?'

'I had the impression that the pub was run by the mother.'

'Exactly. Dorcas is the boss.' Eleanor went into a brown study for a few moments while Miss Pink's eyes strayed to the open windows, her ears picking up birds' songs, muted now as the heat strengthened with the day. The tearoom was closed; it made a pleasant break for Eleanor, not having to cook, being able to sit and relax . . . 'It's funny,' came her voice, softly, as if she were commenting on images: 'funny how the women stand out in Borascal, Dorcas Honeyman eclipsing her son—why does she feed him like that? And Mabel Swinburn: tolerant enough to have her husband's child playing at the farm, turning a blind eye—well, one assumes she does—to Jacob's weekly visit to Sunder to hand over Sherrel's money, and yet, you know'—her expression was puzzled— 'basically Mabel is as much in command as Dorcas.'

'It's not unknown for a wife to tolerate a former mistress.'

A slow smile suffused Eleanor's face.

'You're deep. You're another dark horse.'

Miss Pink merely shrugged and changed the subject, saying she was going for a walk and then regretting it, knowing where she wanted to go.

'You're going to the quarry,' Eleanor said, adding firmly, 'I'll come with you.'

They were differently motivated. Miss Pink wanted to investigate the quarry because it was there and, because she had not as yet been in it, she felt an odd sense of omission as if previously she had been obstructed. There was no reason connected with Phoebe that she should enter the old workings, the dead woman hadn't fallen down one of those man-made walls, she would have had multiple fractures . . . And why did Eleanor want to go there? She asked, and Eleanor said she wanted to see the globe flowers. Miss Pink didn't push it further. As they strolled up the dale, lightly clad, wearing trainers and cotton hats, she said, 'Those letters informing people that there was salmonella at Jollybeard: where did the letterheads originate?'

'Somewhere down south.' Eleanor slashed at a thistle with her stick. 'Lewes, as I remember: East Sussex.'

'Do you remember the department concerned?'

'Environmental Health, of course. He got that right.'

' "He"?'

'One assumes . . . but now you question it, it could have been a woman. Spiteful enough. Why the interest? It can't have anything to do with Phoebe.'

'Not on the face of it.' Eleanor glanced at her sharply. 'Walter Lambert works in the Council offices,' Miss Pink said.

They stopped. The younger woman said coldly, 'So Walter got hold of some letterheads from an office hundreds of miles away and concocted that obscene libel . . . Will you tell me what he has against me to make him do that?'

'I can't. I don't know anything about him, and not a lot about yourself, and nothing of the relationship between you.'

'There is no—'

'Technically. A relationship exists when you know someone, anyone.' Miss Pink started to walk on. 'Suggest a better hypothesis.' Eleanor fell into step, staring at the ground. 'Alternatively,' Miss Pink went on, 'try this: who has a better motive to damage your business than Walter? Dorcas Honeyman?'

'No.' Eleanor was dismissive. 'The trade is different and the only food they serve is hamburgers. Besides, how could the Honeymans get hold of the letterheads, or forge them—if that's possible—on a computer? They don't have a computer.'

'The Swinburns? Blamires? Lees?'

'No, no!' Eleanor was annoyed now. 'It's

90

impossible. No one—none of them could have done it.'

'Someone did.'

Eleanor' s eyes were piteous. 'You frighten me.'

'I want to get to the bottom of this.'

'Why? I can understand you wanting to know what happened to Phoebe, so do I, but the salmonella has nothing to do with her—surely? It's a coincidence.'

'I don't believe in coincidences, not in this context. And it's because the salmonella episode appears inexplicable that I feel the explanation could tie in with Phoebe. Don't ask me why; let's leave it for a while and enjoy the walk.'

The quarry was opening out on their left, less impressive than seen from above and looking down through the vertical walls. From this angle the rock was full in the sun: pearly and smooth, and to a climber beautiful, no longer daunting, in fact quite diminished by the rising fell beyond. Now the place could be seen in perspective: an abandoned excavation rather than a death trap.

Ignoring the Danger notice they climbed the stile and started up a gentle incline starred with daisies. A cuckoo called most musically among the rocks.

'The notice could be there to stop people climbing,' Miss Pink mused. 'Didn't you say it was safe if you kept in the bottom?'

'At the lower level, down here. Right at the back, higher up, there are holes.'

'Shafts? It's a mine then, not a quarry?' They'd come to tumbled stones, an angular boulder field, and Eleanor took the lead. A rock moved under her feet. 'Or both,' Miss Pink muttered, and stopped talking, concentrating on not spraining an ankle. The place might not be a death trap but it was still a bone-breaker.

The cuckoo had flown away, the only sound now was the occasional gentle chock as a stone rocked under careful feet, although increasingly there was the suggestion of a whisper and Miss Pink paused, listening.

'Is that water?' But Eleanor didn't hear. Silly question anyway: Lakeland, there was water everywhere. In fact, there was the beck she'd had to wade across two days ago, the one with the dead sheep plastered against the watergate. That beck flowed into the quarry so where was it? Or rather, where was it in the lower section because with every step it was obvious that she was coming to it. She realized that for some considerable distance it must run underground.

The boulder field ended and they were on turf again: a level floor under a big wall at the base of which was a slit about two feet high and from which issued a clear rill a few inches deep. Miss Pink followed its course to another slit-like cave in the opposite wall where, chuckling to itself, the water disappeared.

Eleanor was amused by her companion's fascination. 'There has to be a tunnel. It's like limestone. No doubt some of the underground channels will be man-made.'

'It's not the same beck,' Miss Pink said. 'Or more likely, the water's been diverted. There's far more going in at the top than there is here.' She walked back to the first cave, stooped and peered into the depths. She stood up and nodded. 'I can hear roaring, like a big waterfall.' She gestured widely. 'Somewhere there's a huge underground channel.'

'That's what I said, and that's where the danger is. I'm not going up there, and neither are you.'

'Going up where?'

They were close to the back of the quarry now and there was no more level ground above. The tall hewn cliffs were behind and below them, and they were in the base of a funnel that was at a transient stage between excavations and natural fell. There were glimpses of the boundary wall on the skyline and a gap where the watergate would be. From where they were standing a narrow path rose diagonally up an overgrown tip. It was no wider than a sheep trod but it was marked by cleated boots.

'Oh, please don't!' Eleanor cried as Miss Pink started forward.

'I'm just going to see where this goes.' Into

her mind came the ominous words of Lawrence Oates to Captain Scott: 'and may be some time'. Not perhaps a good moment to remember that.

Below the watergate the beck poured down the fellside for a hundred yards to a fine waterfall some twenty feet high. Then came a miniature gorge and a natural rock bridge with a mantle of tall grasses, and a rowan sprouting from a crevice, its creamy blooms swaying in cold air currents. Below the bridge there was another waterfall but this one must be even more impressive because it thundered, echoing upwards from a monstrous black hole. Below that, as Miss Pink knew, the quarry was dry except for that trickle in the amphitheatre.

She crossed the bridge—it was wide and safe so long as you had a head for heights— and came to an eroded soilslip dropping straight to the torrent, but it was only a matter of a few steps and without thinking she was across and on another of those turfy levels, and this one ended at a padlocked gate. On the other side was the green path that would intersect the Gowk track.

When she returned Eleanor was pale with worry. 'I know what happened,' Miss Pink announced, in a hurry to forestall an accusation of irresponsibility, although she thought it unlikely that Eleanor had ever seen that lethal chute. 'Meaning,' she went on, seeing that the ploy had worked, 'I see what she could have done.' And she described the setting. 'She could have come down from Gowk, along that green level, over the gate, and she slipped as she approached the natural bridge. Tell me, where does the main beck emerge?'

They looked down past the chasms to the dale. 'We passed it,' Eleanor said. 'It's way back from the track, in a clump of trees. We crossed it by a plank bridge.'

'No watergate?'

'No. You're thinking that, after all, she did come here, and then she slipped. I did wonder, but I wanted to be sure.'

'I think it's highly likely that's what happened.'

They retraced their steps. At one point they stopped, Eleanor staring upwards. Miss Pink looked and saw a gully full of globe flowers. As she was castigating herself for not bringing a camera, thinking that she must come back for a picture, Eleanor said, 'If she fell on Sunday why didn't she—appear until Tuesday?'

'The storm. The body got caught up underground but the rising water freed it.' She looked away from the globe flowers, massaging her neck. 'We need her camera.'

'Why?'

'It would tell us why she came here in the first place.'

'Does it matter?'

'No. All the same it must have been for

something important to make her risk her neck.'

'A flower. She'd have risked anything for a flower.'

*   *   *

Gemma dropped her bike under the laburnum and started towards the porch, silent in her Reeboks. There were people in the kitchen.

As she stepped indoors Isa was almost shouting: '—don't *own* me! What d'you expect me to do: weed the *garden*? Bake *bread*? The one chance I get—'

'I don't give a—' Alerted by her fixed eyes Martin Blamire turned and saw Gemma in the doorway, grinning mischievously.

'You poor thing,' she told her sister-in-law. 'Battered by one guy last night and now getting stick from another one. Is there anything I can do?'

'Battered?' Martin breathed, turning back.

Isa shook her head stiffly. 'You shouldn't listen at—to other people—their conversations,' she blurted.

'Conversation? I could hear you way out in the lane,' Gemma lied. 'You got a problem, Martin?' The tone was deliberately childish, the sentiment wasn't.

Martin said tightly, 'If you have any influence with her or with your brother—stop her driving that car before she's passed her test. She's going to kill someone or land in jail. Or both.' His teeth were gritted.

'Is that all?' Gemma was the picture of astonishment. 'It sounded much more intimate.'

'Don't be so bloody cheeky.' Isa was recovering but still showing the whites of her eyes. 'And what are you doing here anyway? You were supposed to be at the Harbens' all day.'

'Lucy had to go to town with her mother. To see a specialist.' Isa was staring at her. Martin watched Isa. 'Family planning clinic,' Gemma improvised, wondering what she could say that would shake them out of what appeared to be a trance. They looked like dummies in a shop window.

'They phoned through the results of the autopsy,' she said.

'You're making that up,' Isa said weakly.

'No, I'm not! Paul Harben was there: the surgeon—well, he will be when he qualifies. He's cool. He told me.'

'Told you what?' Martin grated.

She glowered at him. 'That she had a fractured skull and water in the lungs. Which means—' she enunciated clearly for his benefit—'that she drowned. I'm going visiting: find some civilized people to talk to.'

* * *

Eleanor and the old woman from Ashgill were sitting on the patio at Jollybeard. There was a coffee pot on the table and a plate with two sandwiches. Dolefully Gemma explained how she'd been meant to have lunch with the Harbens but there had been a misunderstanding and she'd come home only to find Isa had visitors . . . Eleanor got up to make more sandwiches.

'The Harbens?' Miss Pink was mildly curious. 'I don't think I've met them.'

'You wouldn't.' Gemma pushed crumbs into her mouth. 'They live way down the dale. He's a doctor. Lucy, my friend, she's going to be one too, a forensic pathologist actually. She dissects dead animals.'

Miss Pink refrained from looking at the remaining sandwich. 'What do you propose to do?'

'I'm going to be a vet. I'm good at dissection too but I'd rather work with animals. I mean, people are dead.'

'Not always.'

'If you're a pathologist they are.' Gemma reached for the last sandwich. 'The autopsy came through—on Phoebe. Paul Harben told me.'

'The au—' Eleanor was back, putting a loaded plate on the table. 'The report?'

Gemma nodded and swallowed.

'Well?' Eleanor was tense. 'What did it say? How could you have seen it?'

'Grapevine. Medical family. Of course Dr Harben's seen it, or heard what's in it. There's nothing actually. I mean, nothing we didn't know already. She was drowned. What more could there be?'

'She did drown?' Miss Pink pressed. 'There's no doubt about it?'

Gemma stopped eating. 'We knew that. There's water in the lungs.'

'Ah.' Miss Pink sat back. 'Who said that?'

'Paul Harben, he's a medical student.' Gemma nodded solemnly. 'I know what I'm talking about.'

*   *   *

'Miss Pink was right about her arteries,' Sergeant Winder said. 'She was a healthy old lady, for her age. She didn't have a stroke, she just fell in, presumably slipped as she was wading across, lost her balance, and so . . .'

Eleanor replaced the phone. 'Winder reckons she lost her balance crossing the beck,' she repeated to the attentive Miss Pink. Fed and watered, Gemma had left with only cursory thanks for the hospitality.

'It's more likely that she came to grief on the nasty slope in the quarry,' Miss Pink said. 'I wonder where the camera is, and there's her other boot, and gaiter—and her rucksack. She must have had one.'

'She always carried a pack with waterproofs

99

and things. The rest of her gear will be scattered down the course of the beck.'

* * *

The result of the autopsy was broadcast on the local news, with the additional information that a hairline fracture indicated that Phoebe could have struck her head as she lost her balance, and that could have rendered her unconscious and so explained why she didn't try to save herself from a stream that wouldn't be in spate until nightfall. The news went round the village with the speed of a grass fire.

At Sleylands Swinburn said, 'Her never fell in t'Rutting Beck. Her were in t'old quarry, nosying around, looking to see was I tipping there, or worse.'

'Do you?' Mabel asked, rinsing a plate under the tap.

'Do I what?'

'Tip in the big quarry?'

'Don't be daft, woman. I don't need to—' He stopped and his eyes glazed.

* * *

'She were eighty,' Sherrel said, shifting the baby to the other hip. 'That's very, very old.'

'Jacob says Rap's twelve and that's older. He can jump walls.'

'Dogs is different, Bobby. Miss Metcalf

100

would have been rheumaticky too.'

'What happened to her things?'

'Like what?'

'Her—you know . . .' He patted his shoulders.

'Her rucksack? That'd fall off—Bobby Lee, did you find it?' Sherrel was suddenly angry and frightened.

'No, no, I didna! I just wondered—'

'You didn't find nothing: her camera, her wallet—oh no, not money?'

'No, Mam! Honest, on my heart, I never!' Belligerent, he tried to turn the tables: 'Why is it always me? I get blamed for everything. I'm going up t'top. Jacob needs me for t'sheep.'

*   *   *

Honeyman switched off the radio in the Lamb's kitchen. 'Nothing new there,' he said.

'Except the fracture,' Dorcas said, and Misella stopped wiping the interior of the oven.

'The fracture?' Honeyman's eyes disappeared in fat creases. 'I wonder she weren't broke to bits trundled down t'beck in t'storm.' Showing his contempt for women's brains.

'She wasn't—just the head.'

'Well then,' he blustered, 'water would cushion her like, stop t'body smashing against rocks.'

101

But Dorcas was thoughtful. 'I don't like that head wound.'

He stared at her, then grinned. 'You're saying it wasn't an accident?'

They looked at Misella who should have turned back to her work but didn't. She regarded them blankly, no more emotion showing in the gypsy eyes than in Dorcas's lined face. Only Ralph appeared eager, as if waiting for some kind of conclusion, or judgement.

'Someone pushed her?' Misella asked.

*   *   *

Walter Lambert's colleague returned from a late lunch. 'Did you hear the news?'

'No, I had a bite at my desk. What news?'

'The old girl from near you: the autopsy report said she drowned.'

'We knew that already.'

The other shrugged. 'It's just that the autopsy confirmed it.'

'I didn't really know her,' Walter said.

*   *   *

Jean Blamire thought: She could be a real bitch but it was a horrible way to go all the same. I hope she didn't know much about it, but they say time is relative.

*　　　*　　　*

Martin Blamire thought: If they discovered that she was pushed, who'd be the most likely candidate?

*　　　*　　　*

Isa, who didn't drink much and had never before tasted whisky, downed a large measure of Walter's Glenlivet, tossing it back like medicine. It was so revolting that she gagged but managed to keep it down, telling herself that the more disgusting the concoction the more good it would do. She wondered when Gemma would come back; she knew that Martin wouldn't. He said she was going to kill herself in the MG—which was an idea. But he was wrong about her driving, she could drive as well as any woman providing no one was shouting at her. She loved her little car, when she was in it she felt like a queen: on an afternoon like this skimming through the lanes, the top down, her hair streaming, just driving—with music. She refilled the tumbler and turned on the radio.

CHAPTER SEVEN

At six o'clock on the Thursday morning Nick Dolphin, second cowman at one of the big valley farms, came fast down the lane called Waterhouses, braking at the last minute for the T-junction and the swing right to the bridge. He had it gauged to the metre, knew exactly how much pressure to apply to avoid a skid, and he was a good driver. He'd been taking this route to work for two years: over mats of dead leaves in autumn, frost in winter, but this was the last day of May and the road was dry. No problem. Not that he was thinking about hazards, he was dwelling on last night and the chick with the butterfly tattoo at the disco, which was why he nearly didn't make it, because at the turn the scenery changed, had changed out of all recognition.

In this place the river ran below a sandstone crag—not very long, a couple of hundred yards perhaps, and only about thirty feet high. The road called River Lonning ran along the top, bounded by a drystone wall and intersected by Waterhouses Lane where, slewed across the tarmac, Nick now sat trembling in his stalled van, well aware that if he hadn't had good brakes, if he didn't know the road, if it had been frosty, he'd be in the river. The wall was no longer there.

104

'Jesus!' he breathed as he recovered, starting up again and easing forward, so shaken that he'd crossed the bridge before it occurred to him that there were no traffic cones at that place, nothing to show . . . The next guy might not be such a good driver. And then he wondered where the vehicle was that had demolished the wall.

He stopped again. To call the police just because a drunk had grazed the side and toppled the wall would make him look ridiculous; to protest because the break was unmarked was putting on side. Confused, he turned the van and went back.

As he approached on foot it was obvious that nothing had glanced off the wall; the gap was wide and clean, all the stones would be in the river. As was the car: upside down, not quite submerged, water chuckling past one wheel—not much tread left on that tyre, he saw. It was impossible to tell what make of vehicle it was, or even its colour. No doubt it had been stolen although it seemed a risky method of disposal; much easier to torch it if the thieves needed to destroy fingerprints.

Shifting the responsibility Nick told his boss at the farm who reported it immediately, not because he was concerned about a stolen car so much as being worried about the unmarked gap above the escarpment, thinking of the milk tanker going over. A patrol car was there within fifteen minutes, traffic cones and tape were put in place, but they had to wait for a diver to go down and determine the registration. When one did they had a shock. There was a woman strapped in the driving seat.

There were no passengers—at least, none in the car, which was an MG with the top down. Before a search was started for another occupant who might have floated clear the police were on their way to Borascal. Sergeant Rosie Winder was back but this time in the company of the CID: Detective Sergeant Sewell and a DC Holgate. For the car was registered to a Walter Lambert, and there was no identification on the woman behind the wheel. It was possible that a crime was involved.

They drove round the village looking for Borrans, the Lambert house. The Lamb had appeared dead but at Jollybeard House they could see down the flagged path to the open front door. Rosie went to inquire.

Eleanor emerged from the kitchen. 'You're early,' she exclaimed, innocently wondering. 'Come and have some coffee.'

Rosie said they were looking for Borrans.

Eleanor craned to see past her. 'You've brought more—' She checked, then went on flatly, 'You continue along the lane, take the first right, and Lamberts'—that is, Borrans, is the first cottage on your right.' She paused. In normal circumstances one would ask if

106

anything were wrong but when it was the police that sounded like fishing. Eleanor's face revealed her embarrassment.

'I'll see you,' Rosie promised, and meant it. She liked this woman. If it came to that she liked Borascal. She was a town girl and she'd been much impressed by what she saw as the affluence and ease of the lifestyle here: no crowds as in the central Lakes, no crime . . .

'Where to?' DC Holgate asked as she came back to the car. Her mind changed gear and she directed him, remembering to warn him about cats, remembering that she hadn't met the Lamberts when she was here before. Odd that: two fatal accidents within four days of each other—if the woman in the car was from Borascal.

Walter Lambert was about to leave for work. They blocked him in as he was approaching his open gate. He said he didn't know where his MG was, and when asked if he'd lent it to anyone, blurted that his wife drove it—under instruction, he added quickly—and no, she wasn't at home. He refused to go back in his house when requested so they told him there, beside his car, inside his garden gate, told him where the car had been found and described the driver. Then they all went to the house.

Rosie made tea, noting that he'd washed his breakfast things and left them to drain: one side plate, one mug, a cafetière disassembled and rinsed. There was a litre of milk in the fridge, bottled water, Cranberry Pressé and Coke, butter, a jar of Lemon Shred. The freezer compartment was stacked with pizzas and pre-cooked meals. The kitchen was quite neat but then a man who rinsed the cafetière wasn't the type to make a mess. How long had his wife been gone?

'It doesn't have to be her,' he was saying when Rosie returned with the tea.

'What time did she leave, sir?' Sewell asked politely. He was the high-flyer: young, dishy, with lazy eyes. He skied and swam and moved like a cat, the antithesis of DC Holgate, who was putting on weight like a Christmas goose since he married a fat lady and stopped playing rugby. No high-flyer, Holgate, but a steady old gander, always remembering that some people use geese as watchdogs. He didn't miss much.

Lambert was in shock. He tasted his tea, said, 'I don't take sugar,' but when Rosie told him to drink it along with the three spoonfuls she'd shovelled in, he did so without further protest. His face was blank, almost serene.

'What time did she go out?' Sewell repeated casually, thinking that the fellow was worth a bit: that bread cupboard was superb. Still Lambert didn't respond to the question. Sewell tried again. 'Was your wife here when you came home yesterday?'

'No.'

'What time did you get home?'

'The usual. Around half-five.'

'You don't come home at midday?'

'No.'

'Was she here at breakfast time? What time did you leave for work?'

He shook his head as if two questions were more than he could take. There were light footsteps on the stairs and his eyes went to the doorway. 'I'd forgotten you,' he said.

The atmosphere changed. Without making any overt movement the detectives' concentration sharpened, like gun dogs catching the whirr of wings. The newcomer was pretty, cool, nubile. She wore baggy jeans and a skimpy tank top exposing a long brown waist. She was barefooted. She was also very young, but surely not young enough to be Lambert's daughter.

'I'm Gemma,' she told them. 'Who are you, since no one's going to introduce me?' The nonchalance was studied. Since Rosie was in uniform it was fairly obvious that they were all police officers.

'I've forgotten their names too,' Lambert said. 'I can't remember a bloody thing.'

'What's going on?' Gemma started to shrill. 'What's wrong with you, Wally?' She appealed to Rosie. 'What's happening?'

'Hang on, miss.' Holgate came in heavily, raising a meaty hand. He had two teenage daughters. 'Let's start at the beginning. 'I'm DC Holgate from Bailrigg, and this is DS

109

Sewell and Sergeant Winder. You're Gemma. Gemma what?'

'Lambert.' She spat it at him. 'What else?'

His expression didn't change but he was wondering if there'd been some ghastly mistake. Maybe she just looked young. 'You're his wife?'

'His *wife*! Wally, what *is* this?' She swooped on his chair and shook him. 'Wake *up*, Wally! Where's—' She stopped and looked round at them, distressed. 'Isa? Something happened to Isa?'

'Isa is his wife?' Holgate stated with just the suggestion of a query.

'Of course she is. I'm his sister.' She looked from him to Sewell, to Rosie. 'Isa took the MG, didn't she?' She came back to her brother. 'I see. She's crashed it.' She shook her head vehemently. 'She couldn't drive it,' she told him. 'It had nothing to do with you. There was no way you could stop her. Everyone said she'd—crash one day.'

Walter rubbed his knees. 'I should never have given her that car.'

'Give over.' She walked to the bread cupboard and came back with a bottle of Glenlivet and a tumbler. She poured a small measure, went to the kitchen, ran the tap, and returned. The level looked the same. He sipped at it. Evidently even under extreme stress he wouldn't drink a single malt as if it were tea. Behind Gemma's back Sewell signalled to Rosie.

'Is this half-term?' she asked.

Gemma turned, surprised that the woman should put in her oar. She nodded, frowning.

'So you were at home yesterday,' Rosie said.

'Ye-es.' The hesitation was marked, but then it wasn't unusual for a young girl to be wary of a policewoman.

'What time did your stepmother go—'

'Hey! My sister-in-law!'

Rosie blushed at the gaffe and Sewell's eyes gleamed. Holgate was expressionless.

'Sorry,' Rosie said. 'What time did she go out?'

'I don't know! I wasn't home—not all day. I was with my friend—friends; I was all over the place.'

'When did you last see your sister-in-law?' Sewell asked.

Gemma moved and sat down in a chair from where she could keep an eye on her brother. His colour was returning and he looked slightly less shocked. 'It's difficult,' she said slowly. 'We had lunch—wait, did we? No, that was the day before; yesterday I had lunch with Miss Salkeld and Miss Pink.'

Sewell raised an eyebrow at Rosie. 'The tearoom where I asked the way,' she told him.

'Did you come home after lunch?' he asked.

'No.' They waited for more. 'I was looking for a cat,' she said, adding to Rosie: 'Phoebe's cat. He doesn't have a home now, you see, with her place shut up; he can get in of course, there's a cat flap, but the place is empty so he wanders around looking for her. And crying. I thought I'd bring him back here, so I was looking for him.'

Walter was staring at her, blinking at the torrent of words.

'While you were out,' Sewell said, 'did you see your sister-in-law's MG go through the village?'

'It's not—No.' Pause. 'Where did she—' She threw a furtive glance at Walter and stopped.

Sewell nodded to Rosie and the message was unmistakable. 'Come outside, Gemma,' she said.

The girl looked mutinous. 'Can you do that—' she began.

'Go with her, Gemma.' Walter's voice was high and brittle and she went without a murmur.

Outside, beyond the drooping tresses of the laburnum, she said coldly, trying to sound adult, 'She's dead, isn't she? That's why he's gone to pieces. Are you going to tell me what happened or do I have to hear it from him?'

Rosie said, 'She ran out of road at the T-junction where Waterhouses intersects the lane along the top of the crags.'

'What! And went in the river? Down that cliff: straight through the wall? The stupid, *stupid* cow! Why in hell didn't she jump clear?'

'I suppose she couldn't undo the seat belt in

time.'

'Come on! She never—' Gemma gasped and turned away, into the laburnum, lashing out as if the blooms were animate. 'She would never have waited—I mean—she turned back, her eyes fixed on Rosie—'it was deliberate. She was neurotic.'

Rosie returned the stare, trying to appear receptive. There was no responsible adult present, on the other hand there were no witnesses. 'You think it was suicide?'

'She was crazy. She should never have—lived here. She hated Borascal.'

'Enough to—Why did she live here then?'

'Because she married my brother of course! They've only been married two years. It was still the honeymoon period, you know? They're madly in love but Isa, she's a townie; she had nothing to do here so she just used to take the MG and drive. She was a lousy driver, she'd failed her test dozens of times.'

'You're saying she didn't have a licence.'

'Isa wouldn't give a toss for a licence. She was never caught—not by your lot, but everyone said she'd crash.'

'She drove well enough to reach the river,' Rosie pointed out. 'She'd crossed the main road to get there and that's scary. How many fatalities have there been on that road already this year?'

'She was lucky. That's the point about learner drivers: they can manage fine until something goes wrong, then they panic. I bet you'll find the tyres or the brakes, or both of them, are worn. So she skidded and didn't know how to correct, or she over-corrected.'

'You drive?' Rosie was casual.

'I'm fifteen. I don't drive but I know how to. I don't live in a vacuum.'

No, and you're not thick, Rosie thought.

Inside the house Sewell was trying to hang on to his patience. 'What we need to do, sir, is build up a picture of how she came to be there.'

'Why?' There was a hint of belligerence in the tone. Walter wanted them to go away, to leave him alone, or alone with his sister. 'She had an accident,' he went on wearily. 'Can't you leave it there?'

'We have to investigate road accidents,' Holgate intoned.

Some comprehension showed in Walter's face. 'Detectives have to?'

'It's an offence to drive without a licence.'

'Not if the learner's accompanied by a qualified driver,' Sewell put in.

'But she wasn't,' Holgate said, adding, looking at Walter, 'Was she, sir?'

The man seemed bewildered. 'But you said she was alone! You can't mean someone was with her and he jumped clear: survived?' He shook his head. 'That's impossible, he'd have reported it—why, he'd have tried to get her out . . . How deep is it there?'

'Who was teaching her?' Sewell asked.

'Teaching her what?' Bewilderment gave way to anger.

'Instructing her.'

'I took her out a few times,' Walter admitted, 'but I gave up. Husbands shouldn't try to instruct their wives. She was having a couple of sessions a week with an instructor from Bailrigg.'

'In the MG or a school car?'

'Oh, one from the school. Chap used to come and pick her up.'

'We'll need his particulars. When was the last time you were in the MG?'

'Sunday.' He didn't have to think about it. 'She left it blocking the drive and I had to move it so that I could get out on Monday morning.'

There was silence for a moment, then Sewell said, 'You're saying your wife was out in the MG on Sunday?'

Walter swallowed. 'That's right.'

'Alone?'

'I suppose so.'

'Where were you?'

'Here.' He looked around. 'Gardening. I was outside all day—after I read the papers. This time of year the garden tends to get on top of you.'

'You didn't leave the house all day? Where did Mrs Lambert go?'

'I've no idea. I mean, she didn't say.'

'She was gone all day, alone, a learner driver, and you didn't *ask*?'

He looked at them miserably and gave a deep sigh. 'She was unhappy. She used to go to Carlisle a lot. Her family are there.'

'So you did know where she went. Why not say so?'

The atmosphere had changed. There was an air of hostility to the questions but he appeared to be unaware of it. He stared at the bottle of whisky on the coffee table. 'I could accept her driving round the lanes in the MG,' he confessed, 'but going to Carlisle: on busy roads, driving in the city, that was unbearable. I had to block it out.'

'You could have stopped it,' Holgate said.

'She's—she was my wife,' Walter said thickly, 'not my daughter. You think I didn't try?'

'You bought her the MG.'

'And do you think I'd have done that if I'd known what was going to happen?'

'Why didn't you immobilize it? Or sell it?' Holgate was genuinely curious but Walter merely looked at him, and that made him angry. 'Was there another man?' he asked roughly.

'Not to my knowledge.'

*   *   *

'Why didn't he immobilize it?' Holgate asked

as they went down the drive with Rosie.

'She'd have left him,' Sewell said.

Waiting for him in the car they passed round the photograph of the wife which he'd given them. It showed a pretty blonde in a white swimsuit posed on the edge of a pool, long legs swinging. It had been taken in Rhodes on their honeymoon.

'A lot of make-up for a girl going swimming,' Rosie commented. 'Is there a man in this?'

'You mean a proper man?' Holgate asked.

'Walter didn't make a good impression,' Sewell told Rosie, and related how the interview had gone. 'Did you get anything from the sister?'

'I'm not sure. She dramatizes, like a lot of girls of that age. Isa was so neurotic, according to her, that it could have been suicide, but she didn't dwell on that, it was mentioned only once. Apparently the woman hated the country and wouldn't be living here but she married and had to.' Rosie looked at the photo again. 'Looks like a party girl, doesn't she? A lot younger than Lambert too, although Gemma insists it's a love match. Too insistent? Not overly jealous though, I'd say, more— mildly contemptuous basically.' Sewell was staring at her and she fidgeted. 'Gemma maintains everyone said the woman would crash the MG eventually. No surprises really.'

'Funny household,' Sewell muttered. 'I can't imagine any man being so gutless he has

117

absolutely no influence over his wife.'

'It was you said she'd have left him,' Holgate pointed out. 'It was blackmail, of a sort: if you don't let me do what I want, I'm going home to Mum. Or another fellow.'

Sewell pursed his lips. 'So all the feeling was on his side.'

Rosie held up the photo. 'She looks available. I don't see this woman driving around on her own. Did you ask if there was another guy?'

'Not to his knowledge, he said.'

'That's not an answer.' A movement in a mirror caught her eye. 'Watch it, here he is.'

Walter came down the drive having talked to his superior and explained why he wasn't coming in to work. He climbed in the car and Holgate started up, taking him to Bailrigg to identify his wife. Rosie asked about Gemma and he said she would go down to the tearoom; Miss Salkeld would look after her until he returned. Making conversation Sewell asked about the family background; little sisters didn't usually live with married brothers. Without exhibiting any emotion he told them about the earthquake and the death of his father and Gemma's mother. He and Gemma had inherited Borrans between them and, since it was the family home and Walter had never moved out, they went on much as before except that he married. Sewell asked no further questions but Rosie was left thinking that Walter was a good catch: steady job, decent salary, valuable house; that bread cupboard alone must be worth thousands. With a big garden and Lakeland prices you were probably looking at a property in the region of a quarter of a million. Yes, a good catch. What was Isa's background?

*   *   *

Gemma waited until the police car left and then she went down and closed the gate. Walter's Nissan was still blocking the drive so she pushed the seat forward, got in and reversed into the garage. She sat for a moment frowning at the bright garden beyond the dark frame of the doorway, idly running her hands round the steering wheel, wondering how long they were going to keep him, realizing that they would come back with him because he'd gone in their car.

She went in the house, replaced the Glenlivet, smelled the tumbler, grimaced, and took it to the kitchen. Automatically she made toast and ate it standing at the sink looking out at the bronze wallflowers below the cream broom. The air was heavy with scent and loud with birdsong.

She went upstairs and along the passage to what had been her parents' room, then Walter's and Isa's. He had pulled up the duvet and she lifted the far corner to reveal Isa's red nightie edged with something simulating swansdown. His striped pyjamas were neatly folded on the other side of the bed. This was the only feature of the room approaching order. Clothes were tossed over chairs and a pair of feathered mules looked as if they had been kicked across the room. There were two mahogany wardrobes against the wall. She pawed through one and knew immediately what was missing: the Wranglers and the pink T-shirt Isa had been wearing when she'd walked in on them yesterday: her and Martin Blamire.

Gemma sat on the flounced stool in front of the incongruous modern dressing table and stared at the lipsticks, the brushes and pencils, the palette of shimmering eye-shadows, the cream blusher: everything dropped rather than laid down. Carefully she began to tidy up.

When she'd finished, had gone downstairs to drink a glass of milk and returned to go through Walter's wardrobe, she shut the front door and went through the garden to Jollybeard.

Cooper rose from the windowsill with arched back, stretching, greeting her with a silent mew.

'I'm not opening just for the morning,' Eleanor told her as she came in the kitchen. 'It's the inquest this afternoon.'

Gemma gaped. 'It can't be! They've only just found—Oh!' Eleanor evinced mild surprise. One expected odd pronouncements

120

from Gemma—who gulped and said flatly, 'You haven't heard.'

'Heard what?' Eleanor stiffened.

'Isa. She crashed through the wall at Waterhouses.'

'And? Gemma, she's not—Is she?' Gemma nodded. 'Oh, my dear. Sit down. I'll make tea.'

'Don't fuss. I've known for ages. The police came hours ago. They've taken—they've run Walter to town to identify her.'

'Poor Walter.' Eleanor sighed deeply. 'She was alone—of course.'

'Yes. She couldn't undo her seat belt evidently.'

Eleanor looked at Cooper but she wasn't seeing him. 'I never saw her wearing a seat belt; she said, apparently without thought.

'She fastened it when she remembered. She wouldn't want to be stopped, would she, driving without a licence? No way.'

'I suppose not.' As Eleanor busied herself with the kettle and cups there were footsteps in the front room and Miss Pink called ritually, 'Anyone home?'

Gemma blinked rapidly as Eleanor responded. 'You're just in time, Melinda. I was making tea.' She hesitated, glancing at Gemma. It was *her* bad news, but the child was only fifteen. However she was taking it well—

'My sister-in-law crashed her car,' Gemma told Miss Pink whose eyes widened in disbelief. Adolescent girls: fantasy lives?

121

Eleanor signalled frantic confirmation.

'Is it serious?' Miss Pink asked carefully.

'She drowned,' Gemma said, her eyes like a lemur's. 'Just like Phoebe.'

'Well, no,' Miss Pink demurred. 'Phoebe wasn't in a car.'

'All the same: fatal accidents. We go in for them, don't we?'

They eyed her dubiously thinking: shock. The kettle boiled. Tea was made. Miss Pink sat down heavily.

'She went through a wall,' Gemma told her without expression. 'She was a learner, you see, she couldn't drive. She went through the wall, over a cliff and into the river. Couldn't get her seat belt undone in time.'

Miss Pink was frowning. 'What happened to the instructor?'

'There wasn't one.'

'That was Isa.' Eleanor was pouring the tea. 'She drove on her own without a licence. It was bound to—' She stopped herself in time but Gemma had no such qualms.

'Everyone said it would happen. She drove like she was at Brand's Hatch.'

'Without the expertise.' Eleanor couldn't help herself.

They were silent until Gemma put their thoughts into words. 'I don't know what he's going to be like when he comes out of the shock.'

'We'll be here,' Eleanor assured her.

'Anything you want . . .

'Thanks. I suppose the saddest thing is that he never got the chance to say goodbye.' The others exchanged glances over her head. 'She was gone when he came home—how ghastly—he could have passed her on the road . . . Of course, we don't know when she . . . He came in and asked me where she was but she hadn't told me where she was going—I mean, she never did. So we waited supper for a while and when she didn't come we ate, but we didn't think anything of it, you know? She's—she was a free spirit. And then we watched telly, well, I watched, he mowed the grass. We watched a movie together later on and then we went to bed.'

'She still hadn't come home?' Eleanor was puzzled.

'How could she? She was in the river. I'm sorry, that was rude. No, she didn't come home, or come home and go out again. We didn't wait up.'

'You were used to it.' Miss Pink was equable.

Gemma gave a faint shrug. 'I think she went to discos. Wally would never, ever, go to a disco but he didn't mind her going.' Her tone changed. 'I was worried actually, thinking about her driving back in the dark, I couldn't sleep. I woke Wally up when I went down for a drink. Hot night, all the doors were open and later, when I went to the loo, I crept along there like a mouse but he still heard me. I reckon he didn't sleep much himself, just dozing. Eleanor, if you're going to town, shall I take Cooper home with me?'

'Of course you can, dear. And if he doesn't want to come, I'll close up and no doubt he'll find you. If I might suggest it, it would be nice if you were there when Walter comes back, don't you think? He shouldn't come home to an empty house, not today.'

'Oh, that would be ghastly!' Gemma looked stricken. 'He'll have the police with him. Do I—offer them anything? I mean—eats, a drink?'

'Why should he have the police with him?' Miss Pink asked.

'They took him! He couldn't drive. He was in shock.'

Miss Pink nodded, chastened. Eleanor said, 'You don't offer the police anything; they'll just drop him and leave—I mean, they'll deliver—Oh my, I'm making him sound like a package.'

'It's what he looked like,' Gemma said. 'He adored her, you know.'

CHAPTER EIGHT

'I'm not having you along,' Jacob said savagely.

'I'm coming.' Mabel was adamant. 'I need to

hear what you say.'

'Hell, woman! You know what I'm going to say! I saw her pass, I didn't speak, she were too far away. 'Sides, it were misty.'

'There, you see! It weren't misty down here and if you go saying it were, someone else is going to say it weren't, then where'll you be? Shown up for a liar is what.'

Jacob glared. ' 'Twere an innocent mistake. What's it matter any road whether mist were down or up? I weren't measuring it.'

He'd been cutting silage all morning and had come in for an early bite before setting off for the inquest. Surprised to find Mabel in her second-best dress, bag and gloves on the table, her coat over a chair, he'd been astonished at her announcement that she was coming with him, meaning right into court.

'Where did you go after you saw her?' she was asking now.

'I went round t'sheep. What're you on about? You sound like police.'

'It's the coroner will be asking questions. I asked "where", not what you were doing.'

He eyed her, thoughtful now. 'I went down t'dale, looking at lambs.'

'Lambing's over long since.' His jaw dropped. 'That's what coroner will say,' she insisted. 'Even townies know you're not lambing in May.'

'I were looking to see was any of 'em scouring,' he said with dignity. 'You know that.'

'Good. But don't say nowt till he asks. Don't be too ready about anything.' She returned his stare. 'You never went up the way, did you? Over t'top to Closewater?'

'You know I didna. You'd have heard t'tractor grinding up t'slope.'

'Just—you didn't go, and you don't say until you're asked. You were down dale all Sunday, right, except when you come in for your dinner. You never went up bottom road to t'quarry?'

'No, I didna.' Belligerence had given way to trepidation.

'Let's hope no one says owt about where you're tipping, nor about dead animals.' He licked his lips. 'An' about you threatening her,' Mabel added meaningly.

'Her threatened *me*!' He checked, hearing his own words. 'No one's going to say nothing,' he muttered. 'Who cares about the odd sheep and a few empty drums? That tip's miles from t'beck, how could water be contaminated? D'you ever hear of dead fish in it? Stop fretting; only reason coroner got to be interested in me is I were t'last person to see her.'

*   *   *

In the event it was Martin Blamire whose evidence was the most illuminating at the inquest. After Phoebe's body was found the rescue team had returned to the quarry and worked out a scenario that came close to Miss Pink's theory. Knowing now that Phoebe had intended being down by six to feed the cat it was most unlikely that she could have been swept away by a surface stream because the waters didn't rise until after the storm. So, according to Martin, she could have walked along the green level from the Gowk track, climbed the gate and, in trying to reach the floor of the quarry, lost her footing on a smooth slope above the beck just before it went underground. The fracture indicated that she struck her head as she fell.

Eleanor, as her friend—her only close friend as it appeared—was questioned and she suggested that, being a keen photographer, Phoebe could have gone into the quarry to take pictures; there were spring flowers, even the walls would make interesting subjects. The coroner noted that the camera was missing although he doubted that it would have survived intact, falling with her. He didn't even mention a rucksack. He brought in a verdict of accident with the rider that since the Danger notices had no effect on adventurous hikers, the dangerous slope should be adequately fenced. He stopped short of apportioning blame to the owners of the site; everyone knew that upland areas were full of abandoned quarries, one might as well blame the National

Trust when a climber fell off a cliff within its boundaries. And although Phoebe's age had to be mentioned, with their eyes on the press and thoughts on political correctness, everyone avoided attaching any significance to the victim's being close to eighty.

'All the same,' Miss Pink said as they walked back to her car, 'age counts. I find myself thinking twice about exposed paths which I never even noticed twenty, thirty years ago. And I'm willing to bet that if one does stumble at our age, reaction is considerably slower than it used to be.'

Eleanor said nothing until they were in the car but before Miss Pink could start she said, 'Jacob was unhappy.'

Miss Pink's hand was poised above the ignition switch. 'Swinburn? So you noticed.'

'Couldn't help noticing if you knew the fellow. He was in an awkward position: the last person to see Phoebe. Mabel was watching him like a hawk. A good job no one mentioned the friction between them. That could have been embarrassing.'

'The police have never suggested foul play.' Miss Pink thought about that. 'Not to mention anyone.'

'I'm not suggesting for one moment—'

'No, no, of course not.' A longer pause. Still Miss Pink made no move to drive away. 'All the same, given what you've told me about her, their confrontations must have been pretty

128

heated. He could have a motive.'

'Melinda, you have a criminal mind! Next thing we know you'll be suggesting that someone knocked Isa on the head and shoved the MG in the river.'

'And what would be the motivation there?'

'*Melinda!*'

'I didn't see much of her but what I saw in the Lamb two days ago indicated that she was a lively young woman.'

'She was a shrewd little minx who'd seduced an unsophisticated fellow into marriage and who'd have left him already if it hadn't meant leaving a nice home—and worth a fortune where she comes from—and more money for her housekeeping and clothes than her mother would have known in her life. Gemma loathed her sister-in-law.'

'She says her brother and Isa were in love.'

'She's protecting Walter.'

'Protecting him from what?'

'Nothing. I'm tired—I'm rambling, don't know what I'm saying. Let's get home, shall we? I'm dying for a cup of tea.'

*   *   *

Gemma and Jean Blamire were sprawled in the shade under a damson tree at Elfhow, the collie stretched out beside them. Jean had agreed to have the girl to lunch when asked by Eleanor. Her surprise at the request, virtually

129

a demand, was superseded by disbelief when Gemma arrived and explained. Isa drowned in her car, Walter taken to Bailrigg by the police, this child left alone in the house, subsequently to acquaint the neighbours with the appalling news—'They should never have left you,' she blurted, unable to control herself.

'It wasn't like that,' Gemma assured her, as if she were the adult, Jean the teenager. 'Walter told me to go to Eleanor but I couldn't stay at Jollybeard because they had to go to the inquest, her and Miss Pink'—she shrugged and smiled—'then Eleanor thought of you. I won't stay long, I have to be back for Wally; I don't want him coming home to an empty house.'

'Of course not.' How well she was taking it, blocking out the horror; this had to be shock. Jean considered and rejected subjects suitable for chatting; she wished Martin were here but he, too, was at the inquest. She was suddenly startled to realize that this was the second death in four days.

'He'll be lost without her,' came Gemma's voice. She lay on her back, her eyes closed. 'We didn't sleep, listening for the sound of the MG, and all the time she was . . .' Her voice died away.

'But—Waterhouses! She'd crossed the main road. How did she manage to negotiate two lanes of traffic?'

'She managed well enough. She used to go

to Carlisle and that was the route she took. She'd never risk the main roads because of the police patrols so she went by way of the back lanes.'

'The driving's more tricky.'

'But not nearly so many people to see her: driving with the top down and her hair flying.'

'I suppose.' Jean wasn't convinced. 'I think . . .'

'Think what?'

'Well, she was your sister-in-law . . .'

'What are you trying to say?' Gemma sat up, on the alert.

'All that driving, without a licence, in a sports car: it was like, you know, as if she had a self-destruct button.'

'Is that what Martin said?'

'Actually he doesn't know yet; he left before anyone knew, other than you and Walter. But he's said it of her in the past, yes. He wasn't the only one who thought that way, Gemma.'

The girl nodded. 'And he wasn't afraid to tell her either.' She was morose.

'He did?' This morning was full of shocks for Jean—well, surprises. On the other hand Gemma did exaggerate.

'Isa told you Martin said something to her?'

'I heard them—him, rather: bawling her out one time.'

Jean sighed. 'It didn't do any good, did it? If she went to Carlisle so often I'm surprised her mother didn't try to put a stop to it, at least

131

until she'd passed her test. It was her mother in Carlisle, wasn't it?'

'That's what she said. But she didn't have L-plates on the MG so her mother needn't know that she didn't have a licence.'

'I hope Walter isn't going to get into any kind of trouble for failing to stop her.'

'Look, I told that woman sergeant—Rosie something—that he tried but he got nowhere. Isa was like a kid.' Gemma smiled wanly and went on: 'Some teenagers, their parents can't do a thing with them, 'fact, they're frightened—dads in particular—so the kids run wild: play truant, drink, do drugs, you name it. It was like that in our house.'

'You . . .' What was this? 'Oh, Dwayne Paxton.'

'I don't give a toss for him. I'm talking about *her*: Isa. She was the kid in our family. Wally—' She stopped. Jean waited. Gemma went on more quietly, 'That was the trouble: he loved her. Another guy would have knocked her about, stopped her by brute force, punished her. Wally adored her. Funny thing was she loved him too.'

'He's always been a good neighbour.' Jean was circumspect.

'He doesn't have a mean bone in his body,' Gemma said firmly. 'Oh God! There's the car. See you!' And she was gone, Whisk barking and prancing after her: out of the gate and down the lane to where an unmarked car was

132

backing into Borrans' drive. It stopped. Rosie Winder and Walter emerged as Gemma and Whisk arrived.

'Nice dog,' Rosie said. 'Yours?'

'The neighbour's.' Gemma eyed Walter. 'I could use a mug of tea. How about you?'

'I'll come with you,' Rosie said, and Walter frowned at Gemma who thought he was conveying a message. Prudently she said nothing but went ahead of them to the house.

She didn't go to the kitchen but hung back to hear what they had to say. Without a word Walter went to the bread cupboard and took down the bottle of Glenlivet. He was going to start drinking in the middle of the afternoon? This was what she had to be on her guard against.

He held up the bottle. There were about two ounces in the bottom. 'You poured a drink for me this morning,' he told Gemma. 'How much was in there?'

'About twice as much as now.' She was puzzled and sullen.

'Gemma.' Her eyes widened. He sounded like someone's dad. 'Have you been drinking it?'

'Oh, come on!' She threw a glance at Rosie who was attentive, expressionless. 'I hate the stuff. I washed your glass. Even the smell was gross!' Indignation gave place to apprehension. She stared at the Glenlivet and tried to remember if Martin liked whisky.

133

'I told you'—Walter was speaking to Rosie—'it was more than two-thirds full. I can't understand it.' He turned back to Gemma, appealing now. She was wary; she wasn't going to ask the next and obvious question.

'Isa was drunk,' he told her. She waited for the next bit, tense as wire. 'Did you ever see her drinking?' he asked.

'She liked Tia Maria.' Her voice sounded weak, like a little girl's.

They all looked at the open cupboard, at the bottle of Tia Maria among the party drinks, all full or nearly full; this wasn't a boozy family.

'It wasn't Tia Maria but whisky,' Walter said.

How did they know? And how daft can you get? They'd opened her up of course, and she'd stunk of Scotch.

'I'll make us some tea.' She escaped to the kitchen, needing to be out of range of Rosie's feline stare. She filled the kettle and switched on. She reached for the mugs and placed them carefully on the counter, listening for their voices in the other room, but they'd gone outside and she could hear only the humming of insects.

*   *   *

'That's Martin behind us,' Eleanor said. 'You'd

better let him pass. He's a busy man.'

Miss Pink indicated and pulled into a place marked by a white diamond. An old van rattled past with jaunty pips of its horn.

'Nice fellow,' Eleanor commented. 'I do admire him: out in all weathers, always on call. And all without pay.'

'He can't make much from his writing,' Miss Pink mused. 'And I take it Jean doesn't have a job.'

'I suspect Jacob lets them have the house rent-free, and she grows all her own vegetables, sells a lot to me—and to the holiday people in summer. She makes some pin money that way.'

They passed the Lamb and bore left for Jollybeard. Two small figures were walking up the cart track towards Sunder. 'Bobby taking care of his little sister,' Eleanor observed with approval. 'There's another one with a fine sense of responsibility—despite everything.'

Miss Pink drew up at Jollybeard's gate. Cooper was stretched on the cool flags of the porch, waiting. 'You mean, despite being a gypsy child?'

'He's dyslexic or something. He has trouble reading and writing. He's having special tuition now but it should have been diagnosed before. Otherwise he's a very bright child. You'll come to supper? I have pheasant defrosting.'

135

'I heard about it in town,' Martin said as Jean brought him a bottle of Budweiser. 'I'm only surprised it didn't happen before, the way she went through the village. I told her she'd kill one of the Sunder kids if she didn't watch it.'

'Gemma told me.'

'Told you—what?'

'That you were giving her stick for driving without a licence.'

'When was this?'

'After you'd gone to town. Eleanor called and asked me to give Gemma lunch. She was all on her own, Marty, wasn't that cruel? The police took Walter away and left the child alone in the house! Can you believe that? They're heartless—and there was a woman with them too.'

He was astounded. 'They've arrested Walter?'

'No! I didn't say that. They took him to town to identify the body. Naturally. They've brought him back. Why on earth would they arrest him?'

'Gemma came here to tell you that?'

'She came for company basically. Eleanor had to go to the inquest so Gemma came here. She's taking it very well, too well perhaps. But then, like you said, it didn't come as a surprise to anyone, a shock yes, but not a surprise.'

'I tried but I had no influence.'

136

'You wouldn't, would you? We're just neighbours. If her own family couldn't cope with her no one could. I never realized that Isa travelled so far in that car. Gemma says she often goes—went—to Carlisle. Except that there seems to be some doubt about that. It looks as if Isa could have been meeting someone on the quiet. The way Gemma tells it Isa comes over as very immature. Did you think that?'

He hesitated, then, 'She was a nutter. Immature and neurotic. I had a bit of a set-to with her one time—nothing to get upset about'—as Jean registered amazement—'she wanted me to teach her to drive. I refused. She didn't like it.'

'You didn't tell me!'

'It was unpleasant.' He grimaced. 'I wanted to forget about it—and you'd be worried. After all, we live next door, and I was sorry for Walter, married to her.'

'Marty, what are you trying to say?'

He looked so helpless that she had to laugh. 'Darling! She made a pass at you?' She had forgotten that the woman was dead.

'Worse.' He shook his head as if in disbelief. 'She threatened me. Look, what happened was that she told me Walter shouted at her when he was trying to teach her to drive, and she ended in tears, so I felt sorry for her—at first. I did go for a spin with her; I drove the MG out to the old firing range and handed the wheel

137

over to her. She was so bloody incompetent I told her she'd have to enrol at a professional driving school, I wasn't having anything to do with it. So she tried to seduce me.'

'How?'

'*How?*' His temper flared. 'What the fuck do you think she did?'

'Marty! It was a natural question.'

His face smoothed out but his eyes were cold. He licked his lips. 'You want all the details?'

'Well, there couldn't be many.' She gulped. 'Not really. You made—she made a pass. That's it?'

He held her eye. 'She pulled her skirt up. She wasn't wearing any knickers. I got out of the car and told her to drive herself home, I'd sooner walk.'

'You left her there and you say she couldn't drive! Marty, the woman was deranged!'

'There was a stand-off. She said if I walked away she'd accuse me of rape. I said she couldn't, there was no evidence. She said attempted rape then. I said I'd drive her home but if she made any accusation against me I'd come back with a counter accusation. I said there had to be more guys around who'd come out of the woodwork once I went public.' His voice dropped. 'But I did tell her to get psychiatric help.'

'All this and you never said a word.'

'Why should I? It would have made bad

feeling between neighbours. But that woman hated me. You could see it in her eyes. Now what are you frowning at?'

'I was thinking of Gemma and Walter. She's insisting him and Isa were in love. Gemma has to know all about her own sister-in-law; they were close in age, they lived under the same roof.'

'You reckon.'

'I see now.' She was thoughtful. 'She's trying to protect her brother. The husband's always the first suspect.' She was suddenly frightened. 'What am I saying? Marty, suppose Isa's death wasn't an accident?'

*   *   *

Rosie Winder was lost in admiration. 'That looks exotic. What is it?'

'Pheasant in a chanterelle sauce.' Eleanor preened herself. 'And if you so much as *look* . . .' This to Cooper who was pirouetting about their legs in an ecstasy of anticipation. 'I had to defrost it inside a cold oven,' she told Rosie, 'otherwise he'd have been in the window and stolen a breast just for the fun of it. Couldn't eat it till it was thawed of course.'

'You go away and leave your windows open?' Rosie was appalled.

'This is Borascal, my dear. Everyone knows his neighbour's business so they know there's nothing to steal at Jollybeard. But then,' she added quickly, 'there's no petty theft here.' She regarded Rosie fixedly, conveying a message. 'The mothers are very strict.'

'I haven't seen any children.'

'One family only, and if there were any naughty children in it I wouldn't leave my windows open.'

'How different to the city.' Rosie sighed. 'Even to the town.'

Eleanor shrugged. 'Will you stay for supper? Miss Pink is coming down.'

'I'd love to but really I just called because I was passing, to let you know Walter's back and Gemma's with him.'

'Thank you. I'm taking a casserole to Borrans to save them cooking.' The exchange was stilted. If the woman wasn't staying to eat, why did she linger? 'I expect you're dying for a cup of tea,' Eleanor stated heavily. 'Or would you prefer a proper drink?'

'That would be nice,' Rosie said, startling Eleanor, who thought that the police didn't drink on duty. She considered the cooking whisky, dismissed it and produced a bottle of Talisker.

'Isa could have been drunk,' Rosie murmured.

'No, she didn't drink.'

'She was full of whisky, and Walter's missing the best part of a bottle of Glenlivet. Did you see her using a seat belt?'

'Never.' It was jerked out of Eleanor: an

140

automatic response. She was disorientated, first by the information and then by the question.

'That's what Walter says but Gemma says she did wear one.'

Eleanor clutched the bottle of malt to her chest. 'She'd wear one on the main road,' she said weakly.

'Her mother will be able to fill some gaps. They've gone to inform her. I'll know more when I get back to the station. Did you know her mother?'

'No.' Eleanor was mesmerized. 'I never met her. If she ever came here.'

Miss Pink walked in without knocking, redolent of talc and bonhomie, telling Rosie not to get up, eyeing the bottle. 'Most convivial: one of my favourite tipples.'

'How many do you have?' Rosie asked, grinning. Miss Pink beamed, treating the question as rhetorical.

Eleanor produced another shot glass. 'The sergeant tells me Isa was drunk,' she stated, and it was a warning. She flashed a glance at Rosie. 'The autopsy was very quick.'

'It wasn't finished when I left,' Rosie said. 'But as soon as they'—she paused, glanced at Miss Pink—'made the incision, the fumes knocked them backwards.'

'She was drinking alone?' Miss Pink wondered. 'Or with a companion?'

'We've contacted her driving instructor. He

had a full schedule yesterday but it didn't include Isa.'

'You didn't believe her,' Eleanor said when the woman had gone, leaving the two elderly ladies to stroll to Borrans, accompanied by the officious Cooper: 'about the fumes of Scotch knocking the pathologist backwards.'

'She was stretching it. Ingested material passes out of the stomach within four or five hours as I remember—wait a minute though!' She halted. 'Death stops the process so if she was drinking shortly before she drowned, then the whisky would still be in the stomach.' Her glasses flashed as she looked back down the dale. 'I suppose she did drown.'

'You mean—alcohol poisoning?'

'She'd still drown.' Miss Pink was almost inaudible. She moved forward again.

'I never saw her wearing a seat belt,' Eleanor said. 'And Walter told Rosie she didn't. Gemma says she did—and Isa was strapped in when she was found.'

'How sinister that sounds: strapped in. Gemma would say that. Young girls lead fantasy lives, some of them. Rosie Winder is intrigued, no doubt about that—and then there were those two detectives. Why is the CID investigating a road traffic accident?'

142

CHAPTER NINE

Suddenly, at eight o'clock next morning, Borascal was full of policemen: plain clothes and uniforms. Honeyman slept late but his mother saw the marked cars pass the Lamb and was the first of the residents to react with emotions ranging from trepidation to terror. Only the visitors in the holiday cottages were to view the invasion without qualms but then, sequestered as most folk were in their lush gardens, this news seemed to penetrate slowly.

They went to Borrans first and after a while Sewell and Holgate drove away with Walter. Again. Meanwhile Rosie Winder was taking Gemma down to Jollybeard—again. Other police were at the Blamires' house, at the Lamb, and at Ashgill where Miss Pink came to the door carrying a tea towel to regard the two strange uniforms with mild surprise. They asked her if she knew Mrs Lambert. No, she said. They appeared nonplussed. 'Not socially,' she added. 'I've met her.'

'Did you see her on Wednesday, ma'am?' Although she didn't invite them in, she had presence and the courtesy leaked out.

'Not Wednesday,' she said. 'Only Tuesday.'

'Did you know her car, an MG: a sports car?' The younger man was aware that no one of this age knew any make of car.

'No.' Her eyes sharpened as a police car passed her gate. 'You're trying to discover who saw her last. Has there been a development?'

The younger fellow opened his mouth only to be forestalled by his colleague. 'Nothing to bother about, ma'am,' he said firmly, implying that it needn't concern her. 'So you couldn't say when she left home on Wednesday; you didn't see, or hear the car pass?'

'She wouldn't pass here; Borrans is lower down the lane.'

She let them go, turning away but leaving the door open. She wasn't surprised, ten minutes later, walking past the head of the lane, to see a marked car at the entrance to the Blamires' place, and a uniformed figure approaching it, coming either from Borrans or one of the holiday cottages. Phoebe's place was, as always, closed up, and bore that air of abandonment which pervades houses where the owner isn't coming back. No one was interested in Phoebe now. She wondered why they were concentrating on Isa.

At Jollybeard it was a case of déjà vu: Eleanor and Gemma drinking coffee, Cooper on the windowsill. And Walter? She dared not ask.

'We don't know what's happening.' Eleanor answered the unspoken question. 'Rosie Winder came down with Gemma, but she wouldn't say.'

'Even to me!' Gemma was savage. 'They've

144

taken him away *again* and no one'll tell me why.'

'Didn't they tell him?'

'No, he'd have said.'

'We'll find out.' Miss Pink sounded more confident than she felt. This child was getting a raw deal. 'The Blamires must know something; there's a police car at the end of their drive.'

'Really,' Gemma breathed. 'Really?'

'They'll be calling on everyone.' Miss Pink observed her reactions with interest. 'Door-to-door inquiries. They came to me. They're trying to find out when Isa left the village.' She was uneasy, well aware of the customary reason for so many officers to be deployed in order to discover when a person was last seen alive.

Gemma stood up. 'I'll go and ask Jean; she'll tell me.'

'Wait.' Miss Pink was brusque. 'No one will tell you anything while the police are there. Hang on till they've gone.'

Gemma slumped back in her chair. Eleanor looked anguished. 'I'd welcome a cup of coffee,' Miss Pink said, galvanizing her.

It was ten o'clock before they learned the reason for the renewed activity. Gemma had gone to the Blamires', the police appeared to have left the village, Sherrel Lee had arrived at Jollybeard, insisting that she was feeling better, insisting on cleaning, or waiting if

Eleanor were going to open up—and offhand about the police who had called at Sunder, but of course neither she nor her mother knew anything of Isa's movements on Wednesday, nor any other day. She was washing up when the telephone rang.

Eleanor took the call in the kitchen and turned white. Sherrel clattered a saucepan in the sink and Miss Pink turned on her sharply. Eleanor was clutching the phone as if in a spasm. 'Are they sure?' she gasped. 'But who could—Oh no! No, Walter, you must have—yes, yes . . . all right, I'm listening.' She did so, nodding, then pulled a notepad across the counter, scrabbling frantically in a litter of papers.

Miss Pink advanced. 'Slow down. Let me.' She found a pen and handed it over. She watched Eleanor print a name.

'Of course, right now,' Eleanor cried loudly, like a person not used to the telephone. 'I'll ring you back—what? But they must—oh, right. Good b—' She turned. 'We were cut off!' She tried to replace the phone but she was shaking so much she had to use both hands. Sherrel and Miss Pink stared, immobile.

'Something—something was broken,' she told them. 'In Isa's throat: the high—high—a bone?'

'The hyoid,' Miss Pink said.

'What's that?' Sherrel asked, wiping her wet forehead with a tea towel. 'What's it mean?'

146

'She was strangled.'

'I have to call Walter's solicitor,' Eleanor said. 'He wouldn't instruct the man in front of the police, and why should he? It's family business.'

More than that when your wife's been strangled, Miss Pink thought. Aloud she said, 'Sit down and take a breather before you ring him. You've had a shock.' She hefted the kettle.

'I have to do it now,' Eleanor protested, picking up the phone. 'He must get to the station as soon as possible before Walter says anything.'

Sherrel's eyes were wide as she wiped a plate aimlessly. Miss Pink switched the kettle on and took the tea towel from her. She said firmly, 'You can leave this and do upstairs: make a start on Miss Salkeld's room.' The girl glanced at the sink uncertainly. 'I'll finish here,' Miss Pink said, the tone informing Sherrel that she was on a losing streak if she dared protest further.

Eleanor was conducting a shaky conversation, dramatizing, not for effect but for emphasis: '. . . essential you get down there immediately; he's been accused of her murder—what? *I* don't know; what's the difference? All you have to do is tell him to say nothing—isn't that right?'

There was a protracted pause while she listened and the distant voice yapped away.

147

Her shoulders dropped and at length she managed a defeated, 'I'll be waiting for it' and replaced the phone. 'He'll call me back,' she told Miss Pink, 'When he's seen Walter.'

'Walter hasn't been charged.'

'That's what he said: MacLean, the solicitor. He says they need to question him because he's the husband. Is he right?'

'I'm afraid so. When a wife—when anyone's murdered, the people closest are—have to be interviewed.'

'Are suspects, that's what you were going to say. Guilty until they've proved themselves innocent? That's exactly my point: Walter could incriminate himself; he's very naive.'

'There may be other people who were close to her.'

'Gemma? No. *No!*'

'Not Gemma, but a lover. Or lovers.'

Eleanor sat down carefully. Cooper, aware of a possibly permissive atmosphere, jumped on the table. She ignored him. 'Off!' ordered Miss Pink sharply and he flattened his ears, jumped down and stalked out of the kitchen.

'She was discreet,' Eleanor murmured.

'She wasn't. She was flirting—flaunting herself in the Lamb.'

'I don't think she frequented the Lamb. Walter wouldn't like it. Besides she didn't drink.'

'She was waiting on tables the day they were looking for Phoebe.' Miss Pink stiffened and

148

frowned.

'So she was, but flirting is one thing, taking a lover is serious. If she did, she was discreet about that. And we know most of what goes on in a tiny village.'

'Do you?' It was loaded.

'You live in the country yourself. You know how people talk.'

'There's gossip, and there are open secrets, but sexual deviances, extramarital affairs, are usually kept quiet.'

'But people *know*, and a woman has only to be seen talking to the local Don Juan and it's all round the village.'

'And everyone knows it's gossip. You're saying there was no gossip about Isa?'

'None. She was out a lot—and illegally, without a driving licence, but that was the extent of her offences. She hated Borascal so she went home to her mother. No doubt the mother will confirm that.'

*   *   *

Sitting in the car outside the terraced house in Carlisle, Sewell said, 'Now we'll find out what she was hiding yesterday.'

Rosie, in a neat shirt and slacks, said, 'There are three sons, according to Holgate, all long-distance lorry drivers. Their mother could be programmed to stay shtoom where vehicle offences are involved.'

149

'I'm not concerned with a vehicle offence; I want to find out how much the mother knew about her daughter's love life. Stay with the car, Dowling, and watch those kids.'

The driver took him literally, staring morosely at a group of small boys kicking a football against a brick wall at the end of the cul-de-sac. Beyond the wall loomed the bulk of a rusty gasometer.

The house was tiny: two up, two down, but the trim was fresh and neat if in an unfortunate shade of green. The door was opened by a massive fellow, too heavy for his age, wearing a black singlet designed to reveal tattoos that covered most of the exposed flesh. Bristles were appearing on his shaved head lending him the look of a clipped hedgehog.

They were taken into the back room and Rosie regarded Isa's mother with interest. She must have started producing children very young because she wasn't much more than forty now, the years smoothed out by fat. This family had a recurrent gene or lived on junk food, or both. And, remembering Isa, blue-white on the mortuary slab, Rosie postulated different fathers. The mother had been pretty however, and now looked plumply comfortable and as neat as her painted window frames. In the bleached and back-combed hair, in the green eye-shadow and the whole enamelled appearance, there was a glimpse of the daughter's ghost.

They jostled to find seats, the gross son evidently sitting in, and Sewell voicing no objection. Rosie shot a glance round the dim room, the window netted against a sunlit yard. The room was dominated by an oversize television set and a three-seater sofa in blue leather. There was no table, no pictures and no books. This space was for watching telly just and if they ate here it was off their laps.

The family name was O'Neill and the fat boy was Brian. No one was told to make tea; that would have happened yesterday when they first learned of the death.

'So what's it now?' Mrs O'Neill asked, taking the initiative. Her lips twitched. 'Or is it something else?'

'No,' Sewell said kindly. 'It's your daughter. It wasn't an accident, Molly.'

There was no overt change in the rounded face but something happened: an incipient tightening of the mouth, a narrowing of the eyes. Brian looked at his mother. He was uneasy.

'She never killed herself,' Molly said tightly.

'No.' Her eyes flew open. 'She was'—in the face of that stare Sewell hesitated for the fraction of a second—'murdered.'

In the dead silence that followed, through the closed window a pigeon could be heard crooning: part of the sunlit morning and the urban brick yard.

'How?' Molly asked.

'She was strangled,' Sewell said, and then, surprisingly, 'I'll make us some tea.'

Neither mother nor son reacted. Molly looked at Rosie who was fighting to control her expression. 'You got her husband.'

Rosie blinked, cursing Sewell. Her ambition was CID but not to be thrown in the deep end like this. Metaphorically she trod water. 'Why him?' she countered.

'Had to be. The bastard.'

'I'll kill him,' Brian said, but that was automatic for the type.

'It could have been anyone,' Rosie said, knowing Sewell was hearing every word.

'You're saying my girl was promiscuous?'

'How often did she come here?' Sewell cut in from the doorway.

'I told you yesterday! This were her home!'

'Things have changed. Yesterday we thought it was an accident. She was out most days in her car—'

'Oh no, she weren't—'

'Yesterday you said—'

'I were confused! You'd just told me my girl had been in a car crash—Where you going?' This to Brian who had lurched to his feet.

'I'm going to call our Jimmie.'

'He's in Belgium.'

'He's got a mobile, hasn't he?'

Sewell made no move to detain him. 'She didn't dare come here,' he told Molly. 'She'd be too conspicuous, driving through Carlisle in

152

an open sports car.'

'She came at night.' It was quick and as quickly retracted: 'Once or twice.'

'And the other times? All the times she told her family she was here?'

'*We're* her family.' Sewell waited, eyebrows raised. A calculating look crossed Molly's face. Through the wall came the sound of music from next door. 'I didn't ask,' she said.

'But you knew who it was.'

Her silence could have been acquiescence, on the other hand it could be a ploy. 'Don't you want us to catch him?' Sewell asked.

'You said you'd got him.'

'I said nothing of the sort. Did you?' To Rosie. She shook her head. 'Walter's giving us some information,' he conceded, adding quietly, 'He must have known.'

'They're the last to know.' Molly was grim. 'And when they do find out there's hell to pay.'

He studied her, then glanced at Rosie who said, wheedling, 'She told you there was another man, didn't she?'

Molly stared back and blinked. 'Not as such. I guessed. One way and another. She were always miserable living right out there: the sticks, she called it. Then she changed. She were excited—not happy but sort of—sly, like she were playing a game with me, like when she were little, you know? I warned her, I said she'd to be careful.'

'Careful of what?'

153

'Losing it all of course! That big house, the new clothes, pay cheque every month: job for life, isn't it, the Council? Crazy to throw it all away just for a bit on the side.'

'Who was he, Molly?'

She shook her head, cornered. 'I don't know, I tell you. I never asked.'

'Why not?'

She spread her hands. Her head came up. 'I didn't want to know—there! We had words about it. I told her—'

'Mam!' Brian was back. 'Shut up, Mam!'

'She's dead, son. What's it matter now? I never should have—' Tears traced black trails down the plump cheeks. 'It were the last thing I said to her and I'd give my life to take it back.'

'Leave her be.' Brian was suddenly dangerous: a stupid man, frightened and protective. Sewell stood up and the officers allowed themselves to be crowded into the passage.

'Randy little bitch,' Brian wheezed at Rosie who rounded on him in fury. He held up a large hand, palm out. 'That's what she called Isa,' he told her, and nodded unhappily. 'She were right, you know. All the same, she didn't deserve to go and get herself strangled.'

*   *   *

'Well,' Sewell asked, waxing belligerent as they

154

were halted by roadworks in Botchergate, 'what did you make of that?'

'She was the village tart?'

'There's not been the slightest hint of it.'

'Maybe the right questions weren't asked. And you were concentrating on Walter. Does it make a difference: one man or a number of them? If it was your wife, which would be more likely to make you lose your rag: her having an affair with Joe Bloggs or playing the field?'

Sewell glared at the back of the driver's head. 'That's too personal. It depends on the man.'

'Actually I was doing my best to be objective—and you did ask.' She was resentful; he wanted her opinion and objected if he didn't like it. 'As a woman, I'd be much more concerned if my fellow was serious with another girl than if he was sleeping around. But I can't extrapolate to Walter: opposite sex and, I'm sure, a very different temperament to me.'

'What's your conclusion?' He didn't like that 'extrapolate'. Rosie had a degree in English.

She shrugged. 'I reckon Walter would be devastated if she was having it off with one chap.'

'We're back to square one: he strangled her because he discovered an affair.'

'Well,' she was doubtful, 'it could have been

155

the other guy for one reason or another. He got tired of her? She wanted to go away with him, he wouldn't—or wouldn't leave his wife? Emotional blackmail? You pays your money . . . It would help if we could find out who he is—was.'

*   *   *

Gemma had approached Elfhow trying to convince herself that this was the logical thing to do: visit the neighbours to find out what was happening, particularly when it concerned your own brother. All the same she was wary of Martin: arrogant and macho, Mountain Rescue and all that—she found him sexy and dangerous and was working on the delicious feeling that visiting at Elfhow this morning was like walking into a tiger's cage.

Jean was baking. Bread was proving beside the Aga and she was dribbling molasses into a mixing bowl. Martin would be working upstairs because his van was at the side of the house. Gemma sat at the table, found a stray raisin and ate it absently.

'If you're hungry,' Jean told her, 'there's a lardy cake in the pantry.'

'It's all right, I had breakfast at Jollybeard. The police took Walter away again.'

'Oh, Gemma!' Jean threw a glance at the closed door at the foot of the stairs. She hesitated, lowered her voice: 'What d'you mean, took him away?'

'I thought you'd know.'

Jean breathed deeply. 'They didn't—' She stopped.

'Yes?' Gemma looked innocent, appealing.

'They—didn't tell you about Isa?'

'I know she's dead.' Now she was reproving.

'Gemma, dear . . .' The girl's eyebrows shot up, this didn't sound like Jean and the older woman grimaced, embarrassed. 'Isa was str—killed,' she blurted. 'Murdered.'

Gemma stared, frowned, and suddenly appeared strangely adult. Jean muttered something and made a dash for the door.

Gemma's gaze went to the mixing bowl. She scraped a finger round the side, licked it and moved to the foot of the stairs. She could hear Jean's raised voice and a murmur, not a soft murmur, more a hard mutter. She couldn't distinguish any words.

Jean returned after a few minutes. 'Sorry about that,' she announced on a high note, staring as if she were lost in fog and about to collapse. 'Walter's her husband, which is why they have to question him. They questioned us too.'

'What did they ask?'

Jean's mouth opened, and closed with a snap. 'What time Isa—did we hear her leave on Wednesday? We didn't.'

'You're very close, but she's downhill from you—was. You wouldn't hear the MG unless

157

you were listening for it.'

Jean nodded. 'They're asking everyone the same question so I promise you: there's no need to worry about Walter.'

A board creaked. Jean's eyes flickered but Gemma seemed focused on the police: 'Are they asking people where they were on Wednesday night?'

'No, why should they do that?'

'They'll get around to it. After they bring Walter back. Because I know where he was every minute of that night.' She smiled sweetly. 'So what if it sounds incestuous? They'll be interested in every male between sixteen and sixty You know: the usual suspects.'

'It's not a joke, Gemma.'

'Someone did it.'

'No one we know then.' Jean was harsh. 'None of us lives alone.'

'And all our men have alibis. That sounds like a quotation, doesn't it? You're right though, when they find him it'll be a psychopath, a loner, someone she met when she was out driving.'

When she'd gone Jean worked furiously, rolling out her scones, slapping the dough on the pastry board, gouging with the cutters. There was no sound from Martin's study but she wouldn't hear anything with the doors closed. She went out to the vegetable garden and drifted up and down the rows with a hoe chopping the odd weed, coming back to the front of the house to look up at his window, which was wide open. The curtains moved gently but nothing else moved except the swallows swooping into their nests under the eaves.

She was close to the porch when he came down and she followed him to the kitchen having worked herself into a fine state of righteous resentment.

'I *told* you'—he was emphatic—'I will not be interrupted when I'm working. It was bad enough to have you come in ranting and raving; to come down and have to deal with two hysterical women—'

'Marty! She's a child! She's alone and terrified and if you can't spare a moment from your *magnum opus*—'

'Don't be so fucking snide. Why should I be bothered because some dirty little tart gets herself bumped off by her husband? She deserved it. Anyway, Gemma's not exactly virginal herself—her and Dwayne Paxton.'

'That's got nothing to do with it.'

'Hasn't it? How do you know? Come to think of it'—his eyes sharpened—'Dwayne would take anything on offer. Remember what I told you?' He was grimly amused, surprised that he hadn't thought of this already. 'D'you know, I reckon she had it off with Dwayne too.'

'Too?'

He stared at her and licked his lips. 'I won't

be the only one she tried it on with.'

Jean wouldn't meet his eyes. She moved to the cooker and opened the oven door—to be greeted by a blast of smoke and heat. She gasped and grabbed the oven gloves. Snatching at the baking sheet she misjudged it and charred lumps were scattered across the flags.

'Shit, shit, *shit*!'

She backed to a chair, tore off the gloves and threw them at him. He watched her warily. After a moment he closed the oven door, crunching cinders underfoot.

She lifted her face, dry-eyed but anguished. 'You slept with her,' she said dully.

'I told you—'

'You told me a little, a tiny fraction. You left out the important part.'

He turned. 'I'm off.' He paused and regarded her stonily. 'You're fantasizing. I told you the truth and you fabricated a whole drama round it. It's you should be writing the books: a bodice-ripper, that's your style. You're obsessed with sex.' She stared at him, unable to follow his drift but knowing she'd remember every word. 'I can see what's wrong,' he went on, 'it's your time of life.'

'I'm not forty!'

'It happens. What you should do is see the doctor, get him to make you an appointment with a psychiatrist. You can do it voluntary and it's all on the National Health. Now I'm going out; no way can I work here with all these daft interruptions.'

It wasn't until the van had clattered away down the lane that she remembered she hadn't told him what Gemma had said about the usual suspects. She thought that was funny: that she'd forgotten to tell him.

CHAPTER TEN

At Bailrigg workmen drilled out the lock in order to repossess a studio flat and found the decomposing body of a woman with massive head injuries. She was identified as one of the former occupants and a search was started for the husband who hadn't been seen for weeks, neither by the neighbours nor at his workplace. The police were overstretched but fortunately the Lamberts' MG had been recovered and its inspection could go ahead because the technicians involved weren't needed for the Bailrigg murder.

Short-handed then, and with Sewell occupied as he was with questioning Walter, Rosie was sent back to Borascal, in plain clothes and driving her own silver Puma. Her instructions were to find out if Isa had been involved with another man and to try to ascertain Walter's movements on Wednesday night.

'Oh my,' Honeyman breathed as she

approached the bar in the Fat Lamb. 'That's what I call a sexy car.'

'Pretty, isn't it?' Rosie's smile accepted the innuendo as a compliment, knowing that in Honeyman's book sexy cars meant sexy owners. He was leering at her, his eyes like currants in puff pastry.

'Day off?' he asked as she ordered a beer.

She nodded. 'I like this village. I thought I'd rent a cottage later in the year, bring my folks up for a holiday.' She tasted the beer, raising an eyebrow in appreciation. 'I'm looking at some empty places this afternoon.'

His mother came in from the back with a tray and a plate of hamburgers oozing fried onions. Honeyman added drinks and napkins and carried it to a family at one of the tables outside. No one was indoors except Rosie.

'You'll not find any cottages empty this time of year,' Dorcas told her.

'I can walk round and check them from the outside. I have the agents' particulars.'

'You've done your homework.' Dorcas was sardonic. 'You reckon Borascal will suit you?'

Honeyman came back with the tray and eased his bulk behind the bar. He wasn't leering any longer but he was intent on Rosie's reply.

'If I was a journalist I'd say Borascal was unspoiled: pretty; affluent, friendly; that is, everyone's got good manners.' She shrugged. 'It's a world away from what I'm used to:

162

poverty, drugs . . . crime.'

The last word hung in the air. The Honeymans seemed to be expecting more. 'What happened here is in a different league from urban crime,' she insisted.

'We're premier league material.' Honeyman was trying to make a joke.

She ignored it. 'I suppose, even in a village, there's a lot of domestic—er—irregularity? Not real crime though.'

Dorcas uttered an exclamation of either contempt or disgust and went back to the kitchen. He waited until she was out of earshot when he said slyly, 'You don't call murder a crime?'

'Like you said, it's in a different league. What I'm saying is you can't compare a deprived urban area with a prosperous village. Although,' she added thoughtfully, 'sex crimes would be a common factor. There are prostitutes everywhere.'

'She weren't no prostitute!' His fury was startling. 'You think I'd have employed an 'ore in this house? My mother would—'

'What?' Dorcas was back in a hurry, her eyes snapping. 'What's that, son?'

'She says as how Isa were an 'ore.'

Rosie had both hands up, pressing the air. 'I never mentioned Isa! What makes you think— You employed her here? I didn't know that.'

Dorcas asked tightly, 'What were you saying about her?'

163

Rosie shook her head helplessly. 'I wasn't talking about her. I was talking about crime in inner cities as opposed to Borascal and it occurred to me that—' She turned innocent eyes on Honeyman. 'Oh, I *see*! We got our wires crossed. 'Here was me thinking the common denominator was sexual—adventures—'

'Prostitutes! They're everywhere, was what you said,' Honeyman blustered.

'And you saw a connection. Of course she wasn't a prostitute. Everyone would have known.'

'She was friendly,' Dorcas said, so close to her son that she was touching him.

'A looker.' He swallowed. 'She couldn't help that,' he added weakly.

'It's a small place,' Rosie agreed. 'A pretty girl: there would be gossip. Nothing to it of course. The men would discuss her among themselves, they always do. I work with fellows, I know how they talk about any new colleague, even when she isn't a looker. You can't tell me anything about a men's locker room.'

'No one gossiped about her,' Dorcas said with finality. 'There was nowt to gossip *about*.'

*   *   *

Rosie left her car at the pub and, a light Pentax round her neck, trying to present the image of

164

a mildly interested tourist, she turned left towards the houses. On her right was the Rutting Beck and a wooden footbridge which held no interest for her and, on her side of the road, a track with a footpath sign: 'Sleylands. Closewater 3m.'

The road forked, the left lane climbing, eventually to double back on itself, as she knew, and return as the right fork. She turned left, despite her mission, finding a sensuous pleasure in this slow and deceptively aimless amble where before she had passed relatively quickly, incarcerated in a metal box. True, the car windows had been open and there had been scents and birdsong but now there was time to distinguish between different smells and to stare. 'Time to stand and stare', she recalled from her schooldays, stopping at a shabby gate under an arch dripping with the blue racemes of wisteria. A flagged path, rather weedy but cushioned with rock plants, led to a solid porch and a façade in need of whitewash.

Desirable property in need of renovation, she thought, carried away by yet another persona: prospective house hunter. As she leaned on the gate, it opened unexpectedly and at the same moment a lithe young fellow emerged from the porch carrying a haversack. He checked at sight of her and then advanced: no more than twenty, she concluded, and immature. His appreciation was quick and obvious but then she'd dressed carefully; the cut of the slacks emphasizing her long legs, the wide leather belt cinching her waist, the shirt with one too many buttons undone. The wraparound shades added glamour while shielding her eyes.

'Hi,' he said. 'And what can I do for you?' The tone was a caress, his eyes were saying he knew exactly what he could do. Her smile was an acknowledgement of it.

Aloud she said, 'Nothing really, your gate came open as I was leaning on it admiring your cottage. Actually I'm looking to rent one later in the year.'

'Is that so?' She could hear wheels turning in his brain. 'You wouldn't want this place. Alone, are you?' So casual it was ludicrous.

'It depends,' Rosie said. 'Why wouldn't this place do? It's sweet. Are you on holiday too?' Hardly, in those filthy jeans, but the inanity of the question went over his head.

'I live here. I'm Dwayne. I were born here. My folk moved into town and I inherited the old place. It needs doing up. I'm going to get stuck in at back-end when I've finished another house . . . Tell you what, why don't you come and look at that? The owner's after a tenant. Great big kitchen, lounge like a barn, two bathrooms, three bedrooms—the big one's out of this world: parky floor, one wall all glass, balcony to drink your wine on. Suit you down to the ground.'

'You're working there?'

'Well, yeah. I work for meself like. I'm going along there now, it's only just down the road.' He was trying to look boyish and smooth but he couldn't keep still and he was too close to her.

'You show people over it? I mean, you act as an agent or what?'

'No.' He paused, grinned and plunged. 'I just take girls there.' His eyes were sparkling. It was a joke.

'On their own?' She didn't believe this; no one could be so obvious.

'Right.' He exuded confidence. She moved away, trying to avoid stepping on some carmine saxifrage that was invading the path.

She turned and looked him in the eye. 'I wouldn't be the first girl you've taken there.'

He didn't like that and once he stopped smiling he was menacing. 'Who've you been talking to? You been listening to gossip. Were you—' He glanced down the lane. 'You was in t'Lamb! That bastard! Ask him what he gets up to when he's away to the Cash-and-Carry. Takes him all day to pick up a few groceries. And to look at un you wouldn't think un could make it with nowt except a sheep.'

'What was your name again?'

'Who's asking?'

'Dwayne what?' She wasn't going to ask him where he was when the police came calling door-to-door, she wasn't going to ask him if he'd heard Isa leave on Wednesday night, had seen her go, had been with her. But she was going to risk a gamble. 'Were you at that house on Wednesday?'

' 'Course I were.' But the answer had come slowly.

'Wednesday night?'

'No.'

She wished this garden were overlooked by a neighbour but it wasn't and she'd gone too far to pull back. 'So where were you?'

'Who wants to know?'

'What have you got to hide?'

He was quiet and tense, like a cat hearing a rustle in long grass, or was it he who had rustled and now he was immobile, watching the cat?

He turned and went up the path but instead of going to the house he veered to the right to disappear behind some shrubs. A latch clicked. She retreated to the gate. After a few moments a Land Rover emerged from a gap, himself at the wheel. He ignored her, trying to look casual, succeeding only in looking— frightened, she thought. She was left wondering if she'd discovered anything important. A randy young bugger certainly, and one who'd avoided the police until now, but neither need make him a murderer, even if something she'd said had scared him badly.

* * *

168

'That's Dwayne Paxton,' Eleanor said, shunting a batch of loaves on to a wire tray. 'No doubt he propositioned you.'

'Good Lord, how did you guess?'

'I've known him since he was a small boy, which wasn't that long ago. He's not firing on all his cylinders, but you'll have discovered that for yourself.'

'Two coffees and cakes!' Sherrel announced, bustling in from the front. She stared at the stranger suspiciously.

'Have you met Sergeant Winder?' Eleanor asked, but Sherrel hadn't, and shook her head blankly. Rosie asked her if she lived in the village and she said she did, with her family. The atmosphere was electric; Eleanor would have liked to suggest that the visitor go out to the tearoom but dared not say so. On duty or day off, if the police walked in your kitchen, it wasn't a good idea to tell them to leave it.

Sherrel started to assemble a tray clumsily, aware of Rosie's eyes on her. Rosie was considering whether the girl would repay investigation and deciding against it; best results would be obtained from the people she knew already.

Eleanor spooned tea into a pot. 'You don't use tea bags,' Rosie said in wonder.

'This is an up-market establishment,' Eleanor said and then, surprisingly, she winced.

169

'A problem?' Rosie asked, thinking rheumatism.

'Not any longer.'

'There never was!' Sherrel cried heatedly, glad to distract attention from herself. 'That were a trick, Miss Salkeld, and a nasty mean one too.'

'It's over, Sherrel. Folk are coming back.'

'And small thanks to her, whoever.'

'What's this about?' Rosie asked.

'You never heard? I thought the whole county knew. Someone started a rumour that we had salmonella poisoning here. It was a hoax of course, but it wasn't pleasant to know that someone could hate you to that extent.'

Rosie gaped. The Honeymans, she thought, they're the competition. 'I'm surprised you should be the target,' she said. 'The Lamb is much more vulnerable: serving hamburgers on a hot day like this. And presumably microwaved.'

Eleanor giggled. 'Actually they're delicious hamburgers. I have one occasionally although I agree: they're not hot-weather food.' She looked thoughtful. 'Although when you think of it, there's probably more bacteria about than we ever imagine. We must have built up an immunity to it.'

Rosie's lip twitched as she recalled the cat on the windowsill. He had to pass the sink or the draining board to get there—and when he came in: paws all gluey from garden soil.

170

Miss Pink entered from the front carrying a small bundle which she unfurled to reveal a striped apron. 'Day off?' she asked genially, tying the strings.

'House hunting.' Rosie was brazen. 'Just for a short break. I've been offered two already.'

'Which two?' Eleanor was arrested in the act of spooning strawberry jam into a crystal bowl.

'Dwayne Paxton's: his own and the one he's working on.'

Eleanor snorted. 'You can forget both. His must be the last home in Borascal with an outside lavatory—pretty view but—an earth closet? And Blind Keld, at the other extreme, isn't for rent. He's rebuilding the garden wall there, and if he's pretending an interest in it he's suffering from delusions of grandeur.'

'I got the impression the delusion was sexual. He tried to lure me there with a hard sell on the master bedroom.'

'He actually tried to—That boy's impossible! However, if he's courting other girls'—Eleanor was addressing Miss Pink—'let's hope family problems prompted Gemma to give him the push.'

Miss Pink was shaking her head in warning but Rosie's peripheral vision was excellent and even if it hadn't been, Eleanor's sudden tension was significant. 'Did that big party come in?' she cried. 'I'm going to need another kettle if we go on like this. I never asked'—she

171

looked at Rosie wildly—'I suppose you can't say how Walter is?'

'I haven't been in since.' Rosie was ambiguous. 'They must be tied up with this murder in Bailrigg.' They stared at her. 'You haven't heard?' She told them as much as would be released to the media but they were only superficially impressed. They had their own murder in Borascal.

'Was Isa promiscuous?' she asked, dropping it like a bomb out of a blue sky.

The quiet in the kitchen was accentuated by low voices in the tearoom, the gentle clatter of crockery, the scrape of a chair. There was no gasp of shock, no hasty denial. Miss Pink seemed relaxed but attentive; Eleanor was more than relaxed, she looked resigned.

'It crossed my mind,' she admitted at length and then, pulling herself up: 'Oh no, not promiscuous. But . . .'—and then, as if she'd completed an utterance, she busied herself measuring flour into a bowl.

'Her mother says she wasn't promiscuous but . . .' Rosie contributed.

Eleanor nodded sadly. 'Probably.' She sighed and tried to retract: 'Possibly.'

'But of course,' Rosie said, trying to keep the irony out of her tone, 'no one has any idea of his identity.'

Eleanor looked at her blankly. 'Would they say if they knew?'

She dawdled along the top lane, pausing to snap a dazzling white house with crow-stepped gables, working round to include its barn with a sagging slate canopy over its great door, cursing a red BMW which spoiled the effect, then remembering that she wasn't a photographer, only acting the part. No one came out of this house to chat, or chat her up. She strolled on, came to where the lane doubled back at an acute angle and paused to study Phoebe Metcalf's closed house, a magnolia dropping waxy petals on uncut grass, the cat Cooper watching her from a bower of columbines. She took his picture for good measure and then one of Miss Pink's place: a gleam of white walls through silver birch trunks and drifts of bluebells.

Elfhow's gate was closed but she wasn't interested in the Blamires, her attention was focused on Borrans, although she thought it unlikely that a girl of fifteen would be on her own when her brother was with the police. Did Gemma think he was only helping them with their inquiries? If she hadn't left the village she couldn't be far away—unless she'd taken a leaf out of her sister-in-law's book and was driving without a licence—and under age at that.

Gemma was, in fact, polishing her brother's car. Cracks between the stone flags of the drive were still damp and a vacuum cleaner lay on the grass verge along with several attachments. The girl was expressionless as Rosie approached but she hadn't recognized the sergeant in shades and plain clothes. When she did she was hostile. 'Where is he?' she demanded, peering past Rosie.

'I'm sorry?'

'My brother!' She spat it out. 'What've you done with him?'

'It's my day off.' Rosie simulated surprise. 'I was just helping out this morning because they had to have a woman along. Sewell's only talking to Walter, you know; he wants to know about Isa's friends and family.'

'Why didn't he question Wally here?'

'He wanted to spare you.'

'Spare me from what?'

'Embarrassment. About Isa's friends.' Gemma should have asked in what way Isa's friends could be embarrassing but she didn't; she stared at Rosie's dark glasses and waited tensely for the next question.

'I've been talking to Dwayne Paxton,' Rosie said.

The girl's eyes wandered and her lips worked. 'So?' It was too loud.

'Does he come on to all the girls?'

'How the hell would I know?'

'You mean now you've finished with him you don't care if he plays around.'

'Who said I'd finished with him? When did I

174

ever start?'

'He's scared, Gemma.'

She started to nod and then changed it to a violent shake of the head. 'I don't see why. What's he got to be scared of?'

'The police poking around of course.' Rosie moved and peered into the interior of the car. 'Police walk into a village and they're concerned with just one aspect, but they turn over stones, uncover things, find secrets they didn't know were there.'

'Like what?'

'Oh, you know: folk smoking a bit of grass at parties, after-hours drinking in the pub, burying a cow because it shows signs of BSE, driving without a licence, cheating on husbands.' There was along pause. 'Under-age sex,' Rosie murmured.

After a moment Gemma said shakily, 'It's not a crime to cheat on your husband. A sin maybe, not a crime.'

A cuckoo called, threatening to destroy the carefully contrived mood with ridicule. Fortunately Gemma was too young to appreciate the timing.

'And Dwayne wouldn't be bothered about a court case,' Rosie suggested.

'How does a court—oh, you mean like a divorce. No, why should he?'

'Costs?' Rosie was vague. 'I suppose they met at Blind Keld?'

'I guess.' Gemma accepted it as a question,

which she was meant to do.

'How serious were they?'

The hesitation was a fraction too long and then Gemma shook her head. 'Never. She wouldn't want to lose all this.' She gestured to the house.

'Needs a lick of paint,' Rosie said, then turned to stare at the car, P-registered, although coming up bravely under its polishing.

'Borrans is a mansion compared with what she came from,' Gemma said without a trace of contempt, and then, 'Yes, I know what you're thinking: that she'd throw it all away for Dwayne Paxton, but you see, Walter *knew* and it didn't make any difference at all, no more than it did with me. She had the morals of a cat.'

Rosie blinked. 'You're saying there were more boyfriends?'

Gemma was taken aback. 'I'm not saying that, just that she was a slag.'

'You didn't mind living in the same house with a slag?'

'Why should I? She didn't bother me.' Gemma thought about it. 'Matter of fact I was thinking about giving her the push; you know: tell her to go back where she came from.' She glanced at Rosie hopefully. Rosie thought that the girl was getting tired.

'How would you have gone about it?'

'Blackmail.'

'Oh yes. And what crime had she committed that you could blackmail her with?'

Gemma's eyes were shifty and Rosie's mind switched to the other question that needed answering: Walter's whereabouts on Wednesday night.

'Slander,' Gemma said suddenly. 'She started a rumour that there was salmonella at Jollybeard. That's a crime. You don't believe me? She hated Eleanor. Eleanor said she was out for all she could get.'

'I have to go,' Rosie said. 'Shall I put Walter's car back in the garage for you?'

'No, that's OK, I can do it.'

For the life of her Rosie could think of no way of broaching the subject of Walter. 'How could I?' she protested to Sewell on her mobile. 'I got everything else, but no way was I going to ask her if he was in bed all Wednesday night. She'd have lied and turned hostile again and I'd established some kind of rapport which could come in useful. Anyway, you wanted a lover and you've got one—and Walter knew about him. She let that slip.'

'You can come back,' Sewell said. 'You done a good job.'

'Square one again,' he told Holgate when she'd signed off. 'We've got a name for the boyfriend, Dwayne Paxton, but Walter knew about him.'

'If he'd known all along, what triggered him last Wednesday?'

'Not quite square one,' Sewell mused, ignoring him. 'We've got another suspect—identified—and others unnamed? Honeyman's no saint, I wouldn't trust him near my daughter, and there are other men in Borascal, not to speak of further afield.'

'And women.'

'What?'

'If it was a sex murder it could just as well have been a woman.' Holgate spread his fingers. 'Need strong hands though, but these farm women are strong.'

'A lesbian relationship?'

'That hadn't occurred to me. I was thinking of a jealous wife, partner, whatever.'

Or sister, Sewell thought.

*   *   *

In the late evening Miss Pink, fortified by Eleanor's poached salmon but having declined wine, was following a sheep trod along the top of the escarpment where Isa had plunged to the river. Gouges in the far bank marked where the MG had been winched out of the water. Furnished with a large-scale map she had found a gate which gave access to the water meadows and, working her way south, had come to the start of the crag. Here sheep had made a narrow path which she followed, climbing to a long grassy ledge between the wall and the scarp.

The ledge was wide but it sloped gently, no hazard to a person on foot but the angle would have increased the impetus of a car breaking through the wall. Where there were fissures in the crag below small trees were rooted but there was none big enough to stop the MG. One raw snag marked a sapling that had snapped on impact. Above that point was the gap in the wall, the ledge littered with large stones. On the side of the wall that fronted the road a solid metal barrier had been erected, like a double crash barrier. Locking the stable door, she murmured, studying the wall either side of the gap, squinting along the line, looking for bellying. The ground here had been trampled by many people, imprints in the dust clear in the light of the setting sun. And if that hadn't been in her eyes she would have seen a figure sitting in a rudimentary shelter on the far bank of the river, watching with all the interest of a fisherman observing the behaviour of a large trout.

She retreated, climbed the padlocked gate and came back to the gap. The sun was slipping below a wooded hill but the river reflected the sky. Bats were taking over from the sand martins, jinking above the water. A snipe thrummed unseen. Miss Pink, studying tarmac, could see no skid marks on the road, and she saw that where the wall was intact it was solid. The river at this point was deep enough that the driver would have been submerged even if the MG hadn't turned turtle. Strapped in her seat, drunk, Isa wouldn't have stood a chance if she'd been alive. But she wasn't alive, she was dead when she hit the water, in fact she was dead when she went through the wall.

Miss Pink walked back to her car slowly. She stared at the bulk of the fells against an apple-green sky, not seeing them, thinking about the hyoid . . . She remembered Eleanor's saying 'high—high' and herself explaining about the hyoid. How many people knew about it? If he hadn't known, the man who strangled Isa, he would have expected the death to pass as an accident: she was drunk, she couldn't drive well, she crashed through a wall. A wall that was solid, no sign of bellying. He must have started the MG's run from back here, a hundred yards or so up Waterhouses Lane . . . no, too far, only a few yards were necessary; once he'd aimed the car at the gap it needn't be going at more than walking pace—he'd be pushing it—because it didn't have to break through the wall. He'd already made the gap, pushed down the stones.

The murder was premeditated then but the killer was cutting it fine, someone could have come along when he was dismantling the wall, or when he was pushing the MG. What are we looking at here, she wondered: a psychopath? In Borascal? She conjured up images of the contenders, those she had met and those she was aware of. Walter: the husband always the first suspect; Honeyman—her eyes narrowed in unconscious imitation of his; Swinburn and the curiously peasant behaviour involving the weekly tenner to the mother of his bastard. There was Blamire, the mountain rescuer, Dwayne Paxton and his reckless liaison with a fifteen-year-old, now there was one who gave no thought for the consequences. And those were just the men; women could be as tough, tougher, look at Phoebe Metcalf. But Phoebe came a cropper at the end (thoughts going off at a tangent, a corollary of old age), she'd fallen in the quarry . . . down a steep slope . . . and drowned. How odd. It had been a curious coincidence to have two violent deaths in four days but two *drownings*? She shook herself, feeling the cold metal of her car under her hands, recalling her to the present. The first death was an accident, this one was murder, by strangling. A woman could strangle a drunk but could she dismantle a wall? No doubt; if she had the strength to strangle . . . wait, she'd missed something. Another car was needed in order for the killer to get away, moreover someone had to drive the MG to this spot— unless Isa had been strangled here. But even if that were the case the killer still had to get home. Which argued either an accomplice or that he—or she—lived close enough that a second vehicle wasn't necessary. Borascal was about three miles distant. He wouldn't be able to keep to the lanes for fear of showing up in headlights so he'd take to the fields and footpaths. Therefore a local man, not necessarily from Borascal but local.

The stars were starting to appear, Venus brilliant in a tinted shell, no fiery shades tonight. Miss Pink's engine caught and her lights lit up a grove of sycamores. The lights were observed by the occupant of the fishermen's shelter who stood up stiffly and reached for his mobile.

CHAPTER ELEVEN

Walter was home again, exhaustion lines etched in his face. Forcing himself to respond to Gemma's solicitude, he picked at his stuffed chicken thighs until she told him to leave it, wasn't there *anything* she could get for him?

'Another whisky,' he said.

She brought the bottle. He'd already had a large one after the police dropped him off; she guessed a second would knock him out, which was probably for the best. He'd aged ten years in the last two days, and he wouldn't tell her anything except that he'd talked to Sewell, as if she didn't know that. There were a hundred questions she wanted to ask, and some information to impart, but she saw that she'd have to wait. She reached for his plate and started to eat his portion.

At breakfast time he was no more communicative, at least to start with. It was Saturday so she didn't ask if he were going to the office. He looked a little better this morning: bathed and wearing clean clothes, smelling of aftershave rather than someone else's cigarette smoke, but his eyes were washed out and still he wouldn't talk. The initiative had to be hers.

'Rosie Winder came back yesterday.' He looked puzzled. 'The police sergeant,' she explained. 'It was her day off really and she wanted to find a cottage to rent—she *said*. Actually she was after information.'

'It's to be expected. There'd have been more police here yesterday but there's another—death—in Bailrigg. Sewell told me. They're short-handed.'

'Dwayne Paxton made a play for her.'

'For who?'

'Rosie, the policewoman. She looks quite cool in proper clothes, a belt you'd die for. Dwayne was bowled over. Isn't that a scream?'

'Why?'

'Well, he told her he took girls to Blind Keld, asked her to go there with him.'

'He does!' He was concerned. 'Did you ever . . .'

'Go to Blind Keld?' She shrugged. 'I'm not interested in Dwayne. He's history as far as I'm concerned. But he knew Isa.'

183

He looked at her like a sick dog. 'Isa? And *Dwayne*?'

Gemma was frightened but she stuck to her guns. 'You knew—well, if you didn't, you know now. You didn't do it so it was someone else, right? But there was more than one chap, Wally.' The emphasis was not only in the tone but in the fixed stare that was trying to force it home on him.

He sighed. 'Yes, I knew.'

She gaped: the forceful woman reverted to a child. 'You knew?' It was a whisper.

He nodded helplessly. 'Guessed, suspected, who cares? Sewell guessed too. He put it to me that I was condoning it—' He registered her shock and realized with amazement that he was talking to his little sister. He shook his head vehemently. 'It's all over, Gem; we're going to start again. I made a mistake and now we have to forget all about it.'

'But you were shocked just now when I said she was having it off with Dwayne.'

He winced. 'I didn't know about him.'

'So—who . . .'

'You said there were other—look'—but suddenly he was angry, at the end of his tether—'I'm not talking about it, d'you hear? She was my wife and—' Again he remembered that this was a child. 'Forget it, love.' He stood up and said with false heartiness, 'Now I'm going to do some gardening and get some fresh air into my lungs. Why don't you come

184

out yourself when you're finished here?'

Gemma poured more coffee and stayed at the breakfast table, watching him change into his old shoes in the passage, wondering what it was that he knew and she didn't, and how much of it he had told the police.

*   *   *

Miss Pink was watching a tree creeper when a watery crack alerted her to activity in the beck. She was on a track on the north bank and upstream of the house called Sunder. The level of the water had dropped and she felt no anxiety at sight of two small figures intent on constructing a dam; one, a tiny bareheaded girl, the other: young Bobby in a baseball cap.

She was about fifty yards away when the girl looked up and saw her. Miss Pink waved cheerily to indicate that she was no stranger, no paedophile come to Borascal to carry off small children, a hazard they'd no doubt been warned against, although in a dale where doors were left unlocked, it was a moot point that such a warning would be heeded. Different if it were Carlisle. And so ruminating, watching her feet among cow pats and lumpy bedrock, she came up to them, now slowed in their play, idly picking up stones and dropping them where they could serve no purpose except as something to do while they observed her out of the corners of their eyes.

185

Bobby was now bareheaded too. She looked beyond him.

'You've lost your hat.'

'Hat, miss?' No small boy could be as innocent as his expression implied. His sister glanced at him uncertainly.

'Your hat,' she said.

He stumbled, thrust out an arm as he tried to recover, and knocked the child over. There was a scream and a splash, Miss Pink made to start forward but Bobby was already pulling the dripping child to her feet, hustling her out of the water and up the bank. 'You're soaked,' he hissed at her. 'Mam'll kill me! Hurry, we gotta get you into some dry clothes. Give you a hot drink. You're all right, Flo, I'll tell 'em it were my fault.' He looked up at Miss Pink. 'You come too, miss. You tell our nan as it weren't her fault, *please.*'

His sister, infected by his panic, started to sob loudly.

'No harm done.' Miss Pink was calmness personified. 'We'll all go. Of course it was no one's fault and a drop of water's not going to hurt anyone on a hot day. What's your name?' To the girl.

'It's Flora,' Bobby said quickly. 'We was building a dam, see. We're making a paddling pool and then our mam can come down with the littluns and us'll have a picnic like. Maybe we can build un big enough for a proper pool and swim—once us learns how. Oh, I forgot;

186

you go on, there's the house, I gotta go back for me rod.' And leaving them as the wall of Sunder came in sight he darted away up the track.

Flora said between sobs, 'He didn't have no rod.'

'He's gone back for his hat,' Miss Pink said.

'Right. He put it in the water.'

It was odd that such a young child should use the more difficult verb 'put' instead of 'dropped' but Miss Pink had no time to question it as, on the far side of a gate, Misella emerged from the cottage with a load of washing. Her eyes widened.

'Where's Bobby?'

'He's coming,' Miss Pink assured her, unlatching the gate. 'He's fine.' And explained.

'In you go,' Misella ordered the child, in the tone of wry resignation adopted by indulgent grandmothers. 'You know where everything is: the green dinosaur shirt and the red shorts. I wouldn't let her play in the beck on her own,' she told Miss Pink, 'but our Bobby looks after her. He's a great little minder, that one.' She followed the visitor's eyes to a sand pit where two toddlers were playing. Beyond them was a weatherboard fence. 'The littluns is too small to climb the fence,' she said quickly. 'And we keep this gate latched.'

Miss Pink nodded. Forget paedophiles, a beck was the major hazard here. She wondered how soon the toddlers would learn to unlatch the gate but she allowed no disapproval to show, instead she regarded the cottage benignly. The back door opened on a functional verandah roofed by one of those long slate canopies that were a feature of the region. It rose to the level of the bedroom windows and the space below served the dual purpose of drying room and play room, judging by washing lines, and bright plastic toys strewn about the cement.

'So Sherrel's at Jollybeard and you're minding the family.' It was facetious but Miss Pink was at a loss. With the Lees living here rent-free, and officially no father existing for the glut of children, she could think of no subject that wouldn't carry some innuendo. 'Such a shock,' she murmured, casting her net wide: 'Mrs Lambert drowning. It makes you think.'

'I thought she were murdered,' Misella said.

'Drowned, strangled, what difference does it make? She died. I feel sorry for Mr Lambert. And that young girl: only fifteen.'

Misella gave a derisive snort. 'That one can look after herself. I can't say the same for the brother but her! Fifteen?' She frowned at the toddlers. 'Got a sharper brain than our Sherrel and no mistake.'

'That's education.' Miss Pink was earnest. 'Gemma's had advantages. All the same, and judging by appearances, Sherrel's youngsters are bright enough. She's a good mother.'

'With a bit of help here and there but you're right: Gemma Lambert wouldn't do so well if it was her with a load of weans.'

'Time enough yet. She's only a schoolgirl.'

'They start at eleven nowadays, it were on t'radio.' Misella was mildly contemptuous of this old lady, relic of a generation that thought brides came to the marriage bed as virgins. When did they ever? 'But then,' she added darkly, 'what d'you expect with that sister-in-law?'

'But I'm sure Mr Lambert loved his wife.'

'He weren't the only one then.'

'Love?' Miss Pink was bewildered.

'Well, sex they calls it now, like an itch. You gotta scratch it, you know?' Wrong. This old soul had no idea what was being talked about—never had the itch of course, neither legal nor outside wedlock.

'Did she take people home?' Miss Pink asked, seemingly of herself. 'Oh no, never. A hotel then?' She looked hopefully at Misella, childishly eager to be instructed in the conduct of clandestine affairs. 'An empty cottage?'

Misella studied her, not sure about this. 'Who did you have in mind?'

'Heavens! I've no idea who. I was wondering how they could keep it a secret in such a small place. She couldn't have driven far. People say she couldn't drive.'

Misella said slowly, 'What she'd do is drive to meet him and they'd leave his car and go on

189

in hers.' Miss Pink seemed to find this difficult to follow. 'They couldn't leave hers, it were too obvious,' Misella explained. 'Little red sports car. His wouldn't be; leave it anywhere in a lay-by, even on a main road.'

'Why wouldn't his car be recognized?'

'He'd be a stranger, wouldn't he? Not from around here. He could be a truck driver she met in some all-night caff.'

'Ah, I see. I couldn't understand how a local man could get away with it; there'd be a wife to deceive, a mother . . . but of course, if he was a long way from home . . .' She tailed off and after a moment Misella accepted that as the end of the conversation. She bent to her washing.

Miss Pink left Sunder giving no weight to the theory of Isa's lover being a stranger or an itinerant truck driver, but a certain amount of weight to Misella's wanting her to think so. However, Isa was one thing, what was at the forefront of Miss Pink's mind right now was the fact that Bobby had not appeared at Sunder—which he wouldn't do because he'd gone back for a rod, and Flora said he didn't have a rod. He'd gone back for his hat, and this was the second time he'd denied that he had a blue denim hat. What was it about that hat?

*　　　*　　　*

Jollybeard was ticking over nicely. Nine

190

customers in for lunch, Sherrel serving, Eleanor snatching a moment for coffee as Miss Pink tucked into focaccia and olives in the kitchen.

'There are two dead sheep downstream of the Lamb. Would that be Swinburn's land?'

Eleanor sighed. 'The same. Last back-end there were seven. He fattens Scottish lambs in the water meadows and apparently there are always a few who die after the journey.'

'He told you that?'

'He told the police. Phoebe reported it. She was fed up. She'd warned him time and time again that if he didn't bury them she'd inform the police. And she did.'

'That's incredible.'

'Not at all. You didn't know Phoebe, and she was right: it was a health hazard. There could have been more bodies in the beck.' Eleanor stopped short and their eyes met in united recall. She resumed as if kick-started, 'But there was no bad feeling. I mean, we have to live together—and I get my eggs from there.' Her voice dropped. 'Awkward subject,' she muttered.

Miss Pink refused to relinquish it. 'There was a court case?'

'Oh no. He buried the carcasses once they'd been brought to his attention.'

'Lazy shepherding: seven of them. Seven minimum.' Miss Pink thought of the one plastered against the watergate.

191

'Yes, well.' Eleanor swallowed. 'Then Phoebe discovered that he'd merely dumped them on his tip. So she reported that and, granted, he did cover them with earth after a second warning from the police. I'll tell him about the two you found and he'll see to it.'

'Where is this tip?'

'It's an old quarry down the dale a bit. Only a little one, the kind you take just enough stone from to build one or two houses. It's on Jacob's land so presumably it's legal—providing carcasses are adequately covered.'

Miss Pink said slowly, 'Phoebe passed Sleylands the morning of the day she died.'

Eleanor smiled. 'No, Melinda; that hare won't run. She *passed*, she didn't stop, and she waved to him. Does that suggest bad feeling?'

'You've only got his word for it: that she waved.'

'Mabel was there, at the farm. She and Phoebe were friendly. If she says she didn't see Phoebe that day, she didn't.'

'That doesn't mean that Phoebe didn't stop, didn't go into a barn, confront Swinburn. I can't believe they were on good terms, not after she'd involved him twice with the police. Was he at home all that Sunday? Did he go to the tip?'

'Phoebe was found in the beck.' The tone was a warning.

'On Swinburn's land?'

'Mabel would have to know.'

192

'Mabel would protect—her—man.' The quick retort slowed suddenly. Miss Pink glanced at the doorway. 'Where's Sherrel?'

'Why—' Eleanor blinked, and stood up. She went to the front room and after a moment returned. 'She's not there,' she said in wonder.

'Upstairs? Lavatories?'

They both looked. Sherrel had gone.

'She was listening to us,' Miss Pink said, back in the kitchen. 'Swinburn's Bobby's father. He's the Lees' landlord and he contributes to Bobby's support. She's gone to warn him. It's logical but does it have to mean anything sinister?'

'The police must know about Bobby.'

'Not necessarily. Tell me, did Phoebe wear a hat?'

'Always. She couldn't stand the glare so she wore brims and she went in for amusing hats picked up on her travels. She had a sombrero and a cowboy hat and an American trooper's cap with fur ear-flaps. Why do you ask?'

'What about baseball caps?'

'Not exactly, but that type, rather more up-market. The most recent one she brought back from Alaska: little animals embroidered on the front. I don't know if she wore it though.'

'Denim?'

'Yes, like the blue jeans, with a pale brim. But why—oh, you found it!'

'Not me but I think Bobby has, and he's hiding the fact. Can he have found something else? And Misella—and Sherrel—they know what he's found?' She regarded Eleanor absently. 'On what kind of terms were the Lees and Phoebe?'

'Here we go again—but—OK, Sherrel resented her. Phoebe told the girl she was being degraded. No, she said the weekly handover was degrading. It's a class thing; we think of it as humiliating but Sherrel and Misella wouldn't be bothered. It really wasn't anything to do with Phoebe anyway; she should have kept out of it.'

'But that was her problem, wasn't it.' It was rhetorical, Miss Pink's mind had diverged. 'I keep getting my wires crossed. At Sunder I think Misella was trying to mislead me, insisting that the murder was the work of a stranger, but she was talking about *Isa*, and here we're discussing Phoebe.' She pondered. 'Isa was murdered. We know that, although initially it was assumed to be an accident. Phoebe's death was an accident according to the inquest. But was it? Her skull was fractured.'

'She struck her head as she fell.'

'But did she fall? You said there was no reason for her to enter the quarry. You had to contrive a reason: photographing flowers. And Swinburn could have been out that day,probably was, he's a farmer.' There was silence until Miss Pink resumed thoughtfully, 'If Phoebe was murdered, there is surely a

194

connection between the two deaths, between the two women.'

'They were very different,' Eleanor observed, herself thinking hard now, carried along. 'The one a young, flighty baggage, the other a high-principled old lady, one secretive and dishonest, the other too frank for her own good. Maybe.' The last added as she realized the implications of what had gone before. She ended emphatically: 'I can't see Jacob Swinburn being involved with Isa.'

'The connection could be indirect: not directly between Isa and Swinburn but by way of someone else as a link: Isa—Gemma—Swinburn, or Walter as the link.'

'You're reaching, Melinda. It's your criminal mind again.'

'All the same: two violent deaths within four days—'

'Coincidence; you might as well say that the wretched salmonella hoax was connected.'

'Why not?' Miss Pink was resentful and argumentative. 'Who started that rumour? Swinburn? He must have hated Phoebe and she was your friend. He might have found it amusing to mention it in the pub: some reference to his being ill after he'd eaten something Mabel bought here, suggesting it was salmonella poisoning.'

'You see! You have tunnel vision. How can you conceive of Jacob forging a letter from a Sussex Council? A naughty hint in the pub certainly, but that letter was correct down to the last detail.'

'Tell me about it.'

'I thought I did. No doubt with all these murders on your mind you forgot.' Eleanor was patronizing. 'The hoax started with a letter purporting to come from East Sussex Council and it was an excellent forgery—and you'd need a scanner and a printer.'

Miss Pink was gaping. 'Who has a computer?' she asked weakly.

'In Borascal? Only Martin. Walter would have one in the office of course. Are you going to suggest one of those men—of whom I'm very fond'—stretching it a bit—'that one of them tried to put me out of business? That's way over the top.'

Miss Pink wasn't listening. 'The hoax,' she intoned. 'Phoebe's death, Isa's murder.' Eleanor scowled angrily. 'People acting oddly,' Miss Pink continued. 'I wonder what the police thinking is on this.'

*   *   *

A man built like a sumo wrestler walked into the Fat Lamb and eyed Honeyman with contempt. For all his size the publican was smaller and softer.

'You seen Dwayne Paxton?' the newcomer grated.

Honeyman shook his head. Dorcas, wiping

the shelves, paused, studying the fellow in the mirror.

'He's not at his place, his truck's gone and he's not at Blind Keld.'

'Oh, it's you doing the renovating there.'

'Right. I'm Birkett, Builders and Roofers. Paxton's working for me, or he should be. Where's he gone?'

'He comes in but he don't tell us his plans.'

'He's sleeping there. And he didn't expect me at t'weekend, didn't clear his traps away. There's a sleeping bag on t'floor in t'best bedroom. He's been there with a woman.'

*　　　*　　　*

Dorcas pursed her lips and shifted bottles noisily. Birkett glanced round the bar. At three o'clock it was empty although there were a couple of parties at the tables outside. A police car cruised past slowly. The Honeymans stiffened but Birkett had his back turned.

'When you see him you tell him he needn't trouble to come back,' he said viciously. 'Except to collect his stuff, and that's in the stable.' He glowered at Honeyman. 'Where'd he get a key to the house is what I want to know?'

Dorcas turned. 'Why are you asking us, Mr Birkett?' The courtesy made it the more cutting, particularly from a woman of her age and diminutive size. He blinked in confusion.

'Because he's been using the place for his own purposes, missis, and I'm responsible for it. It's in my charge like. How's it going to look if the owners find out and spread it around: one of my men using their nice house? I don't give a damn what my workers get up to in their own time—assuming it was in his own time—but he's got his own place, why'd he not take girls there, eh?' He was shrill with resentment.

'Too near the village,' Honeyman put in.

'Who cares these days? Hell, it's summer; they could do it—'

Dorcas coughed forcefully. 'I don't care for that kind of talk—' She stopped as the police car drew up outside. Both Honeymans were suddenly expressionless but Birkett appeared even more disgruntled, as if he were anticipating yet another problem, but a nuisance rather than trouble. His face didn't change as Sewell walked in, the detective seeming mildly surprised at the company.

'Well, Jackson, afternoon off? Skiving, is it?'

'Looking for one of my men,' Birkett growled. 'And what are you doing here?'

'What'll it be then?' Honeyman asked, straightening a drip mat absently.

'Nothing for me.' Sewell was affable. 'I just called in to speak to Birkett here. Saw his van in the car park. We brought him back,' he told Birkett.

The Honeymans stared. Birkett shook his big head. 'Brought who back?'

198

'Young Dwayne. He's your man, isn't he?' Now Sewell looked doubtful. 'He said he was working for you.'

'Not any more he isn't. He's fired. I told Honeyman here already.'

'You can't do that.' Sewell was firm. 'If we take him in he's got no choice but to go.'

'You took un to Bailrigg? What's he done?'

'What did you fire him for?'

Birkett's temper had been seething from the start but at this point any surviving restraint broke. 'What did—I'll tell thee what Ah fired that randy young tup for: he's been using my property—the one as I was renovating—as a brothel, that's what! Why, even a packet of condoms under the'—a loud crack as Dorcas slammed a tankard on the bar—'under his sleeping bag, there! But that's not the worst of it. Isn't it a crime to have keys cut and enter someone else's premises? Trespass anyway.' He paused for breath.

'He didn't tell us he took women there.' Sewell turned lazy eyes on Honeyman who flinched. Dorcas had kicked him.

'He's young,' she said.

'But he wasn't forthcoming about his girlfriends,' Sewell said.

'Very discreet, our Dwayne.' Birkett's sarcasm was venomous. 'Like they said'—indicating the Honeymans—'he weren't one to shit on his own doorstep. So she were a village girl.'

No one spoke. 'Probably married,' he added.

Standing side by side the Honeymans couldn't exchange glances but Ralph left the field to his mother, as if he'd received a signal.

'Dwayne wasn't choosy,' she said. 'If it was on offer he'd take it.' Which sat oddly with her disapproval of Birkett's vulgarity.

'Did you see her leave on Wednesday?' Sewell asked. 'She had to pass by here and that little car would have been conspicuous.'

'Who are we—' Birkett began, turning to the Honeymans who stood like statues, no way of telling if their brains were racing or immobilized by panic.

'We never saw her,' Dorcas said, only her lips moving.

'Dwayne?' Honeyman breathed.

'Hot-blooded,' Dorcas contributed. 'You can't blame un.'

'We brought him home,' Sewell reminded them. 'Now we're going door-to-door, asking who saw her last.'

'You done that,' Honeyman said, while Birkett looked from one to the other, dumbfounded. He had been focused on one of his lads using Blind Keld for his screwing, they had the chap lined up for *murder*?

'That was before we knew she was murdered,' Sewell said. 'There are other men in the village.' It was as if he read Birkett's mind but he was addressing Honeyman.

Dorcas gave a thin smile and Sewell knew that she would alibi her son for every minute of Wednesday evening and night. He hated remote communities; tracing the missing Bailrigg husband was child's play compared with Borascal where he had a premonition that every one of them would have an alibi. Like bloody Dwayne Paxton who had been drinking in the Grey Goat in Bailrigg.

*   *   *

'My, you're getting through a lot of eggs,' Mabel exclaimed.

'These are for Eleanor. Lovely brown shells,' gushed Miss Pink, who'd kept fowls herself from time to time and was well aware that the only difference between a white egg and a brown one was the colour of the shell. 'I lend a hand at Jollybeard occasionally,' she went on. 'Particularly if Sherrel has to go.'

Mabel arranged the egg boxes neatly in Eleanor's willow basket. 'Had to go where?' she asked casually.

'She left.' Miss Pink was vague. 'A little queasy perhaps. It must be difficult, serving food in her condition.'

'Oh.' Mabel looked up sharply. 'Like that again, is it?' She held Miss Pink's eye. 'There's one in every village.'

'And often good mothers.' Miss Pink was prompt.

'She's all right.' Mabel was grudging. 'It's hard on the taxpayer though, right enough. But then we all condone it as you might say. There's Eleanor paying her in cash—' She stopped short.

'If it's benefit fraud you're thinking of, it'll not be more than a few pounds a week. We can spare that.'

Speak for yourself, Mabel thought. Aloud she said, 'You should hear our Jean on the subject. That girl works her fingers to the bone to keep them in food and she'll go at it even harder if Swinburn do decide to let them have this old place as a hiking centre. Jeannie could do with a little extra a week—' Again she stopped, wondering why on earth she was sounding off like this to a relative stranger.

'Sherrel was up here?' Miss Pink asked.

'No!' Mabel had no time to consider this irrelevant question because the other was explaining—in a way: 'Because you're so angry.' It could have been a child speaking.

Mabel shook her head. How to spell out the facts of village life to an old spinster, and gentry at that? 'Sherrel,' she said patiently, 'is no better than she should be.' Miss Pink was solemn, absorbing this. 'Not a—a street walker,' Mabel elucidated, 'but there's no restraint, you know?' Miss Pink looked baffled. 'She likes men!' Mabel almost shouted, as if the other were deaf. 'Not the only one either,' she muttered, unable to help herself.

202

'Goodness. There are more like her in Borascal? There aren't many young women—'

'Not now. There was.'

'Oh. Mrs Lambert. Well, yes, with hindsight . . .'

'Some poor devil's quaking in his shoes, although it's likely he don't know yet. No reason for him to think, even if the car's been found, that it'd be taken for anything other than an accident.'

'It's in the papers,' Miss Pink said stupidly.

'Not foreign ones, I'll bet. It's only one more death of a good-time girl. Of course he could still be in this country but, like Swinbum says, he reckons that this chap could well be a foreigner or if not, then one of those long-distance drivers as go all over Europe.'

'An outside job.'

Mabel tried to work that one out. 'You could call it that; certainly not a Borascal man. She were too discreet for that.'

Mabel was right there; it wasn't until after her death had been found to be murder that there'd been even a whisper of Isa's promiscuity. And now everyone was full of it.

CHAPTER TWELVE

'We found the Bailrigg man,' Holgate said. 'That is, we found the husband and we're not looking for anyone else. It'll be on the news.'

'You mean he killed her?'

'We're not looking for anyone else, sir.'

Walter led the way to a wooden bench and sat down heavily. 'I wonder why he did it,' he said, not looking at the detective.

'We don't know that he did.'

'He hasn't confessed?'

'In a manner of speaking. He hanged himself.'

'Oh, poor fellow.'

Holgate sat down at the far end of the seat. Neither spoke for a while, listening to the birds, thinking of errant wives, of men driven beyond despair.

'We questioned young Paxton,' Holgate said at length. Walter stared, comprehension dawning slowly. 'Your sister gave us that information,' Holgate reminded him.

'She dramatizes. She's at that age.'

'All the same, Paxton had women at Blind Keld.' The other's silence could have been taken for acquiescence. 'Did you know that your wife went there?' Holgate asked gently.

'No.' There was no surprise.

'But you found out since.'

'Gemma told me.'

'Where is your sister?'

'I don't know.' Walter looked round vaguely. 'She went out. She won't be far away, she didn't take her bike.' His gaze came back to Holgate. 'You can't question her without a responsible adult present.'

The DC smiled faintly. 'Plenty of those around.'

'I mean me.' The tone alerted the detective; Walter wouldn't have any responsible adult sitting in, only himself. Could it be . . . 'Did they have a thing going?' he asked. 'Dwayne and Gemma?'

Walter shrugged. 'They knew each other.'

'Of course,' Holgate mused, 'she wouldn't be in trouble, it would be him.' Walter watched him warily. 'He took women there,' Holgate repeated, 'not just the one.'

'Not Gemma.' It was too quick.

Cooper walked round the corner of the house and across the new-mown grass. He sniffed the stranger's chinos with interest and jumped on the seat, placing himself between the two men. Cooper disdained male laps. Regarding the sleek furred poll Holgate asked, 'Why would your wife suddenly decide to drink a lot of whisky?'

'She was unhappy. You asked me this before.'

And they would keep returning to that same puzzling point until someone broke.

'She wouldn't get drunk to meet a lover,' Walter said. 'She was—eager. She didn't need drink.'

Holgate's jaw dropped. Was this the breakthrough? 'You knew.' It was said with deep finality.

'It's hindsight. She would shower and change and use a lot of perfume and she'd come out'—he turned and stared at the porch—'happy. She was very pretty—not always, but she was then. I thought it was the car: driving it with the top down, people staring, and the danger, the risk of being caught by a patrol; she'd think she could talk her way out of it. She could have done too, with most men.' He stopped.

Holgate, for something to do, put out his hand to the cat. Cooper's spine shivered at the touch but there was no other response.

'I didn't know,' Walter said, and there was all the misery of his situation in the tone. He stretched his legs. There was a long silence which the other dared not break. 'You're right,' he went on, sighing, 'I did know, and I blocked it out. She'd have lied anyway if I'd asked her.'

'Did Gemma know?'

'Oh, I'm sure.' A wry smile. 'She's cleverer than me.'

*   *   *

'There's a call-out,' Jean Blamire said. 'I'm not going, it's only a broken ankle. A botanist slipped in one of the gullies above Closewater. How can I help you?'

She was thinning spring onions, wearing skimpy shorts and a halter top, no hat and her hair tied back with a frayed blue ribbon. All that exposed skin and lack of self-consciousness made Gemma feel gauche and resentful, at a disadvantage until she remembered why she'd come. 'What were you doing on Wednesday night?' she asked.

Jean teased soil out of onion roots and laid the bunch in a trug. 'I've no idea. What makes it important?'

'The question is being asked.' Gemma was belligerent but Jean's face betrayed nothing, not even curiosity.

'I know the police are here again. Why should they be interested in me?'

'Because you'd know where Martin was, that's why!' As if a dam had been breached Gemma became, if not confiding, at least informative: 'It's not personal, they're intensifying their inquiries; they just brought Dwayne back from Bailrigg. They took him away early on for questioning.'

'What did he tell you?'

'I didn't speak to him! No way am I getting involved.' Jean looked wary. 'I found his place shut' Gemma went on, 'so I asked those people opposite, in the holiday cottage, and they told me he'd gone away in a police car. While I was with them the cops brought him back, dropped him off and came on to the village. I kept out of sight, watching to see where they'd go. First place they stopped at was ours. What they're trying to do is break the alibis.' She grinned. 'They'll have a hard job with me. How about you?'

'You're talking nonsense.'

'Oh, come on! All the local guys are suspect. Which is why they'll come back to you, asking about Martin's movements on Wednesday night. And evening,' she added as an afterthought. 'You should thank me; I'm giving you advance warning.'

'Gemma.' It was the admonishing tone of an adult addressing a child. 'Isa was Walter's wife. She may have been a bit—wild, and you didn't have a lot of time for her, but going round spreading stories is going to rebound on Walter. If the police—'

'Walter's fine; I'm his alibi. It's her lovers who are going to have to watch their backs.'

Jean picked up the trug. 'I'm not listening to this; dramatizing is one thing but if I didn't know you I'd say you were trying your best to incriminate Walter—'

'He's safe.' Gemma was smug. 'He's got me—'

'Sort yourself out, girl; if she was a—a—'

'Whore.'

Jean closed her eyes in despair. '—and

Walter found out, it puts him in the frame. He's as likely a suspect as any other man.'

'Actually,' Gemma said quietly, 'I'm not so sure now that she had any more men. What were they quarrelling about on Wednesday afternoon?'

'Who?'

'Martin and Isa of course. He's going to have to explain that.'

Jean gripped the trug in both hands, her knuckles white. 'You told me he was trying to stop her driving. In fact'—her eyes glittered—'he confirmed that himself—to me!'

'That was what he said but—'

'And when he left your place he came home and he was working upstairs all the rest of the afternoon. We never went out, nor that evening either. I was here myself all—What *is* this?' She realized she'd been driven back on the defensive.

'They were fighting. Isa was terrified.'

'You're making that up!'

'Why can't you face it, Jean? You know he's been having it off with her for months. Everyone knows; the wife's always the last—'

'Why, hello!' Jean's shrill cry of welcome cut across the tirade and Gemma swung round, glowering. Miss Pink was coming through the garden, smiling, eyes shadowed by her hat brim and dark glasses.

'Eleanor needs vegetables,' she announced, beaming at them, 'and if Gemma hasn't warned you already, you should know that the CID is going the rounds again.'

Jean tried to speak, coughed and tried again. 'Why?'

Gemma muttered something sullenly and left, treading circumspectly past Miss Pink with a strangled 'Hi.'

'A volatile young lady,' Miss Pink observed. 'Why are the police here? Don't you know? It has to be a new development.'

'Such as?' Jean was trying to control her breathing.

Miss Pink didn't reply directly. 'There are bound to be fresh leads in an ongoing investigation,' she burbled. 'So many questions to be asked, like why had Isa drunk so much whisky when normally she never touched it? Which implies something unusual had happened?' Without a change of tone she added, 'What's the problem with Gemma?'

Jean tried to turn a gasp into a laugh. 'She's in shock. As you said: a volatile girl at the best of times but now—first Phoebe, then Isa: it's brought her close to the edge. I must have a word with Walter, suggest he might send her away on holiday.'

'A good idea. They get strange notions. Isn't there a link between poltergeists and adolescent girls? I could never see it myself but certainly they can be very unstable at that age.' She raised an eyebrow inviting comment.

Jean said sadly, 'How right you are. She's

210

maintaining that Isa was no better than a prostitute.'

'What do *you* think?' Miss Pink was politely interested.

'I think Gemma's been rather naughty; she was seeing a lot of Dwayne Paxton and although it would be him for the high jump if the police learned about it, she's running scared, worried about being put into care. She said the police questioned Dwayne and she's trying to divert attention, implying he was questioned about Isa, not his relationship with an under-age girl. So she's telling people Isa was a prostitute.'

'You're saying she wasn't?'

'Of course she wasn't!' Miss Pink looked puzzled. Jean said, surprised by the thought: 'She couldn't have been! How could she?' She stared at the older woman. 'You mean, the car trips? She went to meet men?' She shook her head in disbelief. 'There's a rumour she was working the transport cafés on the main road: truck drivers. It does make sense when you think about it.'

A stray breeze wandered through the garden ruffling the plumes of asparagus. Jean turned her hot face to it as Rosie Winder appeared at the corner of the house accompanied by the collie. Rosie was in uniform. She smiled at Miss Pink. 'You get around,' she observed.

'I'm living here, temporarily.'

'Not in Waterhouses Lane.' The smile was still there.

Miss Pink hesitated only fractionally; summoning up a mental image of the escarpment, wondering where the cover had been. 'Now why were you watching that place?'

'We weren't. A bird watcher saw you and reported a suspicious presence at the scene of a crime. What were you doing there?'

Good manners might have suggested that Jean make herself scarce, but it was her garden and she resumed her thinning of the spring onions.

'I was working out how it could have been done,' Miss Pink said.

'What was your conclusion?'

'The usual in that kind of situation: put the car in low gear with the engine running and jump clear. Is it in low gear?' Rosie nodded. They were both watching Jean. 'He made a mistake,' Miss Pink said. 'Another one.' Jean's hands were still.

'What were the others?' Rosie asked.

'He didn't know about the hyoid—and he was a local man, didn't realize—'

'How do you make out he was local?'

'Either that or he had an accomplice to drive the other car. If he was alone he had to walk away and he couldn't keep to the roads because he might be seen, so he had to take to the fields.'

212

Jean stood up. 'While you're conducting your interview I'll fill Eleanor's order. What was it, Miss Pink?'

'You do that.' Rosie nodded approval. 'I'm sorry I interrupted,' she told Miss Pink. 'Actually it was Mrs Blamire I came to see.'

*   *   *

It was six o'clock and Miss Pink, seldom at a loose end but giving the impression that she was, drifted down the flowery top lane, binoculars round her neck but having no need of them, her eyes sharp behind the shielding glasses. At the end of his overgrown path Dwayne's door was closed but he could be round the back in the sun because his Land Rover was parked at the side. Further on, beyond the track leading to Sleylands, Blamire's old van was outside the Fat Lamb while, in the field opposite, a tractor was stationary with a shovel mounted on the front.

This early in the evening there were few customers in the Lamb: a family outside, Blamire and Jacob Swinburn in the bar. Blamire greeted her casually and then, evidently remembering that they'd met during the search for Phoebe, he smiled. Swinburn merely inclined his head in something more than a nod. Miss Pink asked Honeyman for draught bitter and observed generally that it was a quiet evening.

213

'And it can stay that way,' Blamire said. 'No more call-outs tonight, please God.' He turned to Swinburn, apparently continuing a conversation: 'Some of the most dangerous rescues are low down: trees, loose rock—a guy could be killed with a rock coming down on his head, even wearing a helmet.'

'But you got that shield thing,' Swinburn said.

'That's for the stretcher; there's no protection for the barrow boy.'

'What?' Honeyman interjected. 'The barrow boy?'

Blamire flicked a glance at him. 'The guy on the front of the stretcher: the one at the sharp end.'

Swinburn said, 'They must be hard chaps as bring a casualty down off Scafell and such.'

'Not really.' Blamire was dismissive. 'It's easier than a little crag—easier and safer. You don't have this problem of loose rock on Scafell—and trees, and of course you're working in the open, you can see where you're going. I'd sooner bring a chap down the face of Scafell than out of one of them gullies above Closewater like we did today.'

'But Scafell's hundreds of feet high,' Swinburn protested. 'You can see the cliff from Wasdale. It's sheer.'

'Five hundred feet, that's all. That's nothing compared with alpine cliffs; they can be thousands of feet. But it makes no difference whether you fall a hundred feet or a thousand, you're just as dead.'

'My goodness,' breathed Miss Pink. 'You've been on alpine rescues?'

He smiled. He'd been having some late nights, he was puffy below the eyes but that could be the result of a strenuous rescue. 'I'm a guide,' he told her, not unaware of her scrutiny. 'Guides help out wherever there's a rescue.'

'You're never off duty.' A careful measure of tribute.

'Right, but it goes with the territory: *noblesse oblige*'—she blinked—'someone will bring me down if I fall. And you, ma'am, are you enjoying your holiday?'

'Oh yes, yes'—indicating embarrassment. And why had he decided to turn the charm on her? A hidden agenda? 'Actually,' she blurted, 'I'm looking for material for a book.'

'What kind of book?'

'A romance,' she confessed. 'I've had one serialized in a magazine.'

'Oh.' He picked up his lager and drank deeply. 'I write,' he said, in the kind of tone that implied *he* did it properly. 'I write mountaineering books.'

'Really.' She was awed. 'I can't say I've read—do you write under your own name?'

'The same. When I've finished what I'm doing now I'm going to write a novel. It will start in the Lakes and it'll feature hard

215

climbing. I'm aiming for TV adaptation.'

'You're on to a winner; you have inside information, and experience. It's not been done before?'

'Not how I'm going to do it.' He leaned towards her, becoming confidential but brimming with excitement. 'It's going to start on Scafell—that's how it opens, and then we go to the Eiger and so to Monument Valley.' He nodded smugly at her amazement. 'You know what I'm talking about?'

'I've seen pictures. That's an ambitious undertaking.'

He laughed delightedly. 'What are you drinking? No, I insist. Ralph, let's have some service here!' Honeyman was deep in conversation with Swinburn but they drew apart at the shout.

Blamire ordered a round. Swinburn edged up to Miss Pink. 'I moved them shearlings,' he told her.

Surfacing from images of Scafell, the Eiger and tall sandstone buttes she said weakly, 'Moved them, Mr Swinburn?'

'Buried un.'

'Deep, I hope,' Blamire said loudly.

'Deep enough.' Swinburn was unfazed.

'That tip's going to have to go,' Blamire said, and Miss Pink thought he sounded as if he were high on something, but perhaps it was no more than strong lager on an empty stomach.

'It's not your land yet,' Swinburn said, and there was something like a warning behind the words.

'Yes,' she murmured: an old lady commenting on her own thoughts, 'I was at your place, Mr Blamire; everyone was there this afternoon.'

Was it imagination or were all three of them suddenly stilled? She cocked her head like a dog.

'Who?' Blamire asked quietly.

'Your wife of course; I went up for vegetables for Jollybeard. And Gemma was there visiting, and Rosie.'

He was staring, as was Swinburn. Honeyman was drawing the beer, making as much noise as a mouse.

'Rosie Winder,' Miss Pink said, flustered. 'The police sergeant. You've been away all day.'

He couldn't walk out although she could tell by his tension that he wanted to, but the round he'd ordered was being assembled, and it had to be paid for, his own drink to be consumed. No one left a full glass on the bar to attract attention.

'Were they at my place?' Swinburn asked.

'The police?' She tried to remember. 'They were calling on everyone so I've no doubt they went to Sleylands.'

He was grinning. 'I'll need to get home. Damage limitation. Good thing I got them

217

sheep underground.'

'I'm off.' Blamire gulped down his drink. 'Gotta get cleaned up. 'Night all.'

Honeyman and Miss Pink faced each other across the bar. He said, 'You ever hear that old joke: you send a telegram saying "All is known, fly at once" and anyone, everyone what gets a telegram like that drops everything and scarpers. You know that one?'

* * *

'What did you tell the police?'

'That you were on the call-out.'

'What did she ask you?'

'Who?'

'That cop bitch: Winder.'

'Nothing they hadn't asked before, like where you were on Wednesday night.'

'And?'

'There was nothing to add to that. You were here.'

Some of the tension left him. He threw a glance at the passage where sunshine streamed through the open front door. 'What else did she ask?'

'There was nothing, Martin, no surprises: did you know Isa, when did you see her last, that kind of thing. I repeated what I'd told them before.'

'So where's the point in asking the same questions?'

218

'It's what they do: trying to catch you out.' Her tone changed. 'Gemma was here again. She's working her guts out to divert attention from Walter. Do you think he did it?'

'Good luck to him if he did.' He went to the fridge and reached in for a can of Carlsberg. Standing at the sink he looked down through the trees towards the beck. 'It seems likely,' he said, considering it carefully: 'if he found out what she was like.'

'He doesn't seem the type to kill.'

He turned and stared at her but she was dribbling oil into the mortar, drop by drop. 'Miss Pink was here too,' she added, putting down the oil, taking up the vinegar. 'She asked an odd question: why did Isa drink Scotch that night?' She looked up at him.

'You're asking me?' He was astonished. 'She liked Scotch, I suppose.'

'Miss Pink said she didn't.'

'I've been talking to the old bat: just now, in the pub. She's senile.'

'And prurient. She's obsessed with Isa's sex life.' Jean mixed the vinaigrette. 'Did you know that there's a rumour going round that she was working the all-night cafés as a prostitute?'

'That doesn't surprise me—although not so much a prostitute, more a nymphomaniac.'

'What's the distinction in this case?'

'It's a more likely motive for murder. A prostitute's not interested in sex, only money.

But once Isa got her claws into a man . . . She was rapacious, a chap might kill her just to get her off his back. She was a—what's the word? An incubus.' He crushed the empty can, stamped on the pedal of the bin and dropped it in the rubbish, heedless of recycling. Glowering, he fetched another, slamming the fridge door. Jean picked up her chopping knife and started on the coriander.

She didn't hurry the supper, lingering outside the porch as she swung the salad basket, thinking that she should be feeling more relief now that Isa was dead; if she'd known what was happening she'd have throttled the slut herself. How could the woman *dare*? And meeting her neighbour every day, smiling, laughing; granted she was always moaning that there was nothing to do in Borascal, but even that must have been an act because she was portraying herself as a gossip when in fact she was so discreet it was criminal.

Jean stopped swinging the basket and stared as a flycatcher pounced and retreated to its perch as if it were on elastic, but she wasn't seeing the bird, she was seeing Isa: pretty and vacuous, giving off none of the sexual aura one would associate with a nymphomaniac. But since she had never met one, how could she know?

She felt his presence behind her, her hair was lifted and he nuzzled her neck. She sighed and saw that he'd brought her a drink.

'For the chef,' he said. 'Supper smells good, what is it?'

He was begging forgiveness, but if he hadn't—responded to the bitch, what was there to forgive?

'Yesterday's cold duck,' she said, searching his face over the rim of her glass.

He was smiling: not amused at her but reassuring, all his feeling in his warm eyes. 'It's in the past, love.' He knew exactly what was in her mind. 'This is us: now. You think I'd have let someone like that come between us?'

'No.' She returned his gaze steadily, thinking that this was indeed reality and no matter what had happened it was herself he loved. If that woman had seduced him she would have killed her—her smile deepened and she closed her eyes to hide that treacherous thought—but here and now—she opened them again, she knew that Isa was nothing. Never had been.

He inhaled deeply; they were both wrapped in their separate worlds of security, both tacitly triumphant. 'Sit down.' He motioned to the garden seat. 'I'll bring the bottle. Supper can wait a while.'

She obeyed, reflecting as he went indoors that, far from Isa's breaking up the marriage, she had brought them together, more together, she corrected herself. Tonight she had everything: an adoring husband, a comfortable house, albeit her father's, a flourishing garden, and this evening: warm sun, wine, and this man whom she'd allow one glass and then take him to bed. Supper could indeed wait. She could even spare a modicum of pity for Isa. It had been a terrible way to die.

CHAPTER THIRTEEN

'It isn't "who" that's important,' Miss Pink said, 'but "why".'

'You can find that out. Eleanor said you'd done this kind of thing before. The cops are no good, they're fixated on Walter—or rather they would be except that I know he never left the house.'

Absently Miss Pink poured more coffee. That Gemma should have come calling at nine o'clock on a Sunday morning was indication enough that she had a problem, nor was it difficult to identify it. She was too young to sustain a suspect alibi indefinitely. And Miss Pink knew, and was well aware that the police knew, that Gemma as Walter's alibi reeked of suspicion.

'It could have been anyone,' the girl persisted, adding quickly, 'You're saying that if you knew the reason why she was murdered, then you'd know who did it. That's obvious: it was a sex murder. One of her lovers did it.'

'All the same, one of them had a special reason for killing her.'

'Such as? What could be so special?'

'You're not using your brain.' It was tart because Miss Pink was faced with a dilemma: how to penetrate the posturing and innuendoes without reference to Gemma's having had a suspect relationship with Dwayne Paxton. Any mention of that and she would close up like a clam. 'Blackmail,' Miss Pink went on, 'is one motive for murder: the victim kills the blackmailer.'

To her surprise Gemma looked thoughtful. 'There's that,' she admitted.

'Greed?' Miss Pink warmed to the theme. 'I don't think so. No one benefits financially from her death—unless there was an insurance policy, but the police would know about—'

'There wasn't,' Gemma said quickly.

'Lust? Desire?' The girl blinked. 'No.' Miss Pink was imperturbable. 'According to you she was free with her favours.' Gemma looked wary but she neither denied nor confirmed the quaint observation. 'I don't see how sex comes into it.' Miss Pink appeared to be nonplussed.

'You're saying it could have been a woman?'

The glasses flashed as wide eyes were turned on her. There was a pause then: 'Is that what you think?'

'God, no! But if it wasn't sexual it had to be—like a jealous wife?'

'Jealousy,' murmured Miss Pink. 'We're back to basics. That was the police theory concerning Walter but'—quickly, seeing Gemma start to react to this—'he's ruled out. So who is it that might be jealous?'

'A guy wouldn't be unless he was possessive. If someone else wants it you let it go. Let her go.'

'You're saying a jealous lover would want to keep his lady but he'd kill the rival. But it was Isa who was killed. Wrong person. So jealousy's out. What else?'

'You're the expert.'

'Eleanor's been embroidering facts.' And you, my girl, came here to tell me something, not to pick my brains. 'However,' Miss Pink went on, 'there is elimination, and fear: the need to silence someone. Hence—blackmail.'

'Walter gave her plenty of money but I don't think she cared for money that much. She bought cheap clothes.' Gemma seemed puzzled. 'She adored the house because she'd never lived in one like ours—and the car, she liked that even better, but I can't see her blackmailing for small sums. Besides, she wasn't clever enough.'

Miss Pink had been listening to this with only half an ear. 'She could have got in the way,' she murmured. 'An obstacle to some project? A scam? So she had to be eliminated.' She gave an odd smile, frowning simultaneously.

Gemma pounced. 'What?'

'My mind was leapfrogging. I was thinking of the scams operating in Borascal and their being difficult to relate to Isa who, so far as I've gathered, seemed uninterested in other people's business. Unlike Phoebe who was the opposite: a human ferret. Now if it had been Phoebe—' She stopped.

'Phoebe drowned. It was an accident.'

Miss Pink was silent, picking up her mug and drinking absently. Gemma followed suit.

'Yuk! This is stone-cold!' Miss Pink was staring at her mug. 'Shall I make some more?' Gemma asked loudly.

Miss Pink surfaced. 'How well did Isa know Martin?'

It was the girl's turn to be silent but she was less adept at concealing her thoughts than wily old ladies. She knew it and stood up, taking the mugs to the sink.

'Even if they were lovers,' Miss Pink said to her back, raising her voice, 'it doesn't rule out Walter. But you alibi him. Was Isa blackmailing Martin?'

Gemma turned. 'We agreed she wouldn't blackmail. But I do know she was terrified of him. The afternoon before she died he was at our place and giving her hell.'

'He was *hitting* her?'

'No, shouting—they were both shouting. He said he was trying to stop her driving without a licence.'

'What did she have to say?'

'Nothing. I walked out. I never saw her again.'

'You left them together?'

Gemma nodded, her eyes searching Miss Pink's face.

'So they knew each other well.'

'Jean says they didn't. She's blind. It's all round the village, and I told her so. I thought she'd kill me but then you turned up and put a stop to it.'

*　　　*　　　*

'Why would Martin Blamire kill Isa?'

'*What!*' Eleanor swung round from the fridge, slopping milk over the floor. Her eyes went to the passage.

'There's no one in the tearoom,' Miss Pink said. 'I asked why *would* he, not why did he.'

'What started this?'

'You didn't know they were having an affair?'

'Certainly not. Who told you they were?'

'Gemma.'

'Oh, Gemma.' Eleanor's knees cracked as she went down to wipe the floor. She pulled herself upright by gripping the edge of the counter. 'Suppose they were having an affair,' she resumed. 'Why kill her?'

'That's what I asked you. Why did she have to be killed? Of course'—Miss Pink's thoughts

226

diverged—'it could have been an accident.'

'Strangling? And putting the car in the river?'

'Yes. They could have been quarrelling and he put his hands on her throat to quieten her'—Miss Pink looked embarrassed—'well, something like that. And pushing the car over the crag was a clumsy attempt to simulate a road accident.' She grimaced. 'The argument against that is he must have knocked the wall down beforehand, or at least have weakened it. No, no accident, it was premeditated.'

' "He?" '

'Blamire?'

'I meant it could have been a woman. Isa was drunk, she couldn't have put up any resistance.'

'I know why she was drunk!' Miss Pink breathed, amazed at herself. 'Gemma walked in on them in the middle of a row. Blamire said it was about her driving without a licence. It must have been after that scene that Isa started to drink. I don't believe the quarrel was about her driving.'

Eleanor said slowly, 'She could be a very demanding person; if they were having an affair . . . suppose she'd wanted him to go away . . . oh no, that's nonsense! Martin would never leave Jean, they're happily married, besides there's their scheme for turning Sleylands into an outdoor centre . . . I suppose it's just possible that Martin—er—slipped up, only the once? And Isa took it seriously? She was rather neurotic. Things could have been awkward for Martin.'

'And she drank because he'd rejected her, perhaps unkindly.'

Eleanor snorted. 'Martin wouldn't mince his words. He has a nasty temper.'

There was a subdued bustle of people entering the tearoom. Eleanor swore mildly. 'Where's Sherrel? Look at me—'

'I'll go.' Miss Pink went out to settle the customers and take their order. 'Jollybeard sandwiches?' she queried on her return. 'For the whole party: six adults.'

'My version of the American BLT. If you'd toast the bread for me . . .'

They busied themselves with salad and rashers. 'Sunday speciality,' Eleanor explained. 'It's too rich for weekdays but people allow themselves a treat at the weekend.'

'It's not that rich except for the cream.'

'Where?'

'In the mayonnaise.'

'Melinda, who brought you up? You don't put cream in mayonnaise. It's the eggs that thicken it.'

'Eggs.' Miss Pink stopped slicing tomatoes. 'Raw eggs?'

Eleanor turned from the grill, frowning. 'Free range, from Mabel Swinburn. Why, you bought them yourself.'

'The salmonella!'

'For heaven's sake!' Eleanor dived for the open door and, about to slam it, caught herself and closed it quietly. 'Are you suggesting those eggs are contaminated?' She was hissing, flushed with indignation.

'It never crossed my mind. Free range eggs are perfectly safe'—maybe, maybe not, but at this moment Miss Pink wasn't bothered if the mayonnaise was crawling with bacteria. 'I was remembering the hoax, and the fact that it had to involve someone with access to a computer.'

'Let's save the post-mortems till we've served the customers, can we?' Eleanor was back at the grill. 'Anyway, we've been over all that, obviously someone had to own a computer—'

'Or had access to one. What about Isa?'

'Melinda! Do you mind? Look'—sweetly acid—'if you want to go away and investigate, leave all this to me. I'll do the tomatoes as soon as I've grilled this bacon.'

Miss Pink continued slicing but she didn't stop talking. 'She could have visited Walter's office, used a computer—or Walter could have done it himself—had you thought of that? And Isa knew about it and had to be silenced.'

'That's ridiculous.' It was a harsh whisper. 'No one would kill just to avoid being exposed as a practical joker.'

'You're right.' Miss Pink was chastened. 'That applies to Blamire as well—the only other chap with a computer—even though

229

he'd make a better candidate than Walter.'

'As a murderer?'

'I was thinking of the hoaxer.'

'But we're on good terms!'

'You think. He could be deranged. You said—'

'Can we finish this order?' It was a fierce demand and had the effect of subduing Miss Pink. She continued to assemble sandwiches but automatically, her brain searching for connections between the salmonella hoax and Isa's murder—until she saw that a yawning gap might be bridged, in time and the mind, by Phoebe's death, which had occurred between the salmonella incident and Isa's murder.

*   *   *

Dwayne slept late on Sundays but by ten o'clock he was climbing into his jeans when he heard the latch click on the garden gate. Innately cautious, he didn't go to the window but faded back into the room hoping that they wouldn't see him, a futile gesture when his Land Rover was parked beside the cottage. It was hidden from the garden but these visitors would have looked first. Two men were coming up the path, one was Sewell, the detective sergeant, the other a stranger. Holgate, the DC, and the woman were walking round the back. Dwayne rubbed his chin, carefully suppressing a forerunner of panic, reminding himself of what he'd told them already but knowing it was hopeless to try to anticipate what new development had brought them to him again—and four of them. Who was the stranger? He swallowed and pulled a clean T-shirt on as they knocked at the front door.

They wouldn't let him wash; not that they refused, his request was ignored. He knew that, stale and smelling of bed, they thought they had him at a disadvantage.

They crowded his kitchen; there weren't enough chairs to go round and Holgate stood, moving about, looking at things. Rosie was in plain clothes so Dwayne guessed she was in line for CID. The stranger was a detective inspector: Gibson by name.

They opened with Isa and he relaxed, still safe. Wearily he denied that he'd ever had anything to do with her, that she'd ever been to Blind Keld or anywhere else with him.

Sewell, sitting across the table from him, said, holding his eye, 'Isa came to Blind Keld.'

He shook his head. 'Never. I never touched her—'

'She was seen there,' Sewell said, without a change in tone.

Dwayne raised his eyebrows and Rosie thought he had just the kind of supercilious looks to charm youngsters, perhaps older women too. 'If she were there,' he said, 'it were at a time I was somewhere else.'

'You were seen there too.'

'Not at the same time.' He considered. 'If you're saying as we was there together, and that that means I were'—he glanced at Rosie—'having a relationship with her, and that means I killed her, shouldn't you caution me?' He addressed the DI, all innocence.

Gibson had the appearance of an Italian footballer with looks. He was young and powerful, prematurely grey hair cropped close as a pelt, and eyes so dark they appeared black. He spoke quietly and Dwayne was frightened despite the words.

'Sleeping with a married woman isn't a crime,' the man said.

Dwayne looked down at the table, then back. 'So what are you doing here?' He heard the bluster in his own voice and tried to tone it down. 'Four of you?'

'We're looking at all her boyfriends.'

Dwayne's teeth snapped. 'What makes you think I'm one of 'em?'

'You were seen—'

'Look, we've had that—' He jumped as, behind him, Holgate moved noisily.

'Her car was seen,' the DI said giving no indication that he was making a correction.

'Her car.' Dwayne stared fixedly at the man, playing for time.

'A red MG,' Gibson said kindly. 'Unmistakable. At Blind Keld.'

'And your Land Rover,' Sewell said.

'No!' It was abrupt. 'Hers maybe, not mine.'

Rosie coughed and Gibson turned his deep eyes on her. She reddened. 'Not your Land Rover,' she told Dwayne. 'You had a van that evening, an old van—' She stopped and Dwayne knew that she was on to it.

'It weren't mine.'

'You're saying that someone else was inside Blind Keld with Isa?' Her eyes sparkled. 'You hired the place out. How much did they pay?'

'No money changed hands,' Dwayne said tightly. He collected himself and they watched him attempt to relax. ' 'Fact I didn't know what were going on. Mind you, I guessed. There was—stuff were disturbed like. I could tell. They musta got in through a window.'

'Who was it with her?' Sewell asked.

'I couldna say.' He was airy, in command now. 'Coulda been anyone—different ones.'

Gibson looked at Rosie and stood up. Chairs scraped on the flags and they trooped out. Sighing, Dwayne filled the kettle and plugged it in. He was standing by it, lost in thought when Rosie Winder came back.

'Coffee!' she announced brightly. 'Brilliant. Now we've got them out of the way we can have a proper crack.'

How obvious could they get: sending the woman back to pump him? He stared insolently. 'I'll wash first. You can make the coffee.'

He stripped off his shirt and sluiced himself

at the sink. He took his time with the towel, watching for her reaction. Rosie made the coffee and they sat opposite each other. He hadn't put his shirt on again and she took time to consider his body: young, hard and beautiful. She smiled, approving it. He smiled, knowing she did.

'Gemma talked,' she said.

His smile faded, leaving him expressionless.

'You were with her on Wednesday night.'

He started to laugh and, furious, she took refuge in a stock observation: 'There's something going on here,' and had the satisfaction of seeing that her mistake was remedied, at least partially. He was no longer amused.

'So?' He was deliberately rude.

'You and Gemma. She's fifteen.'

'There's nothing between me and Gemma, not like that. We're just good friends. If she says anything different it's what she wants, not what she does.'

'Her prints will be at Blind Keld.'

'Why not? I've shown her over. It's a nice house. Folk want to see how rich people do up these old places.'

'And Isa's prints will be there.'

'No, not Isa. She were never inside. I told the others I had nowt to do with her.'

'OK. What was her car doing outside?'

'Ah.' It was an exclamation that he tried too late to turn into a weary sigh. He blinked

234

rapidly. 'Maybe she met someone there.'

'Where did they go?'

He hesitated. 'That's not my business.'

'Dwayne'—heavily: this was Rosie in the role of primary school teacher—'her boyfriend came in a van and left it there along with her MG. What did they drive away in?'

'They'—he gestured vaguely—'they just went out in the fields like.'

Her expression was a caricature of disbelief and he was lost.

'I don't know!'

'They took your Land Rover. You've seen one Land Rover, you've seen 'em all, whereas his van and her MG would be recognized. He paid you for the loan of it. You stayed inside Blind Keld with Gemma.'

'No, she didn't know! Christ, the woman was her sister-in-law! Look, I weren't doing nowt wrong. I worked there, I just let un take my truck while I got on with me walling. Gemma weren't there, ever.'

'Who was he, Dwayne?'

'I don't know.' He was sulking.

'The witness got the registration of the van.' A lie; the informant, who'd been out after rabbits, had recognized the MG, but the van's registration had been hidden by weeds.

'If you know, why ask me?'

'You've been protecting him.'

'No reason to. He weren't doing nothing illegal.'

'Then why didn't you tell us to start with? You've had two sessions with the police and you never mentioned this arrangement of hiring out your van—'

'Land Rover. The van's his.'

'Let's get this straight: the van belongs to Blamire, the Land Rover's yours, and the MG is Isa's, right?'

'Wrong, the MG is Walter's. I mean, someone said it's registered to him.'

'OK. I've got it sorted now.' Rosie stood up, weak with relief, not triumphant, the man was a fool. Stupid people couldn't remember the lies they'd told, especially men. However, that didn't have to mean he was too stupid to have engineered Isa's death.

*   *   *

The front door of Elfhow was wide open but at this time in the morning, the sun reached no further than the flags of the porch, and the passage beyond was dim. DI Gibson gave a tentative cough and Sewell cocked an ear, trying to distinguish interior noises from the clamour of birds. Gibson's eyes, adjusting to the gloom, took in the passage, cluttered with boots and shoes, coats on wooden pegs, the glimpse of a beamed parlour on the right. There was the faintest sound of music and the men focused on the staircase. 'Hello?' Gibson murmured. The music continued. They started

236

up the stairs.

All the doors on the upper floor were open bar one; sunshine, direct or reflected, illuminated white walls, black beams, bedspreads in pastel shades. There was a bathroom, agreeably untidy, a crumpled orange towel on the floor. The music came from behind the closed door, a wide gap at its base where oak planks had shrunk. Gibson gave a perfunctory knock and depressed the thumb latch.

'I'll be down in a minute,' the occupant said, not turning from the computer.

'We knocked and called out,' Gibson said mildly.

Blamire turned, astonished, getting up to approach and peer at Gibson's ID. 'I know you,' he said, casually dismissing Sewell. 'What's this about: first thing on Sunday morning?'

'Nearly noon,' Gibson demurred. 'There have been some developments.'

'Where? What? Look, why don't we—' He looked past them.

'Go downstairs?' Gibson completed genially. 'A good idea.' He turned and Sewell stood aside.

Blamire hesitated. 'What are the new developments?'

'Well, we've been talking to—' DI Gibson was mumbling, walking away, descending the stairs. Sewell stood back, gesturing to Blamire

237

to precede him. He went reluctantly.

In the parlour he didn't ask them to sit down. 'My wife's about somewhere.' He looked around as if expecting her to materialize and play the hostess.

'We don't want to trouble Mrs Blamire,' Gibson said. 'It's about Mrs Lambert, sir.'

He didn't like that, but it could have been the 'sir' that bothered him. 'What about her?'

Gibson studied him, letting the pause stretch. 'The meetings at Blind Keld,' he said.

'What meetings? You've lost me.'

'Your meeting with Mrs Lambert. And goings on in Paxton's Land Rover.'

'He's lying.'

'We have an independent witness.'

'Witness to *what*?'

'You were having an affair with Mrs Lambert,' Gibson stated, not answering the question.

Blamire's eyes were jumpy, shifting from the window to the doorway. 'I'd rather talk somewhere else,' he muttered. 'My wife's had enough distress. I wouldn't want to cause— Can we go?'

'Certainly.' Gibson nodded sympathetically but behind Blamire's back Sewell was swelling with glee.

*   *   *

Rosie had found Jean at the back of her house

sowing carrot seed. While they talked Holgate sat on a pile of slates at the corner of the house, surveying the vegetables with a connoisseur's eye but in a position to give warning of interruption.

Rosie began by saying that there had been a development, they'd been talking to Dwayne Paxton again.

Jean was dismayed but resigned. 'I suppose it had to come,' she sighed, and then, in a bright, artificial tone: 'But there didn't have to be—intimacy; I mean, not to be illegal.'

'Illegal?' Rosie was baffled. Holgate stood up and took a step towards them, intent on a row of sprouting broccoli.

'Definitely not.' Jean was into her stride. 'She's very mature for her age and he's just a handsome boy. No age gap. And they were pals, nothing more.'

'Actually,' Rosie said, 'Dwayne has been telling us about Isa.'

'Shit!' Jean had spilled seeds. She looked at the soil helplessly, pulled out an empty packet and started to fill it with pinches of earth and carrot seed. 'What about Isa?' she asked, addressing the ground.

'You know she was having an affair.' A statement, not a question.

'It's not true.' Jean stood up and faced the other woman. 'I know the rumour's going around, probably started by her—she was a nymphomaniac, did you know that? She slept

239

around—with everyone, anyone—and she did make a play for Martin; she made a bloody nuisance of herself in fact, extremely embarrassing for all of us, but that was it: embarrassment.' She smiled fiercely. 'No affair, I assure you. That kind of woman doesn't have affairs, she was like a bitch on heat.' The smile slipped, became a rictus. 'She ate men, she consumed them. She was the village whore.'

* * *

At the station in Bailrigg Blamire was defiant, casual and confiding in turns. Paxton, he said, was trying to cover his back.

'We know about Gemma Lambert,' Gibson said, as if sex with a minor were a misdemeanour.

'And the VAT fraud?' They listened, knowing that this was par for the course: the accused turning on the accuser. 'He's a handyman,' he went on. 'He charges VAT but he's not registered. And he doesn't give receipts and won't take cheques.'

'Let's talk about Isa Lambert,' Gibson said.

Blamire's eyes were avoiding the tape recorder as if it were a camera. He shook his head. 'She didn't mean anything to me. I was sorry for her. She needed treatment. Everyone's hand was against her.' Gibson raised his eyebrows. Sewell waited. 'Women

240

loathed her,' Blamire assured them. 'She was attractive in a common way—but you've seen photographs.'

'Where did you go?' Gibson asked.

Blamire sucked in his cheeks. 'Out on the old firing range. I was teaching her to drive.'

'You were?' Sewell allowed himself a lewd grin. 'In her MG?'

'That's right.'

'But you left her car at Blind Keld.'

'Ah yes, it *started* with the MG and then we switched to Paxton's Land Rover.' Sewell looked sceptical. 'OK!' Blamire exclaimed. 'I wasn't teaching her—well,' he shrugged— 'I tried. I couldn't get anywhere—' He stopped, then continued, man to man, confessing everything: 'Quite honestly, I wanted out. She'd latched on to me and people were talking. You can't hide a thing like that.'

'When did your wife find out?' Gibson asked.

The fellow looked rueful. 'She knew all along. Of course I denied it but I couldn't stall her, it was only a matter of time. I was dreading Isa coming to the house. Jean's a tiger when she's roused.' His eyes shone with admiration. He was looking down at the table as he spoke and he missed their sudden stiffening, the startled glances they exchanged.

*   *   *

Rosie said, 'He wasn't lying there, sir. Jean knew he was having it off with Isa. You should have seen her—Holgate heard, didn't you?' The DC nodded. The four of them were in Gibson's office discussing the morning's interviews, planning ahead. Rosie went on quickly, 'At the same time that she denied he was having an affair, in the next breath she was slagging the woman off in terms I reckon she'd never used before—except to her husband maybe.' She thought about that. 'Probably,' she amended.

'We've got ourselves another suspect,' Sewell said.

Gibson was silent. They looked at him, waiting for his opinion. He said slowly, 'If it could be one woman, why not another? Another wife? Where are the rest of the boyfriends?'

'Dwayne?' Rosie hazarded. 'No, he was drinking in the Grey Goat. But that was in the evening. He doesn't have an alibi for the night.'

'We're not losing sight of him.'

Rosie was thinking. 'If he was sleeping with Isa, would Gemma be jealous?'

'She's Walter's sister,' Sewell reminded them. 'That would give her a double reason for jealousy.'

'There's the holiday people,' Holgate said doubtfully.

'No.' Gibson was definite. 'He has to be a

local—he or she. After he pushed the car in the river he had to come back across the fields.'

'Not if he had an accomplice.'

There was silence as they thought about couples: the Blamires, the Lamberts . . .

'Swinburn,' Sewell said.

They considered Swinburn. 'And there's his wife,' Rosie murmured but this produced no reaction from Holgate and Sewell who couldn't imagine Jacob and Mabel colluding in *murder.*

'Does anyone care that much these days about extramarital affairs?' Gibson mused.

'If exposure could mean losing your job,' Rosie countered. 'Or losing something else valuable.'

'Such as?' Gibson was interested.

'There had to be a reason for killing her,' Rosie persisted.

'We don't have to concern ourselves with motive,' Holgate pointed out but she was staring at Gibson.

'Rage could be adequate,' he said, 'fury, a blow, an accident. It could be manslaughter.'

'Not a blow, sir; she was strangled.'

CHAPTER FOURTEEN

Sunday afternoon: soft, somnolent, still; even the birds were dozing in this the hottest part of the day. Cooper, stretched in the cool shade of delphiniums, opened a lazy eye as Miss Pink walked down the lane but it was too hot to follow her. It was too hot for walking but she was on the prowl, looking for a computer buff, wary of Blamire's reputed temper but about to play it prudent. And Jean should be at home.

She was, just. They met at her gate. She had been up to Sleylands for lunch, she said, sounding tired and looking haggard. Miss Pink regarded shade under trees beyond the gate and remarked inanely that Sunday was the traditional time for visiting. Jean was forced to ask her in but without enthusiasm, and when her visitor pointed out that she didn't want to disturb Martin, announced with her first show of spirit that he was in Bailrigg with the police.

'Nothing wrong, I hope?' Stopping by a seat under a red oak, Miss Pink sank down, concerned and ready to be enlightened.

Jean laughed harshly. 'It was monstrous! That woman—Rosie—and the fellow Holgate: they kept me occupied in the vegetable garden at the back'—she gestured wildly—'while more police went in the front and took Martin away. You don't believe me? You think I'm exaggerating? He left a note on the kitchen table.'

Miss Pink turned to look at the house. 'What did the note say?'

'Just that he'd gone to Bailrigg with them. I called the station twice. After the second time and I was told the party still hadn't arrived I didn't call again. I went up to my mum's,' she ended lamely.

'I don't think you've anything to worry about.' It was anodyne but Jean felt obliged to respond. She shrugged and said, trying to be casual, 'It'll be about Isa no doubt.'

'Of course, you were her nearest neighbours.'

'That doesn't mean we were on close terms.'

'Everyone is under suspicion after a murder. You must know that.'

Jean bit her lip. 'I do, but it's still a shock, like death. You've been expecting it but when it happens it knocks you backwards.'

'You'd been expecting it?'

'Death—I was talking about death.'

'Ah yes. Why didn't they question your husband here, I wonder?'

'I've no idea.'

'As if they wanted to separate you.' In the face of a tense pause Miss Pink rattled on: 'They did it with Walter and Gemma too, and Dwayne and Gemma; no doubt the Honeymans were interviewed separately. The police are all at sea'—she smiled benignly—

'and all the time it was someone from outside.'

Jean gaped. 'How do you know?'

'It's obvious, my dear. Who could it have been in this little community: Walter, Dwayne, your husband? Dwayne had no need to kill her, and Walter and Martin have alibis. You surely don't think Ralph Honeyman and your father are suspects?'

Jean gave a sickly grin. 'Not my dad, not with my mum keeping an eye on him. And Ralph—well, he's a tub of lard, isn't he? Certainly obesity wouldn't have deterred Isa, but Ralph wasn't capable of the amount of energy involved in that murder.'

'You have a way with words.'

'Do you think so?' Her face softened. 'I write a little,' she admitted.

'That's interesting. What do you write?'

'Only short stories at the moment. I heard that you learn to write as you do it. If I ever manage to sell some I'd like to tackle a novel.'

'I do romances: novellas, nothing serious. Occasionally I'm commissioned to do a travel article.'

'Really?' Jean was awed. 'I'd never have thought—How clever of you! Here it's Martin who does the serious stuff, the guidebooks, while I dream of the great Lakeland novel.' She laughed, it was a joke.

'How does it work: two authors under one roof?'

'I don't write when Martin's here; I couldn't

246

anyway, we only have the one computer.'

They were silent. A blackbird fled shrieking across the lawn. 'Cooper's about,' Jean said, adding dreamily, 'I like to write at night when everything's quiet: in longhand, then I'm not disturbing him.'

Miss Pink regarded the other's big capable hands. 'Were you writing on Wednesday night?'

There was no immediate response. She looked from the hands to the eyes and was surprised to see that Jean was smiling. 'We alibi each other,' she said calmly. 'That was what you were thinking, wasn't it?' She stretched her fingers. 'That I could have strangled her. You're not stupid, you're a very discerning lady. Actually, I would have done worse than that, I would have made her die slowly. It's no secret now'—seeing Miss Pink's astonishment—'I told Rosie this morning and Holgate's ears were flapping. She made a dead set at Martin, you see. Poor chap, he was hag-ridden.'

'Then that explains why he went to Bailrigg.' And why husband and wife had been separated: to check their stories.

Jean was watching her closely. 'You're forgetting that he never left this house.'

'Of course. Nor did you, so you're in the clear too, even though you would have killed her if you'd known. When did he tell you about the affair?'

247

'Affair? There was no affair! You weren't listening. She did try to seduce him, but he wasn't having anything to do with her; he couldn't run fast enough.'

'You knew all along?'

'No! He had to tell me when he realized the police had him down as a suspect. And then Gemma heard them fighting; it was about Isa's crazy driving but Gemma misinterpreted it. So he had to tell me. Like I said, if he'd told me when she was alive I'd have been over there at Borrans and—and beating her with my own hands.' Again she studied them. 'And I'd have enjoyed doing it,' she added defiantly.

Miss Pink sank back on the seat. 'You *have* been through the wringer.'

'Oh, I can take it, but my old man's had a bad time. Imagine: living next door to that harpy after he'd rejected her—'

'He did that?'

'That's what I've been telling you. With her it was either succumb or reject her, there was no half-way house. She had it in for him after that, no mistake about it.'

'He told you all this? Of course he did, you could only get it from him. And all the time it was going on you had no idea?'

'It wasn't over a period of time; just the one episode, but that was bad enough. He couldn't tell me, he was too terrified of my reaction. All part of the macho image: two women fighting over a man. Of course none of it was his fault

248

except that he was weak. He said she was insatiable; he'd never come across anything like it before and he didn't know how to cope. What would it have done to his ego if he'd come to me and asked me to deal with her? I'd have been happy to, but there you are, he was scared of what I'd do. And by the time he did tell me it was too late. She was dead.'

*   *   *

'Hand me t'socket spanner, lad.'

Bobby dived for it, then crowded close as if the removal of a spark plug was the most exciting thing to do on a Sunday afternoon.

'You'm in me light,' Jacob growled, but the light was obscured by men blocking the entrance to the tractor shed. Jacob and Bobby stared, the one expressionless, the other searching for escape routes.

'Your grandson?' DS Sewell asked, advancing.

'This is young Bobby,' Jacob returned with dignity. ' 'Way you go then'—to the boy—'get them calves sorted.'

Bobby slipped between Sewell and Holgate like a hare, followed by the latter's thoughtful gaze. 'Lad takes after you,' he observed.

Jacob showed surprise. 'You come 'ere to talk about me lad?'

'Oh, he's your son!'

'He's me helper. He thinks he's taking over

249

t'farm.'

Sewell said, puzzled, refusing to see a joke, 'Why is it we didn't know that Mrs Blamire had a son?'

Jacob dropped the spanner and leaned against the tractor. He stared at them as he wiped his hands on a wad of cotton waste. 'You know well she don't have no bairns. Bobby be a Lee: from Sunder. Everyone knows.' This with emphasis, implying that Borascal didn't discuss the parentage of its children. Drawing a line under it he asked coldly, 'And what can I do for you gentlemen?'

'Not much,' Sewell confessed. 'We're going door-to-door.'

'How many times is that?'

'Every time we learn a bit more we come back; someone talks, we discuss it, come back again, keep that up till we're satisfied.' Jacob said nothing. 'So?' Sewell asked brightly.

'What was the question?'

'Your son-in-law confessed.'

'Oh, aye.'

'To his affair with Isa Lambert.'

Jacob's face didn't change, and they were watching closely. As if to spare them embarrassment from the lengthening silence he offered some relief: 'And?'

'He *is* married to your daughter,' Sewell pointed out.

Jacob nodded, going along with that and waiting politely to be enlightened further.

250

'You're not bothered?' Holgate put in.

Jacob turned to him, surprised. 'She'm a grown woman; it's her business.'

'And his,' Holgate exclaimed. 'He had reason—'

'Did you know about it?' Sewell interrupted, lurching against the constable.

Jacob sketched a shrug. 'Maybe. It weren't my concern.'

'I wouldn't go so far as to say that.' Sewell was judicious. 'I understand Blamire was looking to start an outdoor activities centre here once you retire: renting the place from you and running courses. You'd be a sleeping partner?'

'Someone's been talking out of turn.'

At last they'd managed to rouse him and Sewell seized his advantage. 'And you wouldn't want to be the business partner of a man who was planning on ditching your daughter for another woman, not to speak of any financial obligations he might have entered into already.' The tone was insidious.

As Jacob considered this, another figure blocked the light and Mabel said coldly, 'Does someone mind telling me what other woman we're talking about?'

No one was happy; everyone, except Mabel, disconcerted. Jacob recovered first. 'Them's come with some tale about Martin.'

Mabel turned on Holgate who happened to be nearest to her. 'Perhaps you wouldn't mind giving me the gossip about my son-in-law.'

Sewell said, 'Did you know he was having an affair with Mrs Lambert, ma'am?'

'No,' she snapped, her eyes flashing at her husband. 'And neither did anyone else.'

'If we had known,' Jacob amended it slightly, 'it weren't nowt to do with us.'

'We didn't know.' Mabel was firm, turning to Sewell: 'Who told you this?'

'He did. Blamire.'

Her hand lifted towards her throat, and dropped, moving aimlessly as if she didn't know what to do with it. 'Does my daughter know? She's never even hinted at it.' Her eyes came back to Jacob.

'Some wives try to block it out,' Sewell said.

'Not—' Mabel checked, then shook her head in emphatic denial. 'Not her.' She thought again, as if recalling conversations and behaviour over the preceding weeks. 'She'd have told me even if it was only a suspicion.'

*　　　*　　　*

'Everyone protecting everyone else,' Holgate said as they came away from Sleylands. 'It's what you'd expect; they're all related.'

'Young Bobby's from that travelling family: the Lees, in the cottage on the beck. Old Swinburn will have had it off with the girl there, the one with all the kids: Sherrel.'

'What's that got to do with Isa's murder?'

252

'Nothing. It's just that Swinburn's a sly old bugger and, of course, Mabel's compliant.' Holgate was staring. 'Bobby'—Sewell was testy—'he's Swinburn's bastard but Mabel goes along with it to the extent of letting the boy come up to the farm. They're very close, all of 'em.'

'That's what I said: too bloody close. Look at the alibis. Christ!'

*   *   *

Flora Lee looked enchanting wearing Bobby's denim cap but at four years old she was too young to be on the wrong side of the beck and alone. Miss Pink, loath to lecture, said that she proposed to visit Nan and perhaps Flora would see her across the beck. The child agreed with alacrity and, hand in hand, they waded to the far bank where Miss Pink studied the little animals embroidered on the hat and the word 'Alaska' in pale grey thread.

'Can I see the hat?'

'No!' Flora snatched it off and crumpled it in both hands. 'It's our Bobby's. I forgot. I gotta put it back. He'll slaughter me.' And before Miss Pink could stop her she'd rushed back across the beck—shallow here and with an adult standing by she was in no danger— and clambered up the far bank. Miss Pink watched, her eyes intent behind the dark glasses. The child disappeared at a clump of

253

brambles and after a moment reappeared, scrambling down the slope. Above the brambles was a mature larch, incongruous among the broad-leaves, easy to remember.

'Where is Bobby?' Miss Pink asked, in no hurry to reach Sunder.

'He's working at Sleylands, mending Uncle Jake's tractor.'

'And you borrowed his hat while he's away.'

'I didn't thieve it!'

'Of course not, you put it back. Who gave it to him?'

'No one. He found un.'

'Where?'

'In t'beck.' The child gasped and clutched at Miss Pink's hand. Bobby was running up the track, pale with some powerful emotion. He glared from his sister to the far side of the water. Flora's hand was as tight as a bird's claw. Miss Pink tried a little reassuring pressure but doubted that it registered; the children were staring at each other and now she realized that they were both terrified.

Flora's nerve broke first. 'I never touched it! Never, ever! I never went there! I been in t'beck—wasn't I?' This to Miss Pink.

'We were both in the beck,' Miss Pink said calmly.

Bobby's face said it all for him: distrust of both of them, and there was still that overriding fear. He pushed past his sister and, starting to run, slowed to the pace of a stalking

254

cat. He came to the stream crossing, turned and looked at them. Miss Pink and Flora jerked into life and resumed their progress to Sunder.

'He'll see I didn't touch it,' Flora said. 'Won't he?'

'Oh yes, he won't be able to tell. What makes it so important?'

'He says I'm not to talk about it.'

Which was no answer, only confirmation of the importance. No, Miss Pink said as Sunder came in view, she wouldn't come in and visit Nan after all; she'd take her tea at Jollybeard instead—saying anything that came to mind, anything to get away and consider whether Bobby's finding of Phoebe's hat had any significance. Not, of course, unless he had found the camera too, but the camera would have sunk, unlike the hat . . . unless the camera had remained attached to her . . . But Bobby was nothing more than a young magpie who picked up trifles; a child of that age could never bring himself to lift a camera from a corpse.

Idly strolling, regardless of heat and the heady scent of hawthorns, of the Lamb tight-closed against the Sunday hush, of ragged robin in the water meadows, she came back to the present when the first waft of foul air impinged on her consciousness and she remembered that this was the field where she'd found two dead sheep. Either Swinburn hadn't removed them or the carcasses had oozed. And there, among the rushes and incongruously framed by yellow irises, was the bloated lump of a sheep.

She was at the gate on the road before she recalled that there had been no sign of a tractor near the carcass, but there were wheel marks at the gate. So Swinburn had taken one and left the other, a gesture only. And where did he put dead sheep? The meadow was boggy and the wheels had shed mud on the tarmac. Grimly determined she followed the traces until they turned in at a gate on the opposite side of the road.

A track climbed through an ash wood towards a crag, diverging sideways to ascend in a wide hairpin and emerge on the rim of what was no doubt a quarry, or the place where the crag had been quarried. In a bay below was Swinburn's tip, an unwholesome cove of plastic and rusted iron, a car chassis, a fridge, a cooker, rotten wood, drums that would have contained oil or toxic chemicals, ragged rolls of wire, some small trees and a load of rocks and soil out of which a sheep's leg protruded. She'd seen worse, at least it wasn't draped down a sea cliff on some magnificent coast. But it was less than a quarter of a mile from the road, and the sheep weren't buried.

*   *   *

256

'I buried un!' Swinburn protested. 'If them's showing again it were foxes pulled 'em out. You didn't ought to've been there anyway, 'tis private land.'

'Hush now.' Mabel was angry and frightened. 'You go back there and you bury those sheep right. You never told me you'd put 'em on t'tip. And that tip—'

'And the one on the meadow,' Miss Pink stormed. 'You didn't take that one.'

'I did then! I took the both of 'em!'

'So another one died in the meadow. And there's one up above the big quarry at the head—'

'Oh no! You'm as bad as that Phoebe—'

'Jacob Swinburn, don't you dare say nowt against the dead! Away you go this minute and you get that sheep out of t'meadow and them two in t'tip—and any more as you put in there, and you dig a pit and you—' but Jacob had gone.

Miss Pink and Mabel regarded each other. Miss Pink wondered how he'd ever dared to *look* at Sherrel Lee. Aloud she said, 'Phoebe certainly got under his skin—and I seem to have taken over from her.'

'No,' Mabel said tightly. 'I have. He's not lazy, just old, and we've got no one to leave the place to, not as a farm, so he's no interest in looking after the land proper. I'll be glad to be shot of it all, I can tell you.'

'Jean said something about turning it into a

mountain centre and running courses.'

'It's not going to work. He keeps chopping and changing, and she's not keen herself—'

Miss Pink shifted her weight and rested a hand on the table. 'Here, sit yourself down,' Mabel fussed. 'We both need a cup of tea, all that shouting builds up a thirst.' She pushed a cat off a chair and filled the kettle. Miss Pink lowered herself on to a warm cushion.

'Mountain activities are all the rage,' she observed, making conversation. 'I'm amazed that so many can keep going, that there are enough customers to go round. The courses aren't cheap.'

'He's got this new idea.' Mabel didn't seem to like naming Blamire. 'At first it was walking parties with himself guiding them, now he's talking about "safaris" with Land Rovers on upland tracks. He says he'll get the folk who want to see the fells the easy way.'

'I wouldn't have thought there are enough tracks where the authorities would allow vehicles.'

'He's finding them. He says there are more than you'd think. I don't see it myself. It's different abroad where there are wild animals to look at but what is there to see here? Walkers like yourself seem to find plenty to interest you, you go slow enough to look at birds and things, but what bird is going to hang around to be gawked at by folk in a noisy truck, and who wants to be thrown around on

258

these rough old tracks anyway?'

There was a long pause during which the kettle started to sing and Mabel regarded it unhappily.

'Jean tells me she writes,' Miss Pink said.

The mother's face brightened. 'Aye, she does. She likes that.' As if Jean disliked the idea of mountain centres. 'You don't have family.' It sounded like an accusation.

'No, only cousins. I never married.'

'We always want the best for our children.'

'Human nature,' Miss Pink murmured.

Mabel warmed a willow pattern teapot, hefting the iron kettle with the ease of familiarity. She made the tea and set it on the side of the stove to brew, brought unmatched cups and saucers to the table, milk and sugar and a canister of biscuits. She poured the tea, passed a cup to the visitor, proffered the biscuits, which were cinnamon and home-made, and sat down. 'The police were here,' she said.

'They were everywhere this morning.'

'They've got Martin in town.'

'They're questioning all the men, the women too actually. They questioned me.'

That brought Mabel up short. 'What could you tell them?'

'It's difficult to remember—but that's how they work, isn't it? They don't interview, they arrive and they talk, and it's only when they've gone that you realize that *you* did the talking,

259

they were listening, and what on earth did you say that they wanted to hear? I mean'—she spread her hands—'I've only been here a week, I'm a tourist; what could I tell them?'

'You talk to everybody.'

'So?'

'You hear the gossip.'

'Is that what the police want: gossip?'

'It's why they came here: because they'd heard that Martin had been seeing Isa Lambert.'

'Seeing her?' Miss Pink might never have heard the expression.

'Going with her. An affair.'

'Jean did mention it.'

'Then you know!' Mabel was mortified.

'I didn't know how much you knew. You wouldn't expect me to repeat gossip about your son-in-law.'

Mabel slumped in her chair. 'I don't know that I care now,' she confessed. 'Jean says she doesn't. It happens; she'll take him back, no doubt.' Her eyes glazed. She could be thinking of her own husband and Sherrel Lee.

'The difference here is that Isa was murdered,' Miss Pink said.

Mabel's eyes narrowed as she caught the inference but she fastened on the more important issue, and without subterfuge. 'You're saying he's a suspect.'

'Apparently it was a local man, because he had no car and must have left the river by a

260

cross-country route.'

'Is that what the police are saying? How do you know?'

'I picked it up. It makes sense.'

'I hope you're wrong, indeed I do. It's not nice, him being questioned by police, and him married to my girl.'

CHAPTER FIFTEEN

Gemma was trying to pull Whisk away from Phoebe's gate; on the other side Cooper spat and swore, his back arched, every red hair on end.

'That dog is heading for trouble,' Miss Pink observed, coming home from Sleylands. 'Are you walking him or does he run loose?' Loose dogs being anathema in sheep country.

'He must have got out, but he'll go with anybody.' Gemma paused. 'Not the only one,' she added darkly, with a glance at her own roof.

'Come and have a cool drink.' Miss Pink was firm. 'I want to talk to you.'

'Might as well.' The girl was ungracious. 'I don't seem to be welcome at Elfhow, and Eleanor's too busy.' She had a grip on the dog's collar as he strained to get back and threaten Cooper. Miss Pink unbuckled her belt and handed it over.

261

'What's this?' Gemma slipped it through the collar. 'It's gorgeous bead-work.'

'I bought it on a Navajo reservation.'

'Oh, wow!' Candid eyes were turned on the traveller. 'You've been around.' But candour was replaced by speculation as Gemma wondered if there might be more to an intrepid traveller than met the eye. She muttered something about getting home to give Walter his tea.

'I won't keep you,' Miss Pink said comfortably. 'I need to talk about Isa.'

They were at Ashgill's gate and Gemma dug in her heels. 'What about her?'

'For instance, did she visit Walter at the office?'

The other blinked. This was unexpected. 'Of course she did. We both did: when we went in by bus and wanted a lift home. Isa more than me actually; there are plenty of men in the office.'

'Would they have shown her how to operate the computers?'

'That's not the only thing—' Gemma stopped. 'You're on to something: something to do with her? And computers? What is this?'

Miss Pink opened the gate and they entered the garden. The collie pulled and the girl released him and returned the belt, her eyes demanding an answer, but her companion wouldn't be hurried.

They sat under a silver birch drinking Seven

Up, Gemma's tension mounting. 'Your brother doesn't have a computer at home?' Miss Pink asked. 'Nor you?'

'Of course not, neither of us. Nor does—did Isa.'

'But could she use one?'

'I wouldn't think so, it would need too much concentration.'

'Did you know she was seeing Martin?'

Gemma gaped, then over-compensated with a mask so blank it was absurd. 'Everyone knew,' she said coldly.

'That's where you're making a mistake.' It was friendly but assured. 'Walter may have suspected, and yourself, but no one knew other than themselves—'

'And her other boyfriends—'

'No! You've protested too much, Gemma; you've been doing it all along. Isa was having an affair with Martin—he admits it himself—but the story that she was promiscuous started with you.'

'She was—'

'Promiscuous is usually taken to mean many men: indiscriminate behaviour.'

'And so she did. She was—'

'She wasn't. You started the rumour because you wanted to divert suspicion from Walter. If she had a reputation for promiscuity you could hope to widen the circle of suspects. It was you who came up with the story of her picking up lorry drivers in all-night cafés.'

'I *knew*.' Gemma was sullen but determined. 'She left the MG at Blind Keld and went on . . .' She tailed off.

'She went on in Dwayne's Land Rover. Dwayne lent it to Martin. Why did he do that? What hold did Martin have over him?'

Gemma snorted, distracted. 'Just a scam here and there like tax fraud, not declaring income, nothing important.'

'And there was yourself. You're under age.'

She shrugged. 'We were friends just.'

'That's it.' Miss Pink nodded, satisfied. 'Two men, each with something on the other, and you and Isa in the middle.' Gemma glowered. 'Martin has a computer,' Miss Pink went on, thinking aloud. 'He'll have a printer?'

'Of course. Jean uses it; she writes—'

'Was he besotted?' Miss Pink wasn't listening. 'Did she persuade him, blackmail him—or did he hate . . . Had Eleanor annoyed him? Or damaged him in some way?'

'What are you on about? What's Eleanor got to do with anything?'

'Nothing—much.' Miss Pink was stunned; she had been talking aloud to a child of fifteen, speculating on blackmail and murder—well, murder by extension. 'What I'm trying to do,' she said, casting about, trying to restore some sense of balance, 'is discover who was behind the salmonella hoax. You remember: forged letters to people and the local paper saying that there was an outbreak of food poisoning

264

centred on Jollybeard? That forgery was done on a computer so I'm considering those people who had access to one.'

Gemma was intrigued. 'OK, so Isa could have blackmailed—no, she had nothing on him—could have persuaded Martin to forge the letters. Isa hated Eleanor because Eleanor said she was a jumped-up little tart'—Gemma caught Miss Pink's expression—'all right then, a gold-digger. But what's that got to do with murder?'

And that was the question.

*   *   *

'I've brought you a visitor,' Rosie said, much amused at finding the old lady dozing under the silver birches. 'Detective Inspector Gibson.'

Miss Pink was embarrassed; dropping off in the daytime was something she associated with old age. To make it worse he was studying her as if she were a rare breed of bird. He was a muscular young fellow with prematurely grey hair. He looked like a nice dog freshly clipped. She started to rise, mumbling about tea.

'I'll make it in a minute,' Rosie said. 'You sit down.'

'Oh yes?' Miss Pink was wary. 'You've got bad news.'

'No, it's just that I don't want to miss this.'

Mystification deepened. Miss Pink turned

back to the man. 'I've been talking to DCI Tyndale,' he told her. 'You've been holding back on us, ma'am.' Tyndale? 'Four years back,' he reminded her: 'you found a child's skeleton in the peat above Orrdale.'

'Of course! I remember Mr Tyndale—he was only Inspector then.' She hesitated. 'And how did my name come to be mentioned? You don't know me.' But her eyes came round to Rosie.

'Sergeant Winder mentioned that your interest in the case was . . .' He was at a loss.

'Suspicious,' Rosie supplied. 'You took more interest than an ordinary tourist would, and it wasn't ghoulish. In fact, the kind of interest you showed was more like a suspect's.'

'The criminal mind,' she murmured, then firmly: 'I'm going to have a drink and so shall you.'

They drank cold lager and she sketched the salient points of the Orrdale murders for them. 'Unsavoury,' she concluded. 'Murders involving small children leave scars for decades, weeping sores in some cases. With some people they never heal, and small wonder.' She raised an eyebrow. 'Fortunately no children are involved here.' But she was disconcerted by her own statement.

'Gemma?' Rosie suggested.

'Actually I was thinking of young Bobby but—no. He's terrified of death, not murder.'

'Is he?' Rosie was intrigued. 'What's the

difference?'

'Now you are not to go to Sunder asking questions; you'll only exacerbate the situation. What happened was that the boy found Phoebe Metcalf's hat. But it's only because it's a dead person's hat that he's frightened, it has nothing to do with Isa's murder.'

'How old is he?' Gibson asked.

'Eight. And he's a nervous child so it's not a good idea to upset him.' She was stern.

'He's too young to have had anything to do with the murder?'

'Far too young.'

'Why didn't he turn in the hat?' Rosie asked.

'He didn't know it was important, that it was Phoebe's. Eleanor told me she hadn't seen Phoebe wearing it.'

'There you are, you see!' Rosie turned to Gibson. 'Like I said: she finds things out; we knew nothing about that hat.'

He nodded. 'You must have talked to everyone, ma'am. Did you learn anything about Mrs Lambert's activities, like names of boyfriends?'

'There were none other than Blamire. The stories about promiscuity originated with Gemma.' He showed no surprise. 'You knew,' she said, adding carefully, choosing her words, 'Is Blamire still in Bailrigg?'

'No, he's at home'—their heads turned automatically to the screen of birches but they were too far away to see or hear any sign of life from next door. 'With his wife,' Gibson added meaningly.

Miss Pink took a moment to catch on. 'You considered her? The jealous wife? How could that be? Jean didn't know about her husband's affair until after Isa died.'

'He puts it differently. According to him he'd already confessed to her. He had to, Isa was becoming tiresome. You look doubtful, ma'am; you don't think a man would kill his lover because she was embarrassing him?'

'There are stronger motives . . . But I'm puzzled because Jean told me she didn't know until after the murder.'

'That's exactly what she would say. If she didn't know then she had no reason to kill the woman.'

Miss Pink pondered this. 'And if she didn't know, it gives her husband a motive for murder: to silence Isa if she was threatening to tell his wife.' She shook her head. 'It's not enough, not with these characters. The man has charm, he could have talked Jean round. She's very loyal, she's been protecting him; whether he's a killer or only a suspect, she's the kind of rather silly woman—I have to say it—who'll stand by her husband come hell or high water. You see the same thing with battered wives—not that there's any indication of that here, even though he's said to have a hair-trigger temper.' She regarded Gibson doubtfully. 'Have you considered that Isa might have been a threat for some reason other than sexual?'

'She had something on him? Something else?'

'The salmonella.' He was bemused. She explained about the hoax and how it was only today that she had realized how it might have been accomplished. 'Isa could have picked up a letterhead from another Council when she was in her husband's office, could have taken it to Blamire and he forged the hoax letter.' Rosie was frowning, Gibson looked sceptical. 'No.' She agreed with their unspoken criticism. 'It won't do. You don't kill someone because she could expose a hoax.'

'What else have you discovered, ma'am?' Gibson appeared to dismiss the salmonella.

She had to admit that she'd learned nothing that might have a bearing on the murder, nothing that they hadn't discovered for themselves. Dead sheep weren't worthy of mention in this context, and as for Bobby's parentage, that had nothing to do with the police. There was one matter to be cleared up: the whereabouts of Phoebe's camera, and in that respect it was possible that Bobby did enter the picture. Not the Lambert murder of course but Phoebe's—death. And not for the first time, an impulse fired in Miss Pink's brain, triggered by those words: Phoebe's death.

*   *   *

'It don't matter who asks him,' Misella said, 'me or Sherrel. He's no thief.'

She sat in a sturdy rocking chair outside her back door, the baby on her lap, rocking gently, her eyes passing vacantly over the little ones playing with colouring books, returning to Miss Pink. Flora stood at her side, twisting one leg round the other, serious and intent.

'He's not in any kind of trouble,' Miss Pink assured the grandmother. 'He only picked it up. In fact I'll offer a reward.'

'Why's it that important?'

'I need to know who it belongs to. It had little animals on the front.' She didn't look at Flora who pulled at her nan's skirt. Absently Misella bent to hear the urgent whisper while Miss Pink affected to take an interest in a small plane droning overhead.

Misella straightened and pursed her lips. 'Where is it?' she asked.

Flora shook her head. 'He moved un.'

'Where's Bobby now?'

'Up to Uncle Jake's again.'

'Then he's not to know who found it. You fetch it here and Miss Pink will give you the reward.'

'How much?'

'A pound,' Miss Pink said smartly.

Flora darted away round the end of the

cottage. 'Coal hole,' Misella observed.

Bobby had put it in a plastic bag to keep it clean. Miss Pink handled it carefully although it could surely tell no stories after the lapse of time; the inside bore no traces, not even a hair as far as she could tell without her reading glasses, only Phoebe's name—no, *figures* on the underside of the pale grey visor. It looked like a car registration and was vaguely familiar if only because it was a local number. She handed Flora the agreed reward.

'Is it only worth a pound?' Misella asked innocently. Miss Pink reached for her wallet and produced a five-pound note. She was lost in speculation, so much so that she had reached the gate before she remembered the other matter. She came back. Flora had disappeared.

'Did he find a camera?' she asked.

'Never! That I would have known. Flo! Come back here!'

Feet padded on stairs. Flora appeared, looking wary.

'Did our Bobby find a camera?' Misella asked, but the child shook her head violently. Misella turned back to Miss Pink. 'I'll let you know if I hear anything,' she said with meaning, but it was obvious that if Flora knew anything more she would have said so; the child was bright enough to know that if the surrender of a hat could produce six pounds, a camera would be worth a fortune.

In the Blamires' garden the four occupants were not enjoying the balmy evening. Jean was livid with anger but doing her utmost to contain it in the presence of Gibson and Rosie Winder. She railed at Martin: 'You're telling me she came in my house and used the computer? She was upstairs—' She stopped herself, nauseated by the image of Isa in Elfhow's bedrooms.

'It was only a computer,' Martin protested. 'I couldn't refuse a neighbour the use of it, now could I?'

Jean was stricken. Rosie felt sorry for her, learning that her husband had actually brought his lover to the house, probably using the marital bed in his wife's absence. The computer was just a handy excuse; if Jean was the killer it was her husband she should have wasted, not the other woman.

Gibson was on his own tack. 'It was Mrs Lambert who forged the letters then?' Martin had denied all knowledge of the salmonella hoax.

The man shrugged. 'I suppose so. I wasn't interested. She could have been printing blackmail letters for all I knew.'

'Who would she have blackmailed?'

'God knows. That was just a suggestion: a shot in the dark.'

272

Jean's eyes were going from one to the other, stunned with disbelief.

'This is shocking,' Rosie told her, speaking quietly as if they were alone: two women sharing confidences. Gibson stiffened and Martin rounded on her, but it was Jean who said feelingly, 'I just can't believe it: here in my own house!'

'You knew,' Martin said. 'It's the invasion of your territory you're objecting to.'

'I'm objecting to—' She checked. 'I didn't know,' she muttered. 'That's the trouble.' She addressed Gibson with a forlorn attempt at dignity: 'My world's changed in the last few days; I don't know where I am.'

'Perhaps we should have a cup of tea,' Rosie said.

Jean burst into frenzied laughter, saw their expressions, and stopped. 'A brandy would be more welcome,' she gasped.

Martin went indoors. Jean said to Rosie, 'Two days ago I was a normal housewife with everything going for me: husband, home, parents close by. Now I'm shattered. It's just one shock after another.'

'You accepted the affair,' Gibson murmured.

'You're mad.' It was unemphatic, no more than a fact.

'You'd known all along.'

'He told me two days ago. Actually he'd skirted round it the day before but then he said only that she'd tried to seduce him—very crudely. Who says I knew?'

'He does.'

'Ah.' She had raged, had controlled the rage, had appeared hopeless and helpless, now they watched her relax. She breathed deeply and regularly, her face softened and the heavy, somewhat masculine features were transformed. She became a handsome beauty. She blinked and it was as if she had closed the door on a bad scene. 'Yes,' she admitted. 'I knew. I tried to kid myself that I could block it out but you can't; wives always know although they swear they don't. It's the little things: a long hair that's not your colour, a smell—she used some cheap scent—absences, lies . . .' Martin was standing beside her with a brandy snifter. 'When they're besotted they can't hide it,' she told Gibson.

*   *   *

'What's this?' Eleanor asked, peering, not taking the hat in her greasy hands.

'It's a registration number.'

'I can see that. It's Dwayne Paxton's Land Rover. Turn it over. Why, it's Phoebe's hat that she brought back from Alaska. What's Dwayne's number doing on it? Where d'you find it?'

Miss Pink collapsed rather than sat. Eleanor was concerned. 'Are you all right? You look a bit pale.'

'I'm hungry.' She was also exhausted. 'I forget when I last ate and this'—indicating the hat—'is the last straw. I'm being crowded.'

Eleanor had her priorities straight. She bustled about the kitchen, filling the kettle, warming soup, assembling smoked salmon sandwiches. Miss Pink propped her head on her hands, her eyelids drooping, brightening up as a cup of coffee appeared in front of her.

She drank the soup, ate the sandwiches, was fortified with more coffee and all the time Eleanor pretended to occupy herself with unnecessary tasks, waiting for the other woman to come back to life. At the end of the scratch supper she offered a drink but Miss Pink said that alcohol would knock her out, she would go to her bed. Eleanor eyed the hat, upside down on the table, the registration number compelling attention.

Miss Pink said, 'Bobby found it in the beck. What I'm wondering is, has he found the camera? I'm hoping Misella will find out.'

Eleanor studied the visor. 'When did Phoebe write that? Could she have met Dwayne on the hill?'

'And there are her binoculars,' Miss Pink mused: 'they're missing. No one thought of those. You think she could have met Dwayne on Gowk Pass? Why should she make a note of his number?'

'Her memory was going.'

275

'All the same, she'd know the number of local cars.'

'She couldn't remember her own.'

'Really?' Miss Pink frowned. 'Well, she was old . . . so she wrote it down because she needed to remember it . . . But she could recognize people?'

'Oh yes, she wasn't gaga. It was just figures, rather like Bobby but at opposite ends of the lifespan as it were. I see, you're thinking that if she'd seen Dwayne himself she wouldn't have needed to make a note of the number. She'd have recognized him, and so it had to be his Land Rover.'

'She didn't see him.' Miss Pink spoke slowly, marshalling her thoughts. 'Only his truck parked where it shouldn't be? Or she saw it from a distance . . . no, then she wouldn't have been able to read the number plate.'

'She saw the vehicle and the number, but not the driver?'

'Possibly—but when?'

'She'd have told me about it.' Eleanor was decisive. 'She couldn't keep anything to herself, that was her problem: altogether too outspoken.'

'So you've said, and everyone else, including Swinburn. Now I wonder if she saw *him* up to something naughty on the hill—'

'It's not Swinburn's number—'

'Right, forget Swinburn. But you're saying that if she didn't tell you what led up to this'—

gesturing to the visor—'then she must have printed it on the Sunday that she died—unless you didn't see her on the Saturday.'

'She called in Saturday evening, which was usual: to tell me where she was going next day.'

'So she met—or saw—Dwayne on top.'

'On top of what?' Rosie asked from the doorway. Gibson loomed behind her.

Miss Pink introduced him. Rosie eyed the hat. 'Dwayne Paxton's Land Rover,' she observed, impressing the two women with her photographic memory.

As Eleanor served coffee Miss Pink sketched the story, giving the police the impression that the hat had been willingly surrendered.

'Could Bobby have printed that number?' Rosie asked.

'No, he's dyslexic. That's an adult hand, it's too uniform for a child who has trouble with his figures.'

'When you said Dwayne was on top,' Gibson put in, 'you meant on top of where?'

'I was assuming he was somewhere near the route that Phoebe was following the day she died, simply because she made a note of his number.'

Eleanor explained why she was sure that had been done on the Sunday. 'But she drowned,' Gibson pointed out. 'Are you suggesting that there was something suspicious

277

about that death?'

'There's a mystery. What made her print that number? It was done not long before she—died.'

They contemplated the hat. 'She was out of doors when she did it,' Rosie said. 'There was no other writing material available.'

'She had the map,' Eleanor said. 'She was a very prudent lady—on the hill; she always carried a map even though she knew these fells backwards.'

'It takes time to get the map out of your sack,' Miss Pink pointed out. 'But she could have had a biro in a pocket, and she whipped off her hat . . .'

'And he saw her do it and killed her.' Gibson raised an eyebrow.

Rosie said reprovingly, 'Dwayne wasn't about to kill because he was out with an under-age girl—which is the worst thing we've got on him, and which she probably knew about already. Anyway, the kids deny the relationship.'

Miss Pink ignored that. 'If he'd seen her write something on the hat he'd have destroyed the hat.' Her eyes glazed. 'The hat went in the water with her—like the camera and binoculars. They'd sink. They could well be in the underground caverns in the big quarry.'

'Dwayne lent his Land Rover to Blamire,' Gibson said, and they all stared at him.

'To go to the firing range with Isa,' Miss Pink said weakly. 'And that's in the opposite direction to the Closewater path. Besides . . .'

'Yes?'

Miss Pink looked at Eleanor. 'What would Blamire have against Phoebe?'

Eleanor shrugged. She was running out of steam, as was everyone else. It had been a long day. Gibson said, 'What's any of this got to do with Isa? We know *she* was murdered; are you implying there's a connection between her death and this old lady who drowned?'

'She *fell* and drowned,' Eleanor corrected.

'Or was pushed,' Miss Pink murmured.

CHAPTER SIXTEEN

The moor below Scoat Pike was already browning in the heat wave but Rosie still managed to find the wet patches. Retreating yet again with mud over the tops of her trainers, she fell in beside Miss Pink, eyeing the other's dry boots with amazement.

'How do you know where to walk?'

'I follow the path.'

'What path?'

'Keep behind me.'

They were on their way to Closewater. Persuaded by the evidence of the hat, by the possibility of a connection between the two deaths, Gibson had decided that Rosie should duplicate Phoebe's route. Miss Pink had volunteered to be the guide and he had agreed: 'She knows the way and she'll see it through a wrinkly's eyes,' he told Rosie. 'You can't; you'll go too fast and miss things.'

He was right. Next morning Rosie had started out at the trot before they reached Sleylands although she did ask Miss Pink if she minded and the other had agreed absently. She was intent on Swinburn chugging across the pastures on his tractor in the direction of his awful tip. When Miss Pink's attention returned to the hill she saw that Rosie was no longer running for which she was thankful; a sprained ankle could have meant postponement of the day's activities. She came up with Rosie who had stopped by some rocks and was trying to control her breathing.

'You're not even panting!' The girl was astonished.

'Old guide's pace.' It was dismissive. 'Is Mr Gibson going to ask Paxton and Blamire where they were last Sunday week? And who was driving Paxton's Land Rover?'

'Probably.' Rosie was cagey—and resentful about the gradient. 'He could be waiting for a report on this track. I'll be telling him that no Land Rover ever came up here; it's desperate for anyone on foot.'

'And he'd have bogged down on top,' Miss Pink said as they continued, Rosie wondering where the bogs were and quickly discovering them. By the time they came out above Closewater the sergeant had learned the first rule of mountain etiquette: that the leader of the party goes first, but it had taken her that long to work out that Miss Pink was the leader. Rosie was the novice.

Salient features were pointed out to her and she tried to concentrate, to see what her companion was seeing and endeavour to interpret those images as they might relate to the progress of another old lady a week ago, and who, shortly after she reached this point, was to die violently.

There were cars parked at the head of the lake but none visible on the track to Gowk Pass. 'I was here the following day,' Miss Pink said. 'By that time a Mountain Rescue Land Rover had gone up and covered any tracks'— along pause—'any tracks left by a vehicle the previous day.'

'Followed exactly the same line?'

'Yes. I paid particular attention although at the time I wasn't concerned with wheel tracks but with the orchids.'

'Orchids?' Rosie had a vision of hothouse blooms, of corsages in old movies.

Miss Pink explained as they climbed. The verges were now imprinted with a multitude of tyre tracks left by trucks, quads, mountain bikes. They came to a steepening with loose stones like a scree slope where they diverged and Miss Pink halted at ruts cut deep in the peat. 'I suppose we could try to transplant,' she murmured. 'Now who was it proposed that?'

'This was where the orchids were?'

'Of course. There's one left.' They moved closer. 'You see: very small flowers but unmistakably an orchid.'

'I'll take your word for it. Sorry! I was thinking of those big multicoloured jobs that come in a see-through box with a bow.'

'There are wild ones similar, but smaller. They're bee orchids.' Miss Pink looked from the gouged peat to the slope of the hill above. 'She couldn't have missed this place; she'd have taken photographs. Or did she find the Land Rover bogged down, the occupants gone for help? But there's no sign of the big holes left by a vehicle that had dug itself in.'

'I think these trucks got through without sticking.' Rosie had experience of police four-by-fours.

They surveyed the slope. A few hundred yards above them the track described a sharp elbow between banks. The surface was pale: another steep gradient of large loose stones. 'He'd have had difficulty there,' Rosie said. 'And there's no way round, it's too craggy.'

'She was a fanatic about the environment. After she photographed this'—Miss Pink gestured to the devastation—'she could well have taken shots of the truck—if one were stuck up there. On the other hand it could have been moving round that hairpin and she saw the number through her binoculars and noted it. How does that sound?'

'She definitely made a note of it at some time. Who was driving the rescue truck that came up here next day, the one that followed the same line?'

'Blamire.' She went on slowly: 'Of course he might not have noticed the orchids, by Monday there were only one or two left.'

They climbed to the stony elbow. Bedrock in the centre of the track was marked with long raw scratches, confirming that vehicles had been forced to keep to the track. On the top of Gowk Pass they came on a Toyota Land Cruiser, without occupants and locked. There was an RSPB sticker on the windscreen, and Rosie said that it had a Yorkshire registration. 'Where are the birds?' she asked. 'I've only heard the cuckoo and skylarks.'

'You're learning,' Miss Pink said absently, thinking of Phoebe. 'There are others around: divers on the tarns, merlin, peregrines perhaps in the quarry.' She frowned at that.

'What?'

'If she did catch up with him after coming on those orchids she'd have been blazing with rage. I would be. And if she told him she had taken photographs . . . and refused to give up the camera . . .'

Rosie shook her head. 'What's the penalty for destroying wild flowers? Come on! You don't kill a person just to escape a fine.'

'He writes books about the fells; he's got an image to protect.'

'So you're thinking it was Blamire in Dwayne's Land Rover, and Phoebe confronted him about some squashed orchids.'

'Suppose Isa was with him?'

'Even if Phoebe saw them screw—making it—he wouldn't kill her just for that, surely? And then put the body in the beck, don't forget.'

They walked on, descending gently as the track improved on the Borascal side, less rocky, dark lines visible in the distance where former dalesmen had obtained their fuel supplies. They went slowly, Rosie starting to take more interest in her surroundings, learning the difference between violets and butterwort, trying to learn bird calls, using her ears. 'And that'—Miss Pink turned—'is the Land Cruiser coming down.'

They weren't concerned, paying more attention to the quarry which was now visible below, only the tops of the sheer walls showing but those impressive enough, hinting at the hidden depths.

The Land Cruiser approached and at that moment the walkers were on a sunken section with grassy banks on either side. Calmly, automatically, they parted, but the next steps were upwards, the grass was dry and polished, and Miss Pink's knees less flexible than she would have wished. She slipped, grabbed at the bank and stumbled back into the path of the truck. It stopped dead.

Rosie jumped down. People called anxiously. Miss Pink swore, flushed with embarrassment.

Apologies and assurances over, they exchanged pleasantries. The bird watchers had seen a pair of short-eared owls and found a ring ouzel's nest. They passed, leaving the walkers to follow at their own pace, Miss Pink silent.

'You didn't hurt yourself?' Rosie was diffident.

'Only my pride.' Miss Pink stopped and looked back. 'Suppose Phoebe had passed the Land Rover because it was stuck, or stopped for whatever reason, had seen Isa and spoken her mind—'

'Rather vulgar of her.' Rosie grinned.

'Spoken her mind about the orchids—and maybe other things as they came to mind, and she walked on, and they came down behind her in the truck and she jumped for the bank and fell back under the wheels?'

'She wasn't run over. She drowned.'

'He could have hit her a glancing blow with the wing. He could have thought she was dead.'

'That would be an accident.'

'He could have run her down deliberately, in a fit of temper, thought she was dead, taken her in the 'Rover to the quarry and dropped her in the beck. I'll show you.'

It was as she remembered it and the features fulfilled all the requirements: the level green path just wide enough for a vehicle (and faintly marked by broad tyres), the locked gate over which a small person could have been lifted easily, particularly with two people on hand, the terrible slope that dropped to a gaping black pit below the waterfalls and from which, even with the water low, came the roar of cascades.

'The camera will be down there,' Miss Pink said, 'but with the film pulled out. And the binoculars.'

Rosie admitted that it could have happened that way; it could explain the registration number on the hat, how the body came to be in the beck. 'But if you're right, then it was murder. He could have struck her by accident originally. And even if he drove at her deliberately, he didn't kill her then. But when he went on to put her down there alive'—she shuddered, staring at the convex slope that plunged like a polished slide into the depths—'I just hope she stayed unconscious.'

'How do you know she was wasn't conscious when he put her in there?'

'Christ! Let's get out of here.' Rosie turned back to the gate and the security of level grass.

'When I was at this spot on Monday,' Miss Pink said, 'first Jean came along and then

Blamire.'

'What was Jean doing here?'

'She was with the rescue team. They were searching for Phoebe, and the rest of them were up there on Blaze Fell.' She pointed. 'He could have sent Jean down to find out who I was and what I was doing, and then became too anxious and came down himself. Jean was bothered about my getting into difficulties in the quarry but he could have been worried that I might come across some evidence of what had happened the day before.' She gasped. 'It was Blamire who mentioned the orchids first. They were on his mind, particularly as they related to old ladies. Someone had made an issue of them, and that could only have been Phoebe.'

They walked side by side on the soft turf. 'There's no evidence,' Rosie said. 'That's the problem. Gibson might consider it as an interesting theory but he'll say there isn't a shred of proof.'

'It goes further.' Miss Pink was unmoved. 'Isa was with him.' She turned to Rosie, astonished. 'Perhaps Isa was driving! Whatever, she thought Phoebe was dead so she helped him get rid of the body, but after the post-mortem, when it was learned that Phoebe drowned and so she was alive when she was pushed in the water, her nerve broke. She panicked and became a threat. So she had to be silenced. On second thoughts it had to be

Blamire driving. If it had been Isa he'd have had no qualms about saying so.'

*   *   *

'I'm going to lose my job.' Dwayne was furious. 'You coming to my workplace and the boss here. He took me back the once, seeing as it were you hauled me to town, but he's not going to stand for it twice.'

The police had found him removing slates from the old outhouse in the garden at Blind Keld. Men were at work inside the house and Birkett was glowering from an upper window.

Sewell asked, almost casually, 'Where were you yesterday week?'

'At home.' He didn't take time to think about it.

'That was quick,' Sewell said.

'It were Sunday; I don't work Sundays.'

'Who were you with?'

'No one.'

'So there are no witnesses to confirm that you didn't leave your house.'

Dwayne was still, smelling a trap, and indeed he resembled an animal, a fine young specimen. He was aware of Sewell's scrutiny and preened himself.

'I coulda been with a woman.'

'Where did you take her?'

Dwayne glanced at the house. 'Can't remember.'

'A week ago? You had a woman on Sunday and you can't— Who was she?'

'I'd rather not say.'

'You don't know where you took her and you don't know who she was—'

'I didna say that!' He hesitated. 'I have a lot of women.'

'That's a lie.'

'No, it in't! I go to discos in town, pick up girls—'

'We're not talking about a quick screw in the toilets, we're talking about bringing women here or taking them on the fells, like last Sunday.'

There was the ghost of a smile on the lad's lips. 'Maybe I did at that; I pick up hikers sometimes, give 'em a lift like.'

He was too confident and Gibson decided it was time to take a hand, go for the jugular. 'Like giving a girl a lift over Gowk Pass from Closewater,' he said.

Dwayne looked away. Gibson went on quietly, driving it home. 'Yesterday week. Sunday: the day the old lady went hiking and was killed. Why aren't you looking at me, Dwayne?'

He raised his head, blinking, licking his lips. He whispered something.

'What was that?' Gibson was politely curious, not unfriendly.

'I said I were home.'

'No. You were seen.'

'Where?'

Gibson looked at Sewell who produced the denim hat from the pocket of his chinos. He held it out: right side up and front foremost. 'Recognize it?' Gibson asked.

'No.' Dwayne shook his head jerkily, recoiling a little although his feet didn't move.

'"Alaska",' Gibson read, and waited. The other swallowed and his eyes wandered.

'It was Phoebe Metcalf's.'

'So?' He was no longer a sexy hunk but a frightened boy.

Sewell turned the hat over and they watched his face. It was as if he felt himself forced to look at the figures exposed. Recognition was followed by blank incomprehension before his face smoothed out.

'Whose number is it?' Gibson asked.

'Mine.' He couldn't deny it; his Land Rover was in the yard on the other side of the wall.

'The Sunday she was killed your Land Rover was on Gowk Pass.' Dwayne stared at him, turning sullen. 'What did you do, Dwayne? Run her down? Push her in the beck?'

'It weren't me.'

'Who was it?'

'Blamire.'

'You were out with Blamire?'

'No, no, t'were Isa with him. He took the 'Rover. I were in me bed—no, I were working here; he come and took it like he always did.

290

They left his van and the MG. They come back in the afternoon, returned the 'Rover.' His voice rose, starting to shrill. 'I told you all this before. I don't know nothing about Phoebe; on my heart I swear I don't know what happened to her. I knew she drowned like, we all knew, but not that he—Blamire *killed* un?'

Sewell was left to watch him, to make sure he didn't use a phone, and that no one went near his Land Rover until it could be impounded. Transport was summoned and more hands called for, while Gibson went to Borascal cursing himself for sending Rosie on the hill. Then he rationalized that she wasn't wasting time; at some point it would have been necessary to retrace Phoebe's route that Sunday.

The situation had changed, like one of those pictures where the mind's eye shifts and you see things differently. Now, with Blamire driving the Land Rover that day, Isa with him, and the registration number being recorded by Phoebe, it was possible that Miss Pink was right and Isa's murder might be explained by Phoebe's death. Always accepting that Dwayne wasn't out to frame Blamire. It was essential to hear Blamire's version of the events of that Sunday. He wondered if Gemma would confirm Dwayne's story. The lad hadn't mentioned her. Out of chivalry? Fear, more like.

It was a short drive to the village. There was

no time to formulate questions, even though he was resolved to ask nothing pertinent until Sewell arrived. His purpose now was to isolate the Blamires from the outside world and to keep the couple under his eye so that they couldn't communicate between themselves. And there was Gemma.

Borascal looked as normal as it would ever look: the Fat Lamb open but with no one outside, purple rock plants draping pale walls, a bank of cardinal poppies, lavender wisteria, a red cat sprawled in the road.

Someone was singing in the Blamires' kitchen: Sinatra on 'Strangers in the Night'. Gibson waited until it finished, enjoying the man's timing, staring sightlessly at the lilacs alive with bees. What was that about Sinatra and the Mafia?

The song ended. 'Hello?' he called.

'Who is it? Come on in.' Sinatra was cut off as he started again.

She was turning meat in a bowl, spooning liquid over small joints. 'Rabbit,' she said coldly, seeing his interest. 'I'm marinading it.' Her attitude was one of barely suppressed hostility and she didn't ask him to sit down.

He indicated the stereo. 'Your husband doesn't object to music when he's working?'

'He likes it himself as background, but he's away right now.'

'When do you expect him back?'

'I don't keep tabs on him, Inspector.'

He should have anticipated this; a glorious day: an innocent man would be on the hill. And a guilty one could be on the run. 'So,' he announced, forcing a light note, 'when you've finished there I'll pick your brains instead.'

'Oh yes? Sit down.' It was grudging and no refreshment was offered.

He asked to use the bathroom, determined to find out if she was lying. She showed no surprise at the request and he found every door open on the upstairs landing, every room empty. Blamire wasn't in the house.

In the kitchen she sat facing the passage and the open front door. Nothing in that, but her position gave the impression of watchfulness. As he allowed himself a brief moment of silence he was wondering what kind of accomplice she would make. That masculine cast to the face might be echoed in mental—and physical—strength. Combine that with cunning . . .

'What was it you wanted to know?' she asked.

'I'm not sure that your husband's been entirely frank with us.'

'About what?'

'The business of the forged letter: the salmonella hoax.'

Her eyebrows went up. She said nothing but then he hadn't asked a question.

'*Could* Isa use a computer?' he asked.

She gave a small gasp of amusement.

'Hardly. She was a bit stressed in that department.'

'What department is that?'

'Operating a computer, thinking up the content of that letter.'

'It's something you could have done yourself?'

'I could, but why should I?'

'If Eleanor had annoyed you?'

'Possibly, but I wouldn't get a kick out of that kind of retaliation. It's petty.'

'How would you retaliate?'

'If someone had annoyed me I'd have a blazing row with them or'—she sparkled and he was struck by the transformation of slightly heavy features into those of an attractive woman—'or I'd put them in a book: get my own back that way. I write.'

He refused to be diverted. 'If you didn't forge the letter and Isa wasn't capable of it—' He stopped.

'He'll tell you all about it when he comes home. I can't speak for him.'

'He's admitted it to you?'

'Not exactly; he's a bit childish like that; he thinks that if he doesn't actually admit something, then he can deny any future accusation.'

'He was quite specific with us; he said Isa forged the letter.'

'No, he said he didn't know what she was doing on the computer. It was rather more than a hint without actually accusing her.'

'I see.' And he did. Hadn't the fellow hinted that his own wife could have killed Isa? 'What other hints has he dropped?' he asked.

'About what?'

'About Isa for a start.'

'Well, he said she was promiscuous, which was predictable; it got him off the hook, letting me know she was no more than a passing—' A shadow darkened the passage and she stood up. 'I have another visitor,' she said, so calmly that Gibson guessed she'd been expecting this. Sewell came in, escorted by the collie.

'Did he get out again?' Jean was fussing. 'I'm going to have to find that gap and plug it. Thank God he doesn't chase sheep. Sit down. I'll make some coffee.'

'Have they taken it?' Gibson asked.

Sewell glanced at Jean's back. 'Yes.'

'And he didn't use a phone?'

'No.' Sewell was mystified. This in front of the woman?

She turned from the stove to reach for mugs. She placed sugar and biscuits on the table. 'Help yourself, the biscuits are hazelnut and date.'

'We've impounded Paxton's Land Rover,' Gibson told her.

'What does that mean?'

'It'll be examined by Forensics to see if there are any traces.' She looked puzzled. 'What were you doing yesterday week?' he asked.

Her jaw dropped. She looked from one to the other, startled, wryly amused, sobering as she saw that they were waiting for an answer. 'I was here,' she said slowly. 'All day. Why?'

'How can you be so certain?'

'We don't entertain much. I'd remember if we'd gone out or had people here. I can't say exactly what I was doing but it'll be in the diary. Everything's recorded.'

'Why is that?'

'You don't garden, do you? How would you know when you'd sown seed, how heavy the crop was—'

'You were gardening all day?'

'That's what I'm telling you. It's a full-time job. I don't write till it's dark.'

'And your husband can confirm that you were here that Sunday?'

'Oh, my God, you think I was up to something! What happened?' She grinned in the face of their silence. 'No, he can't, Inspector; no one can. I was alone all day— except for Whisk here and he's not talking. Martin was on the hill.'

'On the hill?' Gibson repeated, as if he'd never heard the term before.

'He was fell-walking—not for fun, he was working out a route for safari trips he's going to run when my dad retires and we take over Sleylands.'

'So that day he was out in a Land Rover—'

296

'No, I said,' he was on foot. We have a van but it's not four-wheel-drive. So he has to walk, like he's doing today. I don't know what time he'll be back but he won't have gone far because he didn't take the van.'

* * *

'Sunday?' Gemma said. 'I haven't the faintest. Miss Pink was here—Oh, *that* Sunday! How can I remember over a week ago? I'd have been out on my bike: Jollybeard, Ashgill, Sunder, you name it.'

'With Dwayne Paxton?'

They were in the garden at Borrans, Walter hovering unhappily; having taken the day off work. 'You don't have to talk to them, Gemma,' he said.

'Why not?' She stared at him and turned back to Sewell. 'It's not as if I've done anything criminal.' She was contemptuous.

'Did you see Dwayne on your travels?'

She shrugged. 'Probably.'

'Where?'

'I don't know. At the Lamb perhaps.'

'You don't go in the Lamb!' Walter was horrified.

'People sit outside. One sees them as one goes past. It's what he does: sits at a table half-naked, showing off his pecs.' She stared pointedly at Sewell's chest.

'Were you at Blind Keld?' He was harsh.

297

'Maybe.' She caught her brother's expression. 'I was helping him build up the garden wall there,' she said defiantly. 'Anything criminal about that?'

'That Sunday?' Sewell pressed.

'I tell you, I don't know! I was often there.' She glared at both of them. 'Dwayne was my friend, and that's it!'

*   *   *

'There was no camera and no binoculars.' Misella addressed Miss Pink; she had no time for police in any shape or form and ignored Rosie. 'If he'd have found them he'd have told me, wouldn't you, son?'

Bobby, subdued and sullen, glowered and muttered. Misella pounced. 'What were that? Speak up if you got summat to say.'

'It's not fair!' The lower lip was trembling.

'Nothing ever is,' Miss Pink said. 'But if you come up to Ashgill I'll give you another cap. It's a bit worn and it smells of horses. I found it on the Bozeman Trail when we were bringing cattle down off the open range before the snows came.' She took in Bobby's saucer eyes, seeing that, if he didn't believe a word of it, he liked the imagery. 'You can have that one,' she assured him. 'You deserve it for finding the other one.'

'I didna find the camera,' he insisted. 'Nor them binoclers.'

'I know you didn't.'

'You like kids,' Rosie said later. They had walked up to Ashgill and Bobby had been sent home with a cap embroidered with a rider on a bucking bronco and the legend 'Rattlesnake Hills Rodeo' on the front.

'Not really. Treat them like animals, that's the answer.'

'You don't mean that.'

'Oh yes: treat them all the same; animals are people too.'

'I see. Like Bobby and Cooper and the Blamires' collie—and me? You treat us all the same?'

'There are differences. I'm tired. We're both tired. Can I give you a meal before you start back to town?'

'I'd better call Gibson and tell him I'm back. He'll be expecting a report.'

She went out to her car. Miss Pink put the kettle on and poured herself a lager. Cooper entered the kitchen and a few steps behind him came Sewell. 'Just in time.' She stifled a sigh. 'Will you have a lager?'

He sighed. 'I'd love one, but I may be driving later.'

'One lager's not going to hurt. Where will you be driving?' She brought a can from the fridge and handed him a glass.

'We're waiting for Blamire to come home. You didn't see him?' He hadn't answered the question.

'No, we've been on the hill all day.' Didn't he remember they'd gone to Gowk Pass? 'Where's Mr Gibson?' she asked.

'He's back at the station. I saw Rosie on the phone. Isn't she speaking to him?'

'I suppose so.' The words were mundane and uninformative but behind the exchange there was a powerful sense of urgency. 'A biscuit?' she suggested, rather too loudly. 'Or would you prefer a sandwich? You don't know how long you'll be.' She blinked. 'Without food,' she added.

'I'm fine, ma'am. We've asked the lady at Jollybeard to provide us with a meal.'

'"We"?'

'There's a number of us.'

Rosie appeared in the doorway. 'We've to go to Bailrigg.' She was addressing Miss Pink.

'Have a coffee before you leave, and something to eat.'

'We have to go now.' Rosie looked embarrassed. 'He wants to see you too.'

'Me? Why does Gibson want me?'

Rosie gestured limply. She was exhausted. 'We were both up there: on the fell.'

'Hill,' Miss Pink said absently, 'on the hill.' She looked at Sewell. 'Where's Blamire?'

'According to his wife, he's on the hill too, ma'am.'

*   *   *

'That's what she *says*.' Gibson waited while a constable served them with coffee in styrofoam cups. 'And she could believe it herself, but I've got a feeling he's not coming back. Now what did you discover on the pass?'

They managed to give a factual account of their day, Rosie appealing to the expert for the kind of details only a mountain person would register, such as distances and the state of the ground. It was a bleak account and he asked, as they'd known he would, what significance they attached to any of it. At first tentatively, then more firmly, Miss Pink outlined her theory. 'From everything I've heard about Phoebe her reaction would be predictable once she'd come on the ruined orchids. Perhaps she saw the Land Rover's number through the binoculars but then she overtook it and discovered that Blamire was the driver. She admired the man for his rescue work but that wouldn't have stopped her speaking her mind about the orchids. In fact the more disappointed she was in him, the greater the anger. And if he lost his temper as a result things could have deteriorated.' She paused, she had all his attention. 'Although,' she went on, less certainly, 'it's difficult to imagine how matters could have escalated to such an extent that he could run her down—if he did. A sudden flare of rage perhaps—as in road rage?'

They waited for his comments: no evidence,

no proof.

'He had Isa with him,' he said, astonishing them. 'And if Phoebe—already angry as you suggest—if she questioned what he was doing there with his neighbour's wife, there could have been hell to pay. Martin had a lot at stake: he was expecting to take over Sleylands from his father-in-law, but not if Jean kicked him out.'

'I'd forgotten that,' Miss Pink said, adding quietly, 'but where's the proof?'

'We have the Land Rover.' Gibson explained about that. 'They're going over it for traces and tomorrow Forensics will be in Phoebe's cottage looking for matches: hair, fibres, fingerprints. You'll know the drill.'

'You were right,' Rosie said, suddenly fierce. 'The man's done a runner; he'll have walked over the hills and hitched down the A6. He could be in Manchester by now, even London.'

'He can't get away,' Gibson said firmly. 'All the airports and ferry terminals will be watched. Besides, he has no money. We'll catch him.'

Miss Pink was silent, remembering the ones who'd got away.

CHAPTER SEVENTEEN

Blamire didn't come back that night and the police, waiting discreetly in unmarked cars, were kept awake by Eleanor's coffee until, in the small hours, she went to bed, leaving them with full flasks.

Phoebe's cottage had been sealed, even to the cat-flap, and Cooper spent the night coiled against Miss Pink's spine, which was mutual comfort in the cold and dewy dawn.

Rosie appeared at breakfast time, fresh and clean, relieved to find Cooper on hand. It was too soon for a proper report on Dwayne's Land Rover but the lab people had found coarse red hairs, almost certainly animal and very likely feline. She regarded Cooper with satisfaction: 'We're going to need samples.'

'He wanders,' Miss Pink pointed out. 'He could have climbed inside the Land Rover on his own initiative. It's the kind of thing defence counsel would pick on.'

'There will be other traces: her hair, fibres from her clothes. And Blamire hasn't come back. That's the clincher.'

But Miss Pink had slept on her own theory. 'He could have murdered Isa, but you have only Dwayne's word for it that Blamire took the 'Rover on Sunday. And Dwayne has no alibi for Phoebe's death.'

There she was wrong. Gemma, unwontedly scrupulous, had consulted her diary and discovered that she'd been at Blind Keld for part of Sunday morning, and she remembered that Blamire's old van and Isa's MG were there, as was Dwayne of course, but not his Land Rover. They'd worked on the garden wall, she told Rosie artlessly. Rosie didn't believe her but Gemma couldn't be intimidated into retracting any more than she would retract her alibi for Walter on Wednesday night, when she maintained she'd been up and down all night and had heard him in his room.

'They're still sniffing about round Walter,' Gemma protested to Miss Pink. 'They've got their murderer now, or rather they will have him if he doesn't slip through the net.'

'I imagine Rosie was more concerned with Dwayne and the alibi you give *him*.' Miss Pink's tone was loaded.

'Well, he's cleared now, but what I had on Martin could be fatal. I told Rosie . . .'

Miss Pink found Rosie talking to the occupants of a police car and drew her away. 'I've been thinking about times,' she said. 'Gemma told you that Blamire went to Borrans at least twice after Phoebe's murder, is that right?' Rosie nodded. 'The first time,' Miss Pink went on, 'was when he left the team on Blaze Fell. He'd seen me and he thought I was taking too much interest in the quarry. He didn't like that and he came down to the village to warn Isa, to impress on her how essential it was to keep quiet.'

'I suppose that's possible.'

'But he was far more emphatic the second time,' Miss Pink insisted. 'He didn't trust Isa. It was after he learned that she'd been working in the Lamb that he went straight to Borrans and had the row with her that Gemma overheard, or overheard part of. Blamire was terrified that if Isa was mixing with media people she could reveal that she knew more about Phoebe's death than an innocent person could know. I think Blamire told her to stop going to the pub. She objected but she was close to the end of her tether and then, at some point, she learned that Phoebe had drowned, that she hadn't been dead when they pushed her down the slope. She could face disposing of a body but not murder. She would contact Blamire, perhaps suggesting they make a run for it, and they drove to Waterhouses.'

'There's a gap in the timing here,' Rosie pointed out. 'She was gone by the time Walter came home that evening. There were hours of daylight left. You can't tell me they drove in an open-top sports car, in daylight, to Waterhouses.'

'She must have picked him up outside the village and they went—anywhere, a barn or a wood. She didn't go to Elfhow because Jean was there. She could have phoned him and

305

perhaps, terrified of a charge of murder, she was drinking already. That would give him the idea of how to deal with her. When they met he brought more whisky. All he had to do was keep her drunk until dark or—more likely—he strangled her and then waited until dark before driving to Waterhouses, pushing down the wall and sending the car into the river.'

Rosie pondered. 'At least part of it could be true; it's a useful tool anyway, it could be used to break him down, make him confess when we catch up with him.'

*　　　　*　　　　*

That afternoon Jean avoided the watchers in the lane by climbing the garden wall in order to visit Miss Pink. She looked drawn but defiant and, on the face of it, unconcerned that her husband had been out all night. Miss Pink pointed out that when a mountaineer doesn't come home, the first thought is that he's come to grief on the hill. Jean said that Martin could take care of himself.

'Then what do you think has happened to him?' Miss Pink asked. Jean spread her hands. 'Your guess is as good as mine.'

'That won't do. If he were on the hill your reaction would be to call in the rescue team. You haven't, so logic says he isn't on the hill.'

'He could be with a woman.'

Miss Pink said nothing. 'Or protecting a

306

woman,' Jean said.

'He's not protecting you. He tried to frame you for Isa's murder.'

'Isa committed suicide. She was dead drunk.'

'That last is true; she was too drunk to drive.'

'Exactly, which is why she went through the wall.'

'What did he tell you to account for his absence on the night she died?'

'Nothing. He didn't go out that night.'

'How can you go on protecting him? I can understand your taking him back after the affair with Isa but you know he was out the night she died, that he was on the hill the day Phoebe died—'

'That's sheer speculation—'

'They've found traces in Dwayne's Land Rover—'

'Then he was driving it.'

'You're saying Dwayne was on the hill and he killed Phoebe? And Isa? He killed her too?' Jean was silent. Miss Pink studied her, then said quietly, 'And he forged the salmonella letter?'

'That was a joke,' Jean said quickly. Miss Pink gulped and tried to hide it. Jean fidgeted. 'It was cruel,' she conceded, 'but he did it to please Isa. She'd picked up the letterhead when she'd been poking around Walter's office one time and she suggested the hoax to

Martin. She was a very demanding person.'

'He *told* you it was a joke?'

'He didn't think anything of it. He was amazed that anyone else should.'

'You don't think that's significant, that he couldn't foresee the consequences of this— joke?' Jean's eyes wandered and Miss Pink frowned. 'I think Phoebe suspected,' she said heavily. 'I think she tackled him, perhaps that day on Gowk? It started with a confrontation over the orchids and the argument escalated? Is that how it was?' Jean said nothing. 'Did she call him a psychopath? He let her go—go on for some distance, and then he came down behind and ran over her.'

'No.' Jean was shaking her head. 'That's not how it was. Isa was driving and she trod on the accelerator instead of the brake. It was an accident.'

Miss Pink couldn't believe what she was hearing. That Phoebe had suspected Blamire to be the hoaxer was unlikely—she'd surely have told Eleanor—but a nerve had been hit and the result was a revelation: not that Isa had been out with Blamire, had been driving, but that Jean should admit it. And then she knew that this was the purpose of the visit.

Jean was watching her. Miss Pink steadied her breathing. 'Phoebe's death wasn't an accident,' she pointed out. 'She was alive when they put her in the water.'

'We know that now, but they didn't at the

308

time. They thought she was dead. It was when Isa heard that Phoebe drowned that she went to pieces. Martin tried to impress on her that if she kept her head no one would ever know, it would be assumed that Phoebe fell in the beck. But Isa lost her nerve, drank a lot of Scotch and deliberately drove over the cliff.'

'This is the story he's going to tell the police?'

'It's not a story. It's the truth.'

'Then why didn't he stay here and tell them instead of going on the run?'

'He says he has to think things out.'

'Such as why he told the police you knew about the affair with Isa all along? If you didn't know you had no reason to murder her. And you didn't know, did you?'

'I didn't kill her.' She was lacklustre.

Miss Pink said kindly, 'You've rationalized him into a lovable rogue. You've convinced yourself—or he's brainwashed you into thinking that Isa was responsible for Phoebe's death and that the girl couldn't live with her guilt afterwards. You admit he forged the salmonella letter and you deplore the sadism of it but you're probably thinking that a man with a twisted mind can be healed. You're not the first woman to think that way. But when they catch up with him and he confesses, where will you be then?'

'I'm not making excuses for him.'

'You're putting up a good front. You know

everything. Are you going to stick to the version of events you've given me?'

'He's my husband.'

* * *

'I can't make her out,' Miss Pink confessed to Eleanor and Rosie in Jollybeard's kitchen. 'Whether she knows the truth or is believing what she wants to believe, she's still protecting him, but she has to know that if Isa killed Phoebe and then committed suicide, there would be no need for Blamire to have gone on the run.'

'There is,' Eleanor grated. 'He put Phoebe in the beck alive. And of course it was he who killed Isa. The inquest's tomorrow and the verdict will be murder, right?' Rosie nodded slowly. 'He's a cold-blooded killer,' Eleanor went on. 'Society would be well rid of him. At one time he would have hanged.'

* * *

The inquest on Isa was adjourned; it was Gibson's contention that Blamire would soon tire of a precarious existence in a city and give himself up, but he didn't. A factor in his continued disappearance could be his horror of having to face a life sentence. In addition to Cooper's hairs, fibres and grey hairs had been found in Dwayne's Land Rover which matched

310

those from Phoebe's cottage, but the terrible clincher was her fingerprints on a wheel cover in the back. She had regained consciousness at least for long enough to grasp the metal.

When the inquest on Isa was finally held the verdict was as predicted: murder by person or persons unknown.

*   *   *

Martin Blamire had vanished like mist and he never came back. Jean stayed on in her father's house, tending her garden and writing highly charged romantic novels. Jacob and Mabel retired, and a horsey couple bought Sleylands and turned it into a pony trekking centre. They ring-fenced and refenced and made the little quarry wood into a nature reserve. It contained two badger setts. The tip was gone, filled in by Jacob, and the resulting slope was now colonized by tiny hazels and birches.

On holiday in Patterdale some years later Miss Pink rode over to Borascal on a fell pony. She found everyone flourishing: Eleanor in her tearoom, a plumper and less springy Cooper cohabiting, and Jean: now a romantic lady novelist, stylish and confident, a confidence that faltered only slightly when Miss Pink expressed a desire to visit the new nature reserve.

They went together: Eleanor, Jean and the

visitor, climbing the hillside from the gate in the lane, the track now grass-grown since no tractor had used it after Jacob left. It was late spring again, bluebells a haze below trees in early leaf, late primroses pale stars on the banks, young rabbits lolloping silently before them.

The crag rose ahead, little more than a rock step since the quarry had been filled in, the slope gay with pink campion and wood anemones, with one bare chute of soil.

'A young boar making a sett?' Eleanor suggested. 'Or is it the sows who start the digging?'

'Whatever.' Jean was sharp. 'They smell the old carcasses.'

'It was a neat solution to the problem,' Miss Pink observed, advancing to the chute and teasing a bone out of the earth. 'Jacob didn't have to dig a pit to bury the dead sheep, he just tipped rubble down from above. Once I started to find the bodies he was working like a Trojan.'

'No wonder.' Eleanor was tart. 'He was terrified of you.'

Miss Pink turned quizzical eyes on her.

'We all were,' Jean said.

'I only found a few dead sheep.'

'You exposed all our secrets. Only little scandals of course: like Bobby being my half-brother but no one ever talked about it—and Dad leaving sheep to the foxes and ravens.

And there were Dwayne and Gemma.'

'I don't remember saying anything about Bobby.'

They were silent then, each filling gaps in her own way, remembering the secrets that hadn't been little scandals. Miss Pink looked at the bone in her hands: a long bone, a femur, or rather half a femur, broken, shattered when the load—earth and rocks—rained down on it from Jacob's shovel.

'Didn't Martin say something about clearing this old tip when you took over Sleylands?'

'Often.' It was as if Jean had expected the question. 'He said it was difficult to work out how to do it without professional help, which would have been expensive. He was undecided whether we should remove everything or leave the biodegradable stuff like carcasses. There's probably a calf or two in there as well.'

Miss Pink saw that a calf might explain the presence of a femur that was too large for a ewe, a man-sized thigh bone. 'The wire was the worst problem,' Jean was saying. 'It was dangerous, beasts could get caught up in it.'

Miss Pink looked up at the top of the crag. She thought of a beast caught in wire in this old tip and Jacob arriving with the next load of rocks and earth, unable to hear bellows above the noise of the tractor, tipping . . . She thought of Phoebe drowning slowly in the underground caverns, of Isa fastened in her seat as the water rose over the MG. Carefully

313

she pushed the broken bone back in the soil until it was hidden from view.

'She still loves him,' Eleanor said when they were alone. 'Of course she can afford to now that he won't come back and create more mayhem.'

'Memory is selective,' Miss Pink agreed. 'And Jean's a past master at blocking out unpleasant truths. She'll remember the good times.'

'She adored him. As a couple they seemed so right: a marriage made in heaven.'

'That was the trouble; she put him on a pedestal, worshipped him, and when he betrayed her twice she wasn't going to give him a third chance.'

'Twice?'

'First the affair with Isa, and she'd have forgiven him for that, might even have continued to protect him, to find excuses for him, but to frame his own wife for murder, that was when he went too far. He was mad but she wouldn't take that into account. Loyalty is what Jean's about and when he betrayed her he was signing his death warrant. You know that isn't a calf's bone, don't you?'

We hope you have enjoyed this Large Print book. Other Chivers Press or Thorndike Press Large Print books are available at your library or directly from the publishers.

For more information about current and forthcoming titles, please call or write, without obligation, to:

Chivers Press Limited
Windsor Bridge Road
Bath BA2 3AX
England
Tel. (01225) 335336

OR

Thorndike Press
295 Kennedy Memorial Drive
Waterville
Maine 04901
USA

All our Large Print titles are designed for easy reading, and all our books are made to last.